A MODERN GUIDE TO MOUNTAIN LIVING

A NOVEL BY

SHAUNA GLENN

PLAN B PUBLICATIONS

Published by Plan B Publications

First edition, October 2017

The characters and events in this book are fictitious.
Any similarity to real persons, living or dead,
is coincidental and not intended by the author.

ISBN: 978-0-692-83211-0

Library of Congress Cataloguing-in-Publication Data

10 9 8 7 6 5 4 3 2 1

Editor: Jessica Royer Ocken
Cover Design & Book Design by Coreen Montagna

Printed in the United States of America

To all future mountain dwellers.
I wish you good luck and Godspeed.

ASHLEY

I wake up to the sound of my mother's voice. When I open my eyes, the lights are turned on, and they're too bright. I'm not sure what's happening—it feels like I just went to sleep not that long ago. It can't already be morning. When my eyes focus, I see two people I don't know standing next to my mom.

"What's going on? What are you doing? Why are y'all in my room?" Something doesn't feel right. My mom is crying, and I have no idea who these people are.

I sit up, and Mom puts her hand on my shoulder. I'm suddenly very scared. I worry someone has died. I mean, why else would she wake me up like this? I still have no idea who these other people are.

"Ashley, you know I love you more than anything in the entire world. And I just want everything to be okay."

Suddenly my dad enters the room. He came all the way from his place in the middle of the night? His hair is messy, and the jacket he's wearing makes a lot of noise as he fumbles his way around the two strangers and stops next to my mom. They're both standing in front of me now, looking like they're about to tell me something really bad. I hope I'm just having a nightmare. Please don't let this be real.

Dad clears his throat and says, "Ash, this is Marcus and Beverly. They're going to take you to a youth program in Utah. They're going to help you work out the things that are troubling you. We love you, and we'll talk to you very soon."

The room begins to spin. I think I might throw up. I shove the covers back and reach for my dad, but this Marcus person is suddenly right in front of me, holding me by the elbow.

"Let go of me! Dad, tell him to let me go!"

My parents turn and leave the room. I can hear my mom's voice as they walk down the hall. She keeps saying, "*Oh my God! Oh my God!*" I'm alone with these people I don't know, and I've never been this scared in my life. My fear quickly turns to rage.

"Get your hands off me! I don't know you! You can't come in my room and touch me like this! I will call the police! *Mom! Dad! Please come back and help me!*"

The woman—Beverly, I think my dad said—hands me a pair of jeans and a T-shirt. "Please put this on, Ashley. We have a plane to catch."

What is happening? I don't want to go on a plane. I want to go back to sleep and wake up in the morning and tell my mom about my bad dream. I'll be nicer to her, I swear. I won't argue anymore. I won't get in trouble. I won't drink or smoke weed. I'll do my research report without complaining and hang out with my sister more. Please, just let this not be real.

Marcus is talking to me, but I can't understand what he's saying. There's a loud ringing in my ears that's keeping me from hearing. They're both standing there waiting for me to do what—get dressed and go with them? There's no fucking way that's happening.

I throw the clothes on the floor and try desperately to get past them. If I can get out of this room, I can run and find my mom. I just need to talk to her, to fix this.

Marcus grabs me by the arm again, and this time I'm ready. I fight to try to free myself from his grasp, but he's way stronger than me. He reaches around his back and pulls something out. It's handcuffs. The sight of the shiny metal rings makes me queasy.

"We can do this the easy way, or we can do this the hard way," he says as he holds them in front of my face. I suddenly give up. I don't want to be handcuffed. I don't know exactly what's happening, and I'm scared shitless, but I'll do what these people tell me because I'm afraid not to.

Beverly picks up my clothes off the floor and hands them to me. She motions to Marcus to stand out in the hall, and he does.

But Beverly watches every move I make. I have zero privacy. She watches me take off my pj bottoms. She watches me fasten my bra. She watches me slip on my jeans. She watches me pull my long sleeve T-shirt over my head. It's a strange feeling having someone watch you like a hawk. I don't like it at all. I thought this was America, not some communist country. A person should be able to get dressed without an audience. She seems like a pervert, the way she's staring at me.

"Can I at least brush my teeth?"

She's ready for the question because out of nowhere she holds out a toothbrush. I take it from her and head to the bathroom. She's right behind me.

She even watches me pee.

I'm given five minutes all together to get dressed, wash my face, and pull my hair back in a ponytail. I'm not allowed to take anything with me except a baggie my mom evidently prepared in advance and my jacket. Inside the baggie are a handful of family pictures—me and my sister, Annabelle, last Christmas; my mom and me looking like we actually like each other; my dad standing with me on the first day of school, and even an old one of all four of us together, back when we were really a family—plus my asthma inhaler. Who packs shit in a baggie? This has to be the weirdest thing anyone's ever given me. And what's the message here? Think of us and don't die? Nice.

As I follow Beverly and Marcus to their minivan (which is baby blue and hideous, by the way), I can't help but think about one thing: my parents schemed and planned this behind my back. Did AB know? They were probably all in on it together.

They're seriously sending me away. What assholes. I may never speak to any of them ever again.

THREE MONTHS EARLIER

CHAPTER 1

Sarah

This never happens. Getting upgraded to first class these days is a myth or an urban legend. Like Bigfoot, but with hot, moist towels, free booze, and mini bowls of mixed nuts. And yet…The agent behind the counter at gate B4 at Los Angeles International Airport just handed me my new boarding pass, which says it all: LAX to DFW, Flight 2445, Seat 5F. I almost feel important.

I hadn't been to LA (or anywhere else, for that matter) since my divorce nearly six months ago. Lately I've hardly had the energy to wash my hair, much less do any traveling. Putting on a bra feels like work. And don't even ask me when I last shaved my legs. I've decided shaving my legs is so very 2014, and I would just as soon have 2014 deleted from my memory's hard drive.

So my trip to Los Angeles was quite a departure from my "new" normal life. But when an old writing partner, Jen Waitte, asked me to come to LA for a few days to collaborate on a web miniseries she's creating, I said yes without thinking about it. It was almost a reflex. And it was good to get back on that horse I used to be so comfortable riding. It felt good to be using that part of my brain. I started to feel alive again.

I began losing control of my surroundings and the people who inhabit them twelve months ago. Traditionally, I am known to be a humorist. I write mostly essays about motherhood and parenting and the lighter side of domestic life. People have come to expect that from me. Sarah Lange: humorist, author, doting wife, and mother of two teenage daughters. That's been my bio for the last four years. Today it reads more like this: Sarah Lange, not so funny anymore, divorced, detached, hairier than normal.

When I'm not this version of me—when I am the old me, the funny me—I can walk into a room and consume the entire space. I am a quick-witted, sharp-tongued lady who can make jokes without making fun of anyone but myself. I'm always the butt of my humor. I love being the center of attention. People respond to me. I have spoken at mom-blogging conferences and appeared on local morning news shows. My essays have been published at *The Huffington Post* and *The New York Post*. I even submitted a story about raising girls in a post-*Cosby Show* world to *The New Yorker*. They loved it. After it was published, I saw a man reading it in a hotel lobby. I watched his face, waiting for some kind of reaction. He smiled and then laughed, and that was the best feeling. My life was going according to plan. No, scratch that. My life was going way better than I'd ever imagined. Until it wasn't.

"*Now boarding all first-class passengers on flight twenty-four forty-five with service to Dallas-Fort Worth.*"

The woman's voice over the intercom startles me. I loop one arm through my Marc Jacobs ivory leather hobo, pick up my laptop bag with my free hand, and make my way down the jet bridge and onto the silver, red, and blue 727 aircraft.

I now regret having had the taxi driver stop at In N Out on the way to the airport. The burger (ordered up the way I like it: animal style) now weighs me down, almost like I swallowed one of those kettle bells my trainer forces me to use during my workouts. But I couldn't help it. We recently got In N Out in Texas, but it's a kind of tradition that when I'm in LA, I eat there at least once. This trip had me on a pretty tight, no-time-for-silliness-like-eating-fast-food schedule, so my only option (if I wanted to keep with tradition) was to stop there on the way to catch my flight home. I had no way of knowing I would be upgraded to first class where, undoubtedly, food will be served.

The longest relationship I've ever been in is not with a man or even another person, but with food, so I will most likely, definitely eat again in the very near future—even though I'm so full I could almost vomit. This day will end badly, no question.

At my seat, 5F, I place my laptop bag in the compartment above my head. Being five-feet-one-and-three-quarters inches tall doesn't make tasks like this easy. Standing up on my tiptoes and audibly grunting is generally involved, not to mention the trail of sweat that begins just under my bra strap and makes its way down my spine. Yes, despite the extra work, I wear a bra in public, mostly.

When I've shoved my bag in the overhead bin, I try to appear as normal as possible so my seatmate doesn't find me offensive. Maybe no one can tell I'm on the verge of an emotional breakdown. What they *can* see, however, is the gigantic cold sore that has appeared in the center of my upper lip, almost like magic, but with less confetti and more middle finger. I'm taking it personally.

I pull my handbag into my lap and dig through until I find my iPhone. I have to get a handle on the damage that's taken place on my face. The rational side of my brain reassures me that the cold sore is not that noticeable. The crazy-pants part of my brain (who regularly binds and gags the rational side) screams in my ear that it's the size of a porcupine and has teeth. And a pulse.

"Can I help you with that? I don't mind taking the picture for you."

When I hear these words from my right, there are no words to describe my humiliation. And I'm a word person. No, on second thought, here it is in a nutshell: It is spectacular. I didn't know I could be this embarrassed. There should be a song written about what exactly I'm feeling at this moment.

But instead of composing lyrics to the Humiliation Song, I turn to face my seatmate: a man, probably in his late forties, casually dressed, working on what appears to be a Sudoku puzzle. It's the first time we've made face-to-face contact, my seatmate and me. It's then that I notice his ball cap. It reads *Betty Ford Clinic*, which means he has either a wicked sense of humor or a drinking problem. The idea that both might be true is not lost on me.

"I'm not taking a picture of myself, thank you. I'm using the camera to look at my face."

He lifts his eyebrows, the crook of his smile turning upward. He puts down his puzzle and offers his full attention.

"What I mean is, I have this giant cold sore, see? And I wanted to see if what other people see when they look at me is what I imagine it looks like."

"What do you think it looks like?"

Humiliation levels rise yet again. *She's going for a new world record, folks!*

"As if a porcupine has given birth on my upper lip."

He turns away from me, picks up his pen and Sudoku puzzle. "Oh. Well, it's not that bad. I didn't notice until you pointed it out."

"What a relief. Thank you."

"I just thought you were taking a picture of yourself to send to someone. Your husband or boyfriend or whatever."

Oh God, this is worse. People think I'm conceited. Well, I'll have you know I don't do selfies. I'm not a teenager! Good Lord, is that what everyone in first class thinks I'm doing? Taking cellphone pictures of myself and texting them to people? Should I stand up and announce that I am, in fact, *not* doing that very thing?

I hate technology. I know what's going on these days. Don't forget I have two teenage daughters, seventeen and fifteen. I follow them on Instagram and Twitter and Facebook, though I'm not exactly sure why. Most of the crap they post is pictures they take of themselves in the bathroom mirror. They make these weird, pouty faces and hold up their fingers, flashing what I can only assume are suburban gang signs. So no. Me taking pictures of myself? *As if.*

I don't know why I feel so inclined to explain myself to the guy next to me in 5E, but I do. "Excuse me; sorry to bother you."

The door to the plane closes, and I can feel the aircraft backing away from the gate.

"I just want to be clear that I'm not in the habit of taking pictures of myself. And I certainly don't send pictures of myself—that I took of myself—to other people. I truly was using the camera as a mirror. I just wanted you to know that."

Once again, he puts down his pen and puzzle and makes direct eye contact with me. A trail of sweat is forming just under my bra, making my back itch. I wriggle in my seat to try to make it go away. I'm also beginning to question my choice of clothing: a long, striped cowl-neck sweater and jeans tucked into Ugg boots. What is it, like, two hundred degrees on this plane? Air. I need some fucking air. I think I might pass out from heatstroke. Why is no one freaking out about the sudden lack of air?

"Are you a celebrity? I feel completely stupid asking that question," he says. "But it is a flight from LA, and you kinda look like you might be on some TV show, possibly one of those reality ones."

Is he serious?

For the first time since I entered the plane, I laugh—mostly at his expense—which is a refreshing change of pace.

This must insult him because he mutters something like "sorry" and reaches in his backpack for a newspaper.

I touch his arm, which is alarming to both of us. I pull my hand away as quickly as I've done it, like I've just happened upon a stovetop that's still hot. He looks down at his arm where my hand touched him, and then up at me.

"Sorry. So sorry," is the only thing I manage.

And then I stick out my hand. "Hi, can we start over? I mean, it's a long flight to Dallas, and I don't want to have this weird thing between us. I'm Sarah, from Fort Worth, and I'm not usually this crazy. Let's just pretend that I'm normal, and you're normal, and we're two normal people who happen to share the same row on an airplane. I'll mind my own business, and you can have your little space over there with your hilarious hat—it's a joke, right?—and your Sudoku, and this will all be a funny story you tell your wife. '*Honey, you won't believe the sweaty woman I sat next to who wouldn't stop talking.*' She'll love it; you'll both laugh. It'll be great. You'll see."

I have no idea what has gotten into me. It's like I'm one of those Chatty Cathy dolls from my childhood, the one with the string in the middle of her chest. You pull the string and Cathy blurts out, *"I want my mommy. I want to hug you. You are my best friend. I think I'm a lesbian."* Okay, I'm pretty sure she didn't say that last thing, but you get the idea. My point is I seem to be channeling my inner Chatty Cathy, and my string is broken, and I won't shut the fuck up. What am I even saying? I'm my own worst nightmare. Plus, I'm just realizing what a cliché I am in my UGG boots and long sweater. No forty-something woman wears UGGs. What the hell is wrong with me?

"Folks, this is Captain Stallings from the flight deck. We've been cleared for takeoff."

I don't know what it is about first class that brings people together. Is it the extra legroom and over-exaggeratedly leather seats? Maybe it's the hot towels and free headphones. I can't quite put my finger on what makes us click, but I'm telling you, we're a real community, bound together by a see-through curtain and non-plastic flatware.

After we've taken off, the flight attendant hands each one of us a rolled-up hot (from the oven?), wet towel. It's meant to be used to wipe your hands and maybe your face. That's it. Nothing more. After an appropriate amount of time has passed, she comes around to collect the used towels. She does this with a pair of silver tongs, because honestly, you'd be surprised what people do with these little white rags, even though most civilized people know the rules. You couldn't pay me to touch those used towels with my bare hands. I think some people forget they're not at home in the privacy of their own bathrooms, where no one is just three feet away, staring in disbelief and judging them. Turns out, our flight is no different. I watch the man across the aisle from me take off his shoes and use the towel on his bare feet. His bare feet! Disgusting, yes, but also an icebreaker between Betty Ford Clinic and me.

As if it is a normal occurrence, I turn to my seatmate and make a face. He must also have been witness to the feet guy because he makes the same face back at me. And this is when I really notice Betty Ford Clinic for the first time. His face is slim, his nose perfectly placed, his eyes the color of sea glass. He seems really tan for the middle of February, but he could have just come from somewhere exotic like Hawaii. Or Bora Bora. Not that I am interested in him or in finding out why he is so tan, or in the story behind the Betty Ford Clinic hat (a minute ago, when he turned to look out the window, I was able to read the word *Outpatient* printed on the back of it, which made me laugh). I am interested only insomuch that I have three hours to kill and airplane rides can be boring.

So far I've learned that his name is Daniel Griffin, and he's an aeronautical engineer. He lives in Irving, a city right in between Fort Worth and Dallas, and has two teenage daughters, like me. He's said nothing so far about a wife, but it's not like I care anyway. My interest in a man at this juncture in my life is about as wanted or necessary as an extra arm growing out of my forehead. Or perhaps a porcupine staking claim of my upper lip.

The food service begins, and I am given the option of a chicken Caesar salad or beef fajitas. Neither one sounds all that appetizing—or I could just be full from my burger and fries—but the flight attendant is waiting for my answer so I blurt out, "chicken Caesar salad." Daniel opts for beef fajitas. Feet Guy is currently asleep and snoring, loudly.

Over the dinner course we exchange tidbits, whatnots, and mostly benign information about each other's lives. When he first told me he was an aeronautical engineer, I called bullshit; that's no one's real job. I assume it's a cover for what he really is: an air marshal. I don't know why I've convinced myself that he's on board for the sole purpose of keeping us safe, but he seems like some kind of federal agent. Maybe it's the fact that he's wearing this cool leather jacket and sneakers. The hat with the jacket with his obvious big, muscle-y arms and broad shoulders just screams *air marshal* to me. Somehow I feel safer sitting next to him. I want so badly to ask him if he is, in fact, an undercover agent working to fight terrorism, but I'm worried that kind of thing is illegal. You can't yell *Bomb!* in an airport. What if you can't call out an air marshal when you see one? You know, for security reasons. I'm not going to take any chances. His secret is safe with me.

Though I'm not hungry, my wine glass seems to keep refilling itself. Every time I take a swig, the tall, blond flight attendant is right there, topping it off. Normally I wouldn't mind, but I do have to drive home once we land in Dallas. For the moment, though, I'm caught up in what feels like my own comedy variety show. Turns out, Daniel is funnier than me. As quickly as I'm making jokes, he's beating me to the punch line. And his anecdotes are so much wittier than mine. I find it rather attractive.

A little while later, our trays have been collected, and now Blondie is shoving warm cookies in my face. I wanted two, but I only took one. There's no reason to reveal the whole truth about my love affair with food; I barely know the guy. Anyway, I start to tell Daniel some of the usual things I find funny about air travel:

You have to pay for everything now: a blanket, five dollars. Headphones, two dollars. Pretty soon they'll charge you for using the toilet. There'll be a credit card swiper machine outside the door. Going number one will cost you five dollars. Gotta go number two? You're out ten bucks. Plus a mandatory extra dollar for air freshener. And the bonus is…everyone knows exactly what you're doing in there, because it scrolls across the television monitors. This is the airline's way of keeping it real.

Daniel is laughing so hard his face is a deep shade of red, like a plum, and he's crossed his arms around his waist. And then he stops laughing and looks at me real serious like. He tells me I'm funny. "*Really* funny," he says. No one has accused me of being funny in months. Sure, I am still me in my head. I'm still slinging pithy anecdotes right and left; it just doesn't come across on the outside. The outside me is a total downer these days. But the inside me is scratching and kicking to get out. She just doesn't know how.

It's been quiet for a while—well, except for Feet Guy's snoring. Daniel has gone back to reading his newspaper, the sports section, I think. I really need my day planner so I can review the week ahead, but it's in my laptop bag, which is stowed in the overhead compartment. There's no way I'm going to go through that whole process again until I absolutely have to. And even then I'm hoping someone will help a short girl out. So I'm just sitting here, staring at the back of the seat in front of me. I consider popping headphones into my iPod and listening to music, but it feels like a lot of trouble. I would have to reach into my purse, dig around for my iPod, locate my earphones, plug them *into* the iPod, turn it on…It's this whole process. You wouldn't understand.

I'm about to laugh at my own absurdity when I suddenly feel someone really close to me. It's Daniel, and he's only inches away from my face. I can feel his warm fajita breath on me.

"Are you married, Sarah?"

I'm a little taken aback by his question, which, I might add, by the way, came out of nowhere.

Still, he leans back in his chair, never taking his eyes off me, and seems to be waiting for my answer.

"I, uh, was married. For nearly twenty years. But I'm not anymore."

The words come out choppy, like I'm chewing glass and cutting them as they escape my mouth. They're more like word shards than actual words. I wonder if he thinks I'm having a stroke.

His eyes widen as he shakes his head. "I can relate. I was married for twenty-two years before getting divorced a year ago. Don't you find it strange being single at our age?"

"Yes, *very*."

Daniel turns to his right and stares out the window. I wonder if he's thinking about his wife (I mean ex-wife) or the death of his marriage.

I think about my own failed marriage and taste a familiar bitterness on my tongue. Steven is not a bad guy, just a terrible husband. And it's not all his fault, even though blaming him makes me feel a lot better about myself.

Steven Lange and I met my sophomore year in college. It was a blind date set up by one of my roommates, Michelle. Well, calling it a blind date (or even a *date* for that matter) is stretching it. She liked this frat boy named Lane, but was having a hard time getting his attention. She wasn't really his type. He seemed to be into really tall, skinny, blond girls, who were a dime a dozen on the University of Texas campus. There are more blond girls in Texas than there are cows. And there are a lot of cows in Texas.

Michelle was short, with red hair and pale skin. She had these amazing green eyes, and when you looked really deeply into them, you could see flecks of brown and gold. I wouldn't call her a freckle-face (to her face), but she had just enough peppering the bridge of her nose and cheeks that one might describe her as a girl having freckles. Some people assumed we were sisters. And I admit, we do resemble each other in a "we're both short" kind of way, but my eyes are dark brown, my hair is brown and wavy, and there's not a freckle to be found on my face.

Apparently Michelle felt she would have to do or say something outrageous to get Lane to notice her, so she made up this crazy story about how she and her roommate (that would be me) sometimes made out with each other. That basically we couldn't decide if we were straight, lesbians, or bisexual. She wanted to know if he would be willing to go out with her to see if she could be attracted to the opposite sex. This got his attention. That Lane, he was no dummy. I mean, the possibility of watching two chicks get it on with each other? Who would pass up that?

Of course Lane agreed to hang out with Michelle, but only if her (sometimes) lesbian lover came too. He then asked his buddy Steven to come along as a witness. And that would be how I came to meet my future husband and, eventually, ex-husband. Of course it's not the story we tell our girls. Not yet, at least.

I wanted to kill Michelle. The whole thing was absurd. I told her there was no way I was going along with this. I reminded her, "We don't make out, *ever!* We're not lesbos!"

She begged and pleaded and swore she would make it up to me. I didn't know what more she could do. She was already doing my laundry for a whole month in return for my having taken her shift as a lifeguard at the YMCA near campus because she was too hungover. (I wasn't an employee there, nor a certified lifeguard.) A few weeks later I kept her friend Keith's pet snake for a whole weekend while they went tubing down the Brazos River. She knew I hated snakes, so to get me to do it she had to promise to pay my part of the electric and phone bills the next month. Just last night I'd agreed to read four chapters in her chemistry book and take notes. "Notes so good it's like I read the chapters myself," she'd demanded. So she's buying the groceries this week and getting the things I always want but can't always afford: a good razor, dark chocolate, and mangoes.

And now there's this.

Michelle assured me we wouldn't really have to make out. Or if we did, it would only be a little kiss here and there. She was certain that once she had Lane away from his friends and the frat house, he would see what a stone-cold piece of (non-blond) ass she was, and then…well, she would take it from there.

Based on the track record I've just described, you know I couldn't say no to Michelle. I was terrible at it, and she knew just what to do to get me to say yes. I would go along with most anything she cooked up, because that's just the kind of friendship we'd built. She yelled jump; I jumped before asking how high.

As I stomped off to my room to get ready for our "date," I pointed my finger in her face and yelled, "*No tongue!*"

"We are beginning our initial descent to Dallas-Fort Worth International Airport. The captain has turned on the fasten seatbelt sign. Please stow away any electronics at this time and raise your seat backs and tray tables to their upright position. We should be on the ground shortly."

The flight attendant's voice startles me for a second time today, and I realize I've been sleeping. It's one of those moments when for a split second I had no idea where I was. I stretch my arms up over my head and breathe out a heavy sigh. I turn to see Daniel watching me.

"Did you have a nice nap?" he asks.

"I guess so. I don't remember falling asleep."

"You were only out a half an hour. You slept on me just long enough for me to finish the business section but not long enough to need a raincoat." He points to his left shoulder and what is apparently a wet spot. I drooled on a person's shoulder. A person I hardly know.

That's it. No more drinking for me. Or going out in public.

"Oh my God, and to think I thought today couldn't be more humiliating." I bury my head in my hands, hoping and wishing I could somehow vaporize.

He places his left hand on my back. "Seriously, it's no big deal. It happens."

I snap my head up to look at him and ask, "So, what, you've fallen asleep on some random person on an airplane and then drooled all over him?"

He seems to wince at this. "Well, I like to think I'm not some random person you drooled on. We have a history, you and me. Caesar salad and beef fajitas, that's us."

"You may be more deranged than me." I laugh. "But thanks for making me feel like less of the idiot I know I am. And thanks for not being creeped out by having my DNA on your leather jacket."

"There's no need to thank me. Just agree to have dinner with me."

The very thought of having dinner with a man (that means a date, right?!) scares me more than the thought of accidentally falling off a ten-story building to my death. And know this about me: I'm terrified of heights. Even thinking about being on a mountain top or hanging off a ledge or being trapped on a Ferris wheel makes me break out in actual hives.

Before I have time to answer, Daniel follows with, "I won't take no for an answer. It's the least you can do. My jacket isn't waterproof."

Oh, for fuck's sake. Why not? I mean what could go wrong? He takes me to a really nice restaurant, and I sneeze and accidentally shit my pants at the dinner table?

The exchange between us at baggage claim feels a little awkward, mostly because I'm not sure what to do or say. I hardly trust my body to keep me standing upright, as if I recently got new legs, and I'm not sure how to operate them. Three hours ago I didn't know this person, Daniel Griffin, and now he's writing my cell number on the back of one of his business cards. I watch how he carefully prints each letter of my name, followed by ten numbers that alone mean nothing, but when written in a particular sequence connect him to me via…I don't know, wind chimes or outer space or something. As is my nature, it would be very easy for me to let my mind wander and question how telephones are able to work, but I feel I should stay in the moment. So I fight back the urge to say something to him like, "Doesn't the invention of the telephone just blow your mind? I mean how does it even work?" Instead I try to focus on Daniel. Okay. A-ha. Here's something: He has beautiful penmanship.

He slips the business card into his inside jacket pocket, smiles at me, and asks, "You okay? You look like you're deep in thought about something."

Oh yes, Daniel. You definitely need to know that while you're being all attentive and seem to want to get to know me better, I'm wondering how telephones work.

I smile and shake my head, trying to erase all the stuff in my mind, like my brain is made of Etch-A-Sketch. Daniel places a hand on my lower back, which puts the thousands of tiny hairs on my body on full alert. I haven't had this kind of intimacy (and I realize this isn't much) with a man in a very long time.

I am overwhelmed, my anxiety level off the charts. This is really happening. I have just given a man my phone number for the purpose of going on a date. And now he's touching me. If someone sees this, they'll automatically assume we're together. To strangers in Baggage Claim C19, we look like a couple that has just returned from a trip.

It's all happening so fast. I wasn't expecting this. And I am definitely not prepared. Had I known the universe had this in store for me when I woke up this morning, I would have rethought my outfit. Oh God, I am starting to sweat again.

While on the inside I'm in full-on panic mode, I think the visible me somewhat resembles a woman who's got her shit pretty much together. How I'm able to be two different people right now defies any kind of reason or logic. Is this what schizophrenia feels like?

The bags finally appear, and I point out my grey Tumi bag (although technically one could not really call my bag "grey" anymore). Purchasing a grey suitcase was one of the more terrible decisions I've made in my life. It was a pristine shade (gorgeous, really) until the first time I carried it on a flight. Now the poor thing looks like someone found it in the bottom of a mineshaft. It's like a sad hobo. Or a mangy dog. Daniel helps to retrieve it from the baggage carousel, and I stand with him while he waits for his to come down the belt.

There are moments of silence and a few feet of distance between us. If I wanted to, I could easily slip away and run like hell to the parking garage. This would be the time to do it. By the time Daniel turned around and noticed I was gone, I could be halfway through the tunnel with my SUV in my sights. Part of me thinks this is the best idea I've had all day. Yes, it would be a crappy thing to do. And he *does* have my phone number. That's easily fixable though. I would just get a new one! *You still have time to get out, Sarah,* I repeat to myself.

And yet, I do nothing.

Because the truth is, I want to go through with this—or at least I think I do. If I've learned nothing else from the last six months of extensive therapy with Dr. Kouros, I know this: It is okay to be uncomfortable, and excited, and worried, and not in control of everything all of the time. This is harder to practice than you might think. I suddenly wonder if Dr. K would take my call. I think this qualifies as an emergency.

Daniel has his bag and is saying something to me. *Focus!*

"Where are you parked? I'll walk you to your car."

"Oh gosh, Daniel, that is so sweet, but totally unnecessary. I can make it from here." *Paging Dr. K! Dr. K, are you there?*

A look of disappointment scribbles his face. "No, really. I want to. It's late, and you shouldn't walk to the parking garage alone. Let's go."

As it turns out, my earlier plan to run for my life while Daniel wasn't looking would have totally backfired. My silver Jeep Cherokee is parked directly across from his black Land Rover Sport in the exact same garage—literally twenty-five feet apart. We stand there, surrounded by thousands of cars, encased in a dimly lit concrete structure and laugh. This is too weird. Do you know how big DFW International Airport is? It's big. Gigantic even.

Without warning, Daniel pulls me in and hugs me tightly against his chest. The smell of his cologne overpowers my senses. I close my eyes and breathe in the spice and the forest and the mint from his gum and let out a sigh.

"I will give you a call tomorrow, if that's okay," he says as he releases me.

"Okay."

I climb in my car, lock the doors, and when I'm sure the coast is clear, scream like a fourteen-year-old girl.

As I exit the parking garage and turn onto the airport parkway, my phone buzzes in my purse. I reach inside to find it. I'm sure it's one of the girls wondering why I'm not home already. When I left two days ago, I taped a printed copy of my flight itinerary on the refrigerator in the kitchen so they would know when to expect me. Next to the itinerary was a note that read: *Please make sure the house is picked up before I get home. This means dishes in the dishwasher, not the sink.* I can see Ashley, my seventeen-year-old, rolling her eyes as she reads it.

The girls have been with my ex-husband, Steven, for the two days I was gone, but I told him he could drop them off earlier this afternoon so they could settle back into their routines. They hate being shuffled back and forth. My fifteen-year-old, Annabelle, often proclaims, "It's like we live out of suitcases. It's not fair."

You're right, AB. It's not fair.

I glance at the phone screen. The text message is not from my girls. It's from Daniel. It is three little words:

Best flight ever.

CHAPTER 2

Daniel

After sending Sarah a text message, I put my phone in the cup holder and turn up the volume on the radio. That Maroon 5 song about Mick Jagger's moves is playing, and normally I would switch the station to AM radio and catch up on sports news, but February isn't the greatest month of the year for sports. The Super Bowl was two weeks ago, but I didn't have a dog in the fight; haven't had a dog in the fight since the mid-nineties. I was glad the Giants beat the Patriots because I'm not a fan of Tom Brady, and I absolutely despise Bill Belichick's wardrobe.

I grew up a diehard Dallas Cowboys fan and a believer in the late, great Tom Landry. Coach Landry would never show up for a game wearing such ridiculous clothes. Every time I see Belichick on the sidelines wearing hooded sweatshirts with the sleeves cut off, I want to yell at him through the television screen: *Have some respect for the game, dickhead!* Anyway, after the Super Bowl to the opening day of baseball season is a somewhat depressing time of year for me, although today has been a pretty good one. I'm finding my spirits suddenly lifted.

When I walked on the airplane earlier today, I had no idea I would meet such an interesting person. Although calling Sarah *interesting* is like calling a rabid dog *spirited.* That one, she's something. I haven't been able to get her out of my head.

After she finally got settled in her seat, I was able to really study her profile—without her noticing, obviously. She was too busy looking in the camera of her phone, making this really cute pouty face with her lips pursed, almost like she was blowing a kiss. I hadn't meant to embarrass her when I offered to take her picture; boy, she hated my ass. I just thought I could help her out. How was I supposed to know she was using the dadgum thing as a mirror? I won't pretend to understand what goes on in a woman's head.

She was ice cold after that for nearly the first hour of the flight. I tried to ignore the fact that such a beautiful woman was sitting inches from me, but her smell (I can't put my finger on what it was exactly…vanilla…cotton candy?) was distracting. Every once in a while our elbows would touch, and each time a knot formed in my stomach. I couldn't solve that stupid Sudoku puzzle to save my life.

It's not like I haven't been on dates with hot women. There was the Pilates instructor I met at the gym and also a teacher at my daughter Bridget's school (not *her* teacher of course; she would be horrified), but nothing happened after a couple of dates. I stopped calling them back. It was the whole it's-not-you-it's-me thing that's usually a chicken-shit way of letting someone down easy. But in those cases it was really true. They were gorgeous, fit, and interesting enough, but nothing about them made me feel what I felt when I started talking to Sarah. There's something about my recent seatmate that unsettles me. She's like an illness or an infection you don't want to cure.

It's not like me to get this excited over someone I just met. I haven't been single that long. After Jackie and I split, I went through a period I call All Women Are Bitches and Liars. My days went something like this: get up, go to the gym, work all day and into the night, grab something to eat, slug a few beers or maybe a vodka and OJ, watch sports (or the Food Network), go to bed, start all over again the next day. On the weekends I spent time with my girls, Bridget and Emma. But at eighteen and sixteen, they're mostly into hanging out with their friends—not eating Mexican food and chitchatting with Dad.

This routine was comforting for the first few months of my newfound single life. For more than twenty years I'd been operating on autopilot, going where I was told to, fixing this, buying that, vacationing here, hanging out with this couple…My life wasn't my own, and I certainly didn't have a say in it. Then one day Jackie told me she was leaving. She was in love with someone else.

I was completely blindsided. I mean, I wasn't happy. *We* were not happy. We hadn't really talked to each other in years, besides the obligatory exchange in the morning and maybe a "could you pass the salt" here and there at the dinner table. Our sex life was non-existent, like a figment of my imagination. It had been so long since I'd seen Jackie naked that I'd forgotten what parts of her body looked like. I could no longer close my eyes and see the curves of her hips, the fullness in her breasts…In fact, had Bridge and Em not been living in the house with us, I would've wondered if we'd ever been intimate. But they were proof that we used to fuck.

Still, I never considered leaving her. Jackie was like an extension of me; we'd practically grown up together. Twenty-two years is a lifetime to spend with someone. She was still funny, still had that bubbly personality and kind heart that had made me fall in love with her. When I was in my office, I could hear her in the kitchen on the phone with her friends. When she laughed, it still made me smile; she has the best laugh. That's the only time I felt like we were okay, hearing her laugh. But it was stupid of me to think I had anything to do with any kind of happiness she was feeling.

Jackie left me for Susan. Jackie is apparently a lesbian.

CHAPTER 3

Sarah

In my dream I am standing in front of a huge audience—more people than I can count—giving a speech about breastfeeding, while breastfeeding. There's this annoying ringing in the background, and I yell out into the audience, "Would someone please turn off that ringing?"

I sit up in bed then, realizing the ringing I'm hearing in my sleep is my front doorbell. I turn to the clock beside the bed: 3:12. Surely it's not three o'clock in the afternoon. There's no way I slept all day. Plus it's pitch black in my room. But being three o'clock in the morning is worse. That means something bad has happened. I climb out of bed, nearly falling down. I've somehow managed to get tangled up in the bed sheet, my feet bound together. There's knocking now, and I scramble to get to the door. I can't help but feel sick to my stomach.

"Who is it?" I ask as I press the side of my face against the cold mahogany.

"Officer Kent, Mrs. Lange. I have your daughter Ashley."

You watch this kind of drama unfold on the Lifetime Channel. It's a show about a seemingly normal family who lives in Happyville, USA. Dad's a banker. Mom stays at home. Amy and John are good kids who never give their parents any trouble. And then *Bam!* Amy gets knocked up, and John goes to prison for selling pot. Dad leaves Mom for a stripper, and Mom gets addicted to painkillers. You shake your head after the final credits roll and wonder What Is Wrong With America?

When I got home from the airport, both girls were in their rooms. They barely looked up at me as I asked the obligatory mom questions: *What are you doing? Are you hungry? Do you have any dirty laundry? What's that awful smell—is that your tennis shoes?* They were preoccupied and not at all interested in talking to me. Seriously, I could have been on fire and they wouldn't have noticed—or cared. Normally it might have bothered me, but not tonight. I was a little preoccupied myself.

I've been home from my trip for less than twelve hours. I haven't even finished unpacking. I went to sleep happy, thinking about my funny, handsome seatmate, Daniel Griffin (who may or may not be an air marshal), wondering if this was a sign that things were getting better.

Now I can feel the other shoe dropping.

I open the door, and there are Officer Kent and Ashley in handcuffs. I can't believe what I'm seeing. It's a scene right out of a parenting handbook titled *Worst Nightmares.*

When Ashley looks at me, she immediately begins sobbing. Her whole body shakes, and she no longer looks her age. She seems like a little girl, the little girl who wore her hair in pigtail braids every day of second grade.

Officer Kent removes the handcuffs from Ashley's wrists and asks if he can come inside. I can't put words together. But I open the door wider and watch, silently, as Ashley leads him into the living room. I have no idea what is going on. I'm scared for my daughter. I'm scared for myself.

The two sit next to each other on the leather sofa, and I manage to make it to the wingback chair opposite them. Finally, I break my silence. "What happened?"

Officer Kent scoots to the edge of the sofa and begins telling his story. "I received a call shortly after one AM that there had been a break-in at Sherman's Pharmacy on the square."

I nod my head. Yes, I'm familiar with Sherman's. They've been in business for more than fifty years. Nice couple, the Shermans. They still run the store themselves. Mr. Sherman is a pharmacist, and Mrs. Sherman manages the cash register. I get all my prescriptions filled there, even though it's five miles out of my way. It's one of the few places left in Fort Worth with any kind character or charm. It's a place you root for; you never want Walgreen's or CVS to force them out of business.

"Another officer and I headed over there and found your daughter and a boy—" He takes a notepad from his shirt sleeve and flips a page. "—named Russell Berry inside the store. Apparently they broke in and intended to steal drugs. They were unaware they had tripped a silent alarm."

Ashley will not look at me. She is staring at a spot on the rug, wringing her hands and crying. I, on the other hand, cannot believe what I have just heard. Ashley (*my Ashley!*) breaking in someone's place of business, and stealing? *Drugs?*

Suddenly, I'm pissed. "Look at me."

She does nothing.

"Look at me right now, Ashley Dawn Lange!"

Ashley lifts her head and looks in my eyes. Hers are filled with more tears. Her face is splotchy, and her mascara smeared.

"Is what he's saying true?"

Her voice cracks as she says, "Yes, ma'am."

CHAPTER 4

Ashley

My room feels like a prison cell. All I have to stare at are my four walls. Okay, I can see out two windows into the side yard. But there's nothing out there except the neighbor's trashcan and their orange cat that licks his balls 24/7. My mom took my phone and my laptop and even the cord to my TV. She'll probably starve me to death just to further prove her point that I'm a screw-up.

Or maybe she's Googling *example of a prison meal* right this very minute. She'll realize she has to feed me the bare minimum so she doesn't get in trouble for child abuse. Any second I expect my door to open and a tray to slide across the floor. On it will be a sandwich with turkey on white bread—no mustard. Mustard would be too extravagant. And an apple and a small glass of room-temperature water—tap, not bottled.

I'm not on drugs.

I like Russell. A lot. He was dating Skylar for, like, the past year, and when they broke up last week, he started texting me. I was happy he was finally noticing me. I didn't really want to break into that pharmacy, but he's really persuasive and super hot. Plus, it's not like we're dealing heroin or something major like that. It's prescription drugs. They're legal.

Russell is not a bad guy. Yes, he drinks beer and smokes pot sometimes, but a lot of kids in my school party. I tried pot once last summer, but I didn't like it. It's not a big deal.

My mom totally freaked out after the cops left. She took my phone and grounded me for, like, the next year. I hate her. I don't blame my dad for leaving; I'd leave too. She is ridiculous and embarrassing. And she completely overreacted about what happened last night. But apparently the old assholes, the Shermans, are pressing charges against Russell and me. My dad is coming over this morning to figure out what to do. It was dumb what I did, and I wish I could take it back, but everyone is acting like I freakin' killed someone! I can't even deal with this.

My sister, AB, is mad at me too. But I'm really not surprised because she's like a mini version of my mother. The two of them act like best friends, and it drives me crazy. When everything was going down with the police last night, AB woke up, stormed into the living room, got right in my face, and called me a shithead. Mom just stood there and let it happen. Then AB rushed to my mom's side, threw her arms around her neck, and my mom started crying. It was disgusting.

I feel so alone.

My mom and I were close when I was younger. She would let me help in the kitchen. She called me Susie the Sous Chef. I acted like it annoyed me, but really, it made me happy. She taught me how to cook, and when I was old enough, she let me make dinner one or two nights a week. I liked being able to plan the menu. My dad would come home from work and gush over me and tell me he was proud. Mom and Dad would sit at the table and talk while AB set the table. When dinner was ready, I would serve everyone, and then we would spend the next half hour laughing and talking. This was my family. This was my life. I never wanted it to end.

One night last year I baked my very first lasagna. It wasn't fancy, but I found a recipe online and went to the grocery store myself. I spent over an hour in the kitchen, browning meat, sautéing mushrooms and onion and garlic, and boiling noodles. I loved putting all the layers together. I let AB sprinkle the cheese all over the top. When I took the lasagna out of the oven, it looked and smelled amazing. I couldn't believe I'd made it all by myself. I had seriously never been prouder. AB set the table as usual, but Mom was in her room with the door closed, and Dad was late getting home.

When Mom finally came out of her room, she headed straight to the refrigerator and took out a bottle of wine. After she poured some into a glass, she sat at her regular spot at the table. She didn't look well. It was obvious she'd been crying. Her nose was red, and her eyes were puffy and swollen. She didn't say two words to me. I heard the garage door then and was relieved to see my dad. I didn't know what was going on with Mom, but I knew Dad would make it better.

It just got weirder from there. Dad didn't seem to notice (or care) that Mom was upset about something. Nobody said anything at dinner. AB tried to make conversation and complimented me on the food, but the meal was basically a disaster.

Mom pushed her lasagna around on her plate, and Dad finished his helping in record time. I was getting madder and madder watching them. I decided I wasn't going to sit there another second with these assholes. I scooted my chair back and picked up my plate. That's when my dad finally spoke.

"Sit down, Ash. We need to talk."

I was so pissed off I was seeing stars. Who did these people think they were? I mean, no one was going to say *"good job"* or *"great lasagna!"* or anything? I'd never had my feelings hurt like this before. The last thing I wanted to do was sit back down with these dicks.

I rolled my eyes so he would take notice before I sat back down. My mom stared down at her plate. She still hadn't said one word.

"Listen, girls. Mom and I need to tell you something. First, we love you both very much. You know that. And I love your mom, and she loves me. But your mother and I are going through a kind of rough patch right now. We have been talking and think it's best if I move out for a little while. Temporarily."

At this point everything went black. There was a loud ringing in my ears, and I had to blink my eyes really quickly over and over again to try to make it stop. I felt like I might pass out. I heard screaming and realized it was coming from me. I couldn't believe what my dad was saying. And Mom was still staring at her fucking dinner plate.

I looked over at AB, and she was hysterical. She got up from her chair and rushed to my mom's side. The two of them bawled and held on to each other. I made eye contact with my dad and he mouthed the words "*I'm sorry.*"

I'm sorry, my ass.

I slid my chair back, picked up the pan of lasagna from the center of the table, charged over to the trash can, and dumped the whole thing in there, pan and all. I ran to my room and slammed the door. I cried myself to sleep.

The next day, Dad and his things were gone.

CHAPTER 5

Steven

When my phone rang at six o'clock this morning, I knew it had to be Sarah. She's the only person who knows I'm up and moving around at that hour. Even on a Saturday.

But I didn't have a clue about why she'd be calling. As I heard the words *Ashley*, *police*, *drugs*, and *breaking in*, my chest tightened. Sarah was pretty hysterical on the phone. Several times I had to tell her to slow down and start over because I couldn't understand what she was saying. But I knew one thing for sure: this was bad. I grabbed my keys and cellphone and headed out the door.

As I pull up in the driveway on Hackberry Lane, it's as familiar to me as if I still lived here. The only thing different is now I ring the doorbell instead of putting my key in the lock—or I will when I get out of the car. I'll be the first to admit it makes me a little sad. I miss some things about my old life. I miss the smell of the fancy candle Sarah burns every morning. I miss seeing the girls before they head off to school. I miss the way Sarah folded my shirts. I can never get them to crease the way she did.

We made some really great memories here. I taught the girls how to ride their bikes right in the middle of the street. The traffic coming in and out of the neighborhood isn't that bad, so you don't have to worry about your kids so much. The trees we planted are huge now, nothing like the twigs they started out as. There was the year of the fire ant infestation, the time Ashley tripped on the front steps and broke her arm, and the many Sunday afternoon picnics we enjoyed under the pecan tree—not to mention the bike rides through the park.

Sarah and I bought this house a year after we got married. It's a 1920s Spanish Tudor with white stucco walls and a red tile roof. Sarah has a fancier description of it because she cares more about that kind of stuff than me. For years I listened to her describe the wood beams and ironwork and hand-painted tiles in elaborate detail, and I learned something about myself: I'm not as observant as she is. To me it was an overpriced, run-down old house that definitely needed new electrical and plumbing. But the way her whole face lit up when the realtor showed it to us, I knew I was doomed to say yes.

Shortly after we moved in, Sarah presented some grand ideas of ways we could update the place, although it seemed perfectly fine to me now that the toilets worked and I no longer feared we'd electrocute ourselves. I'm a numbers guy, and I know a thing or two about remodeling and adding on. I may not know how to do the work myself, but I know it costs a shitload of money. The last thing I wanted to do as a newly married, newly employed stock trader was get myself in debt. Sarah pouted when I put the brakes on her plans, but in time she was able to finagle a project out of me here and there. Over the past eighteen years she's added on to the master bedroom and closet, built a second bathroom on the second floor, turned an extra bedroom into a movie theater, updated the kitchen with professional appliances and granite countertops, and put in a swimming pool. I guess it's fair to say she won the battle of wills. To be honest, I hardly minded. I always told her, "I want to build a successful business and have enough money so I don't end up like my old man: in debt and broke all the time. My dad may have been a great man, but he was terrible at managing money. So as long as I can afford it without compromising those objectives, we'll talk."

She would reply, "I just want this to be our forever house."

I fucked up her forever plans.

CHAPTER 6

Sarah

I look out the front window and see Steven sitting in his car. What is he doing? He's been sitting there for ten minutes. If he's replying to fucking emails, I will kill him. I need him to come inside. Even thinking about Ashley right now makes me sick.

I feel the back pocket of my jeans buzz, and I reach around and pull out my phone. It's a text message from Daniel.

God, I'd forgotten all about him. It's amazing how quickly your life can change in just a few hours.

**Hope you had a great night.
Would love to see you tomorrow for lunch
if you're available. Call me. D**

Lunch *tomorrow*. I can't wrap my brain around how to get through *today*. I'm dealing with a family crisis right now, and the last thing I need is to jet off to Sunday lunch like a person with not a care in the world. Don't get me wrong; I would be giddy about the idea of seeing Daniel had last night not happened. But I'm facing possible legal problems and a teenager who seems to be spiraling out of control.

It's still hard for me to believe this is actually happening. My daughter, my first-born, is in big trouble.

I hear the front door open, and Steven pokes his head around. "Hey," he says. "Where is she?"

"In her room, chained to her bed."

He lets out a heavy sigh and heads up the staircase. I type a quick response to Daniel's text:

Something terrible has happened.
I'm okay, just my oldest daughter is in trouble
with the law. I'll call you later. Sarah

I slide my phone back in my jeans pocket and make the long, heavy walk to Ashley's room. Thank goodness AB is out of the house right now. She's gone a lot these days. Three days a week she goes to school early for Student Council and yearbook committee meetings. And on Saturdays she helps out at the homeless shelter, in the women and children's building, with her friend Rachel. Rachel's mom is also her biology teacher, and we take turns driving on Saturdays. I'm grateful today is her turn to drive.

"What were you thinking, Ash?" Steven is asking her. "This is by far the stupidest thing you've ever done. Stupider than the time you took my car without permission and drove through the garage door."

This is true.

"*And*, you're in trouble with the *law*. The *police* are involved. Do you realize your mother and I are going to have to hire an attorney to try to keep you out of jail? *Jail!* Does any of this register with you, or are you just going to keep acting like what you did was no big deal?"

Up to this point, Ashley has been stone-faced, sitting on the corner of her bed, hugging her knees to her chest. She looks absolutely pitiful. I know for a fact she never went to sleep. I was awake too.

"I know what I did was wrong, Daddy, okay? I said I'm sorry a million times. It was stupid and…and…I don't know what else you want me to say."

Steven whips his head around to face me. "Have you called the boy's parents? We need to talk to them."

His question catches me off guard. "No, I hadn't even thought about that."

He puts his hands on his hips all self-righteous-like and says, "Goddammit, Sarah. Why not? Are you really this irresponsible?"

I see Ashley's eyes widen and her mouth open. I look back at Steven; my hands are beginning to shake. "Irresponsible? Are you kidding me? Look, I know you're upset, but this is not on me." I point to Ashley. "This is who you need to be directing all this anger toward. Not me. I guess I didn't think to call Russell's parents because the police are handling it. My only concern is what to do from here. They're pressing charges, Steven."

He puts his hands up to his head and presses them against his temples. His eyes are closed, and he's just standing there...maybe counting to ten or repeating some mantra? Ashley and I watch him. It's odd, and I don't exactly know how to react to all this, so I just remain very still. I'm pretty sure I've even stopped breathing.

After half a minute he puts his hands back on his hips, looks at me, and says, "You're right. I was out of line. This isn't your fault. I think I'm just freaking out."

Right now Steven is the most vulnerable I've ever seen him. He almost appears broken. While normally he is the go-to guy when there's a crisis, today he seems completely at a loss.

This is new territory for both of us.

I guess I'll take it from here. "Steven, come downstairs and let's talk; I'll make coffee. Ashley, stay in here until I come get you. And clean up this room. It's a pigsty."

Once back downstairs, Steven seems to have composed himself. He tells me several times how sorry he is for the angry outburst in Ashley's room. I assure him that while it was intense, I totally understand his sudden lapse in judgment.

I pour us both a cup of coffee and join him at the kitchen table.

"We need to hire a lawyer," he says as he sets his mug on the table. He raises his eyebrows. "A good one."

My phone buzzes in my back pocket again. I retrieve it and see another text from Daniel.

Now I'm worried. Is it weird that I'm already worried about you and we just met yesterday? Please call when you can. D

I smile and even laugh a little.

I look up and see Steven staring at me. "Right. An attorney."

"I say we call your brother."

Somehow I knew he would say that. My brother, Benny, is a fabulous attorney. I'm not sure he's ever lost a case. So calling him up and asking him to help his niece seems like the most logical, best decision ever. Right?

The problem is Benny isn't speaking to me—*hasn't* spoken to me in nearly two years. All because of an essay I wrote about my (our) childhood. I didn't think (I *still* don't think) it was wrong for me to share my experience of growing up with a mean alcoholic for a father and an abused, broken-down woman for a mother. But after the story ran on *Huffington Post*, my brother waged a holy war against me. He called me, screaming, demanding that I take down the post and write a retraction. He wouldn't meet with me to talk about it. He just doled out his demands and hung up before I had to chance to say anything. I couldn't believe or understand why it had upset him so much.

Everyone who knew us was aware of the kind of house Benny and I grew up in—it was hardly a secret. The people at church could see the marks my dad left on my mom. Dad couldn't hold down a job because he was always wasted. My father wasn't a nice person—he never once told me he loved me. Not once. Benny and I were left to fend for ourselves a lot of the time when Mom was so depressed she couldn't get out of bed. Neighbors would bring us food and make sure our mom was okay. Poor Mom; she was so beaten down from the years of my father's wrath that I think she was actually relieved when her body succumbed to breast cancer.

She died my senior year in high school. Benny was just fourteen. Dad packed his clothes in a bag and left town. He didn't bother telling us he was leaving, and we haven't seen him since. A lawyer knocked on the door a week after Mom died and told Benny and me she had set up a trust in our names. I think somehow she knew she would die too soon (probably at the hands of my father), and we'd be left with nothing. She'd taken out a life insurance policy worth a quarter of a million dollars. It wasn't a lot of money, but it would pay for Benny and me to go to college. Mom also owned the house outright. It had been left to her when her parents died, and she left it to Benny and me.

Since I'd already turned eighteen, I was able to stay in the house and take care of Benny, temporarily. Over the next few months we cleaned up the house, fixed the things that were broken, and sold it. I looked after Benny the best way I knew how, but after graduation

I moved to Austin to attend the University of Texas. Benny moved in with our church pastor's family until he finished high school.

I called and checked in on him a lot in the beginning. I missed him—I missed having a family. I needed to feel connected to someone who'd seen what I'd seen, who shared my same pain. Feeling like I belonged to someone, that someone else out there had similar DNA to me, was comforting. But over time I got busy with my studies and my social life, and the phone calls became less and less frequent. Benny and I always saw each other at Christmas, but there was a strange unfamiliarity about it. I no longer found it comforting. It actually made me remember things I was trying to forget. Benny was part of a past that brought on feelings of pain and anger and self-pity. After a few years I don't think either of us particularly enjoyed spending those days together; we may have even dreaded it. Eventually I know I did.

I watched him graduate from high school (with honors, I might add), and I hugged him and told him I would always be around if he needed me. I'm not sure it was convincing to either one of us. He waved goodbye and joined the group of people he now called his family. I watched as they huddled around him—a loving dad, an attentive mother, and twin sisters—and I knew he would be okay.

I, on the other hand, was an orphan.

The rest of the weekend involved playing bad cop, and even more bad cop. There was nothing good about it. Ashley mostly stayed in her room with the door closed. There was a lot of crying—mostly by me. Steven tried his best to be supportive, but I don't really like Steven right now, so any goodwill from him is met with a certain degree of hostility.

What I mean is, I don't want to be comforted by him. Sometimes even the sight of him makes me angry. I realize I have to put my feelings aside so we can make reasonable parenting decisions together, but it's hard. It's so very hard.

I briefly spoke with Daniel. It was kind of awkward for a couple of reasons. A, I don't know him well, or at all, really. And B, who wants to share their kid's fuck-ups with a potential new friend? I don't want people to think poorly of Ashley. And I'm guarded, mostly.

The other thing still weighing heavily on me is the thought of calling my brother and asking for help. That makes me want to vomit.

It's early Monday morning. I've had more cups of coffee than normal, but nothing feels normal anymore. Plus, I have to call Benny, who's going to be less than excited to hear it's me on the other end of the line, so the extra boost of caffeine can't hurt. I pick up my phone and scroll through the contacts. Well, here goes nothing.

"Good morning. Berkeley, Shaw, and Shapiro, how may I help you?"

"Hi, yes. Um, I'm holding what I believe to be a winning lottery ticket—it's a scratch off. Says I won five million dollars? I think I need a lawyer. Is Bernard Shaw available?"

It's a lame cover, I know, but I'm desperate. I need to know for sure that he'll take the call.

"One moment, ma'am. I'll get Mr. Shaw."

"Hello, this is Bernard Shaw."

"Benny, I need your help."

"Christ, Sarah. What do you want? I'm guessing you're not really holding a winning lottery ticket."

"I'm not. I'm sorry. I just knew you wouldn't take my call."

"I'm hanging up now."

"Wait! Please, Benny. It's Ashley. She's in trouble. Please. Just let me talk for five minutes."

I hear Benny breathe heavily into the phone. "Okay. I'm listening."

For the next twenty minutes or so I have my brother's undivided attention, and it's unbelievable the positive effect his voice has on me. I can feel my anxiety levels lessening. He's like the human form of Xanax.

He asks lots of questions about Ashley's recent behavior: *Have her grades slipped?...Do you trust her friends?...Have you drug tested her?... Yadda yadda.* At times there are long pauses, and I assume he's taking notes. I wonder if he's as comforted hearing my voice as I am hearing his. I realize now I have missed having my brother in my life.

"All right, so here's what we're going to do. I will call the District Attorney's office and speak to the ADA to find out their case against her. You make sure Ashley stays out of any further trouble. Maybe even keep her home and definitely off social media. In fact, you might delete her Facebook page, et cetera, so there's nothing—no evidence of past inappropriate or questionable behavior. And for God's sake, Sarah, don't fucking write about this on the Internet."

I guess he's still upset.

CHAPTER 7

Daniel

I'm early and sitting at a table. But that's nothing new for me. I'm always early, wherever I'm going. You never know what the traffic is going to be like, so I give myself plenty of time. It seems like every major freeway in and around Dallas and Fort Worth is under construction. You can expect to be delayed as long as two hours sometimes. It's a real ballbuster if you're in a hurry to make an appointment.

My being early everywhere used to drive Jackie nuts. But I guess the fact that I *have* nuts drove her nuts too, now that I think about it. *Lesbian jokes never get old.*

I look over at the entrance and see Sarah. God, she's more beautiful than when I first laid eyes on her just over a week ago. My heart belly flops into my stomach as I stand up and wave her over. She smiles at me, and I thank God and American Airlines for introducing us.

Before I can offer her a friendly peck on the cheek, she practically jumps in my arms and buries her face in the brand new John something-or-other black shirt I bought special for today. We stand there like this, in the middle of a crowded restaurant, surrounded by people eating sushi, for more than a minute.

When she finally pulls away, I see tears in her eyes. "Sit down; talk to me," I tell her. "What's going on?"

Sarah takes off her jacket, throws it on the seat, and sits opposite me in a semi-corner booth. She unrolls her napkin, dabs her eyes with it, and then folds it carefully across her lap.

She sighs. "You must think I'm a crazy person—and rude. I'm sorry I haven't talked to you since we left the airport. Things have been…I don't even know the word…*catastrophic?*…at my house."

I reach a hand across the table and then quickly take it back. *Too soon.*

The waitress appears and takes our order. When she walks away, Sarah begins to tell me the events of the last several days, and I can't believe it. It's a parent's worst nightmare.

The food comes during her story, and she eats a few pieces of her rainbow roll, but leaves most of her lunch on her plate. She apologizes, saying she doesn't have much of an appetite. But it doesn't faze me. I'm just glad to be sitting here, spending time with her, despite the not-so-hot circumstances. Even in the midst of a crisis, everything she says and does is fascinating to me.

It feels different with Sarah. I've known her for seven days and have seen her twice in that time, but she has this way of making it seem like we've known each other for years. There are no games, no pretense. She gives every indication of being a what-you-see-is-what-you-get kind of girl. That's exactly what I need.

"Let's talk about something other than me," she says as the waitress clears the plates. "Tell me something funny, or interesting, about you."

All right. She wants a story? I've got a story.

For the next twenty minutes I talk about my ex-wife, Jackie, the (now) lesbian. I tell her how Jackie broke the news to me that she's gay and how, looking back, I should have seen it coming. *Daniel, you know I have a hard time giving you blow jobs? I have a super-sensitive gag reflex—my doctor told me, remember?*

"So basically," I tell Sarah, "my ex-wife had a doctor's note excusing her from sucking my dick." It's crass, I know. I regret the vulgarity the second the words come out of my mouth.

But then, as if the floodgates are opened, Sarah laughs. It's like it's been bottling up inside her and someone (me?) flipped the switch. And when I say she starts laughing, I'm not talking the low-volume, inside-voice kind. It is a no-holds-barred, cheerleader-voice laugh. It's exactly the kind of laugh you want your second wife to have.

Whoa. Stop thinking like that, Daniel.

Sarah suddenly stops mid-laugh, reaches across the table, and places a hand on my arm. "Oh God, Daniel, your daughters! How did they react? Are they okay?"

I love the way she seems genuinely concerned about my girls. Her face softens as soon as she starts asking questions. She's the nurturing type—it's obvious—and thinking about her this way makes my heart ache. I want to kiss her mouth so badly I have to fight back the urge to jump across the table and tackle her to the floor.

After another half hour, during which I down more iced tea than I have in my life, Sarah tells me she has to get home. She doesn't want to leave Ashley alone for too long. I get that. And I need to pee like a racehorse.

I walk her to her car, and when we get to the driver's side door, I pull her to me, wrap my arms around her waist, and hold her for a good minute. We don't say anything to each other; we just hug. I do my best to memorize everything about this moment: the way her long hair feels against my neck, the flowery smell of her perfume, and the firmness of her breasts against my chest.

When we finally break away, she smiles and stares her big brown eyes into mine. "Thank you, Daniel. You have no idea what today has meant to me. I know we just met, and it's crazy, but I like you, and I feel like you're someone I can trust. You have that kind of face. I can tell you're a great dad by the way you talk about your girls. This, right here—as weird as it's going to sound—is the best thing going on in my life at the moment. So…really…thank you."

Then she does something I'm not expecting: She leans in and kisses my lips.

And now I fear the worst: I'm going to fall in love with this girl.

CHAPTER 8

Sarah

I'm driving, but I haven't been able to stop thinking about Daniel—and, even more, about the kiss. I don't know what got into me; I've never been the aggressor. Ever.

But he was standing there in front of me, looking at me like no man has ever looked at me before. It was like he could really *see* me, into my soul. He has these amazing eyes that sparkle in the daylight. He licked his lips once—and then again. And then he smiled and opened his mouth like he was going to say something, and I suddenly became overwhelmed and just leapt at him. It wasn't a long kiss, and it wasn't overly passionate; it's not like we made out in the parking lot of Sushi Samba. It was sweet and soft and...perfect.

And now I pull up at home, a place I've come to dread. My home used to be my place of respite, the place I felt the safest. I still love the smell of the old magnolia tree that someone planted too close to the house years before we bought it. The aromatic white blooms tickle my nose as I make my way up the front porch steps. When we bought the house, the front porch was nothing but a cement slab with a rusty handrail. Now, with the addition of Spanish tile, cozy outdoor seating, and hanging baskets, my front porch all but screams *Welcome Home*. But since Ashley's run-in with the law, my house feels more like a prison than a sanctuary.

I haven't let her leave the house, or talk on the phone, or be on a computer. So she spends all day moping and pouting. When I ask her to do things like unload the dishwasher or vacuum the downstairs, she makes faces like I'm annoying, which makes me want to punch her. I can honestly say I don't like my daughter very much right now. I'm sure that makes me a terrible person and an even worse mother, but I can't help it—that's how I feel. She doesn't really seem like my daughter these days. She's more like an unpleasant houseguest who won't leave.

Steven offered to let Ashley stay with him at his house for a while, and I'm sure she would prefer that. But Steven is away often on business trips, and Ashley would have zero supervision. Well, except for Monica, the new whore (I mean woman) in Steven's life. She's the reason we're divorced, actually. That tired old story. Boy meets girl. Boy marries girl. Boy and girl have kids and a mortgage. Boy gets antsy and feels like no one understands him. Boy has affair with much younger girl. Boy is a fuck-head.

So excuse me if I'd rather Ashley not stay at Steven's house for an extended period of time. Call me the bitter ex-wife, but that's exactly the opposite of what she needs right now. So she's stuck with me. And vice versa.

Benny has been in touch with the Assistant District Attorney, and we're meeting tomorrow to go over the State's case against her. But he thinks since it's her first offense she'll most likely get deferred adjudication and two years' probation—and maybe drug counseling. I hope he's right.

Meanwhile, with so much attention being paid to Ashley, Annabelle has become the forgotten child. I forgot to pick her up after her acting class on Tuesday. It just totally slipped my mind. I was sitting at my desk (well, it's more like a small nook in the kitchen), reading story after story online of parents who've been through what I'm going through, and I completely lost track of time. My phone rang, which startled me, and it was a number I didn't recognize.

"Mom, where are you?" Annabelle sounded frantic.

"What do you mean? I'm at home."

"Oh my God, Mother. It's after six. You were supposed to pick me up at five-thirty. Mr. Zachary is ready to leave. And he can't until you *pick me up*."

I rushed to my feet, grabbed my handbag off the back of the dining room chair, and turned a few circles trying to remember where I parked my car (in the garage or out front?), all the while apologizing over and over. And I was suddenly feeling dizzy. "I'm so sorry, AB. I'm on my way!"

Wednesday was the deadline for softball tryouts, which I also forgot. We were a no-show to her orthodontist appointment on Thursday, and I promised to take lunch to her at school on Friday—which again, totally slipped my mind. I think I'm a shoo-in for Shitty Mom of the Week.

I've begun to worry that while I'm trying to fix what's wrong with Ashley, I'll screw up AB in the process. Parenting is the least fun job I've ever had. It's a wonder any kid survives childhood at all.

I can't apologize enough to Annabelle for being late. She keeps saying it's okay, but I know it's not. It's not even close to being okay.

It was quiet on the car ride home. Too quiet. I begged her to tell me what she was thinking.

"You want to know what I'm thinking? I'm thinking Ashley has really done it this time. Not only has she screwed up her life, she's seriously messing up mine. It's not fair. It's not fair that I always do the right thing, and yet I end up with the short stick. And I imagine it's going to get a lot worse before it gets better, which pisses me off. And no offense, Mom, but I feel like you are two different people these days. Some days you're suffocating. I can't breathe. You hold me too long and too tight or hang out in my room like we're best friends. Then you seem fine and do stupid shit like forget to pick me up or take me somewhere. You're all over the map. One minute you're attached to me at the hip, the next you forget who I am."

Hearing her say these things brings tears to my eyes, but I refuse to break down. I grip the steering wheel tighter in hopes that will keep the tears from spilling down my cheeks.

Then she adds, "It's no secret you've been totally depressed since Dad left. I know you take medication for depression. Everyone sees your unhappiness; it's not like you can hide it. Our neighbors, the teachers at school, even the man who owns the deli—they all treat you like a car crash victim. You know what I'm talking about? Someone gets in a bad wreck and they get out of the car all dazed and confused, blood gushing from a gash in their forehead. They're all like, 'Where am I? What happened? Is that blood coming from *me?*' That's *you* most days."

She barely takes a breath between sentences. My tears are flowing now. I can't stop them. Annabelle doesn't look at me. The whole time she's looking straight ahead, waving her arms around. I want to tell her to stop, but I don't. I think I need to hear this, as hard as it is. And it sure seems like she needs to say it.

She goes on. "Want me to slice your ham extra thin this week, Mrs. Lange?" She mimics the deli guy. "The way he whispers to you across the counter like you're so fragile the slightest sound might cause you to split apart where the stitches are healing, to start bleeding again. I don't blame you, Mom. And I know I'm being a jerk. I'm sorry for lashing out. But you asked what I'm thinking."

I nod because it's true. She reaches over and puts her hand on my shoulder. She wipes the tears off my cheek.

She's softer now. Her voice is lower. "I'm sure it's hard finding out your husband of a billion years is in love with a woman half your age. You think I don't know all about how Monica came in the picture, but I do. That's not a secret either. The rooms in our house may be separated by walls, but they're not exactly soundproof. I heard everything that night. You were yelling at Dad, calling him names I'd never imagined would come out of your mouth. He didn't yell back, not that I could hear. His voice was low, and I had a hard time making out what he was saying. I had to press my ear to the wall and squint my eyes shut, but I listened to him repeating the same thing over and over again. 'I'm sorry. I didn't mean for this to happen.' The last thing I heard him say was, 'I'm in love with her.' Then I heard you slap him."

We pull up in the driveway, and I put the car in park and turn off the ignition. Neither of us gets out. We sit there for a minute just staring at each other. I really need to blow my nose.

Annabelle smiles and says, "You're a mess."

I open the middle console and pull out a paper napkin with the Whataburger imprint on it. I dab my eyes and wipe my nose.

"Mom, Dad was an asshole for what he did to you and to our family. And I thought it was pretty cool when you slapped him. I remember the perfect outline of your handprint on his cheek. He deserved it."

Yes. The fucker absolutely did.

A new health club had opened up a few miles from Steven's office. He popped in there the week of the grand opening and accepted their offer for a one-week free trial. He came home after his first day working out raving about the place. "You should see their facilities, Sarah. Everything is state of the art!"

I was slicing a cucumber while Ashley and Annabelle set the table for dinner. He threw his bag on the table, which led me to stop mid-slice and scold him. "Seriously, Steven, do you have to put that smelly duffle bag on the table? We're about to eat."

That's all I said in the way of joining his conversation about the new gym. Looking back, it seemed to deflate his excitement. He never talked about it again. But every day he packed a duffle bag with shorts and a T-shirt and sneakers, and he would work out during his lunch hour. He kept at it after his free week was up, and he started looking more fit than he had in a long time. He looked good—younger. There was definitely something different about him—his whole outlook on life changed. Turns out the reason for the change was a trainer named Monica.

I didn't suspect anything, which makes me crazy sometimes. I mean, how did I not see? Steven was the same as he'd always been—maybe a little happier, but still the same guy. He still teased me and flirted with me. He would lean over while we sat on the sofa watching TV and kiss my cheek. He was still around for the girls and talked sports with Ashley. We all rode our bikes through the park on Sunday afternoons like we had for years.

The big blow came one night in June. Steven was in the shower, and his phone lay on the bedside table. It dinged once and then a second time. I was folding laundry on the bed and ignored it. I was used to the sound of it beeping. It was always work-related. But then it beeped a third, fourth, and fifth time. I stopped what I was doing and picked it up. I worried something bad was happening at work. Who texts that many times in a row unless it's bad? When I pressed the home button, I saw an unfamiliar name: Monica. Was that someone new at Steven's office? He hadn't mentioned anyone named Monica. That's when I got a sick feeling in my stomach. The texts were a punch to the gut.

Yesterday was amazing.

I can still smell you on me.

Are you there?

Are you at home?

Is your wife nearby? I guess you can't talk right now. XO

The rest, I guess, is what you call *history*. Things pretty much exploded upon impact.

Steven moved out, I fell down a well, Ashley turned criminal, and Annabelle became the forgotten child.

CHAPTER 9

Daniel

The girls and I are shoe shopping. It's not my favorite way to spend an afternoon. I never would have done this in my former life. Jackie was in charge of all this kind of stuff. Now the girls come spend time with me and ask me things like "Can we go to the mall and look for skinny jeans?" or "I need a new hair straightener; can you take me to Ulta?"

There's nothing I want more in life than to make my girls happy, so I take them where they "need" to go. Today it's looking for something called *wedges*. I don't mind this new role, even if they just see me as a way to get places—and their own personal ATM. Although more and more lately they also ask for my opinion on how they look. Women's shoes, by the way, are not cheap.

When your wife leaves you for another woman, you start to doubt yourself. You ask yourself a lot of questions you don't know the answers to. And God Almighty, you hope you're wrong. *Am I not the man I thought I was? Am I not a good lover? Do I not know how to satisfy a woman? Is my penis not doing the trick? Am I not putting my mouth/tongue/fingers in the right places?* At one time I thought I would kill myself if the answer to any of these questions was *no*.

"Dad, are you listening to me?"

What? "Oh, sorry. My mind was somewhere else." I shift in my seat. The shoe department at Dillard's is busy. I was lucky to score a chair.

Emma rolls her eyes and says, "Which shoe do you like better?" Then she turns her feet from side to side.

They look exactly the same. But I can't say that because I know it's not the right answer. "That one." I point to her left foot.

Bridget makes a face and says, "No, the right one."

"That's exactly what I was thinking." Emma nods. She turns back to me. "Can I get these, Dad? They're eighty-nine dollars, on sale."

I reach into my wallet and pull out my Visa. "Sure. And then are we done?"

While Emma pays for the shoes, Bridget plops down on my lap. "Almost. I need something to wear for Saturday. That okay? Won't take me long. You can sit here, if you like." And before I can say anything, the two of them take off toward the women's clothing department, leaving me holding the bag of shoes.

I struggled for a long time after Jackie and I split. I couldn't quite wrap my brain around what was happening. I could hear the words coming out of her mouth, but it was like they'd been translated into Chinese by the time they reached my brain. I had to ask her a handful of times to say it again, just so I could fully understand her. She thought it was my way of being cruel, making her say the words over and over. But that wasn't it. I needed clarification.

"Daniel, I love you. You're all I've known for more than half my life. I can't explain what's happening to me. Trust me, I've agonized over this for years."

Did she say *years?*

"I want nothing more than to be a family with you, but I can't physically do it any longer. Dr. Anthony says I need to own this, the truth, and that I need to be honest with you. He says living a lie will only hurt you, and I don't want that. I wish I didn't love you so much. This would be a lot easier if I didn't, or if you were an asshole. But the truth is you're the best guy a girl could ask for. I just can't be that girl any more. I'm sorry."

She broke down right there in the middle of our bedroom, sobbing and shaking, covering her face with her hands. I sat on the edge of the bed, staring at her, a sense of numbness washing over me like morphine through an IV. I couldn't believe this was now my life.

Dr. fucking Anthony. Jesus Christ, what I wouldn't give for five minutes alone with that prick. I blame him for Jackie leaving—I really do. He put all these ideas in her head. She told me he's the one who helped her realize she was a lesbian. I'm sure after this breakthrough he hugged her goodbye, closed his office door, and sat behind his desk, jerking himself off to the image of Jackie and Susan getting it on. The guy is an obvious sex fiend who preys on dissatisfied, unfulfilled housewives. Jackie was no more homosexual than I am. We fucked like crazy the first fifteen years of our marriage. And yet, six sessions with Dr. Anthony and she's all *Eureka!* I like pussy! I should report his ass to the AMA. And I probably would if I didn't find the whole thing humiliating.

Telling the girls their mom was gay was the second-hardest moment I've had to endure in my life. I don't know what was more devastating to them: that we were getting a divorce or that she was attracted to women. It didn't really matter; the outcome was the same. We were a broken family however we wanted to spin it.

I think it would've been easier on me had she left me for another man. *You say you've fallen in love with a filthy rich entrepreneur who owns a villa in Tuscany and has a shlong the size of a baby walrus? Best of luck to you!* A man can almost understand losing his wife to that. Hell, he can probably appreciate it—help her pack her bags, maybe even want to see the guy's baby-walrus shlong for himself. But your wife leaving you for tits and ass is a tough pill to swallow.

This past week I've found myself spending way too much time thinking about Sarah. This has trouble written all over it. For one, I just met her and have seen her in person exactly two times. Second, it sounds like she's got a lot of shit going on in her life, and normally I don't particularly care to take on other people's problems. I've finally gotten to the point in my muddied-up thing called a life where I'm feeling like my old self again.

And yet I can't stop thinking about how she could be someone special. And her problems don't make me want to run. There's no doubt in my mind I want to see her again. Thinking about her face and her lips rouses the sleeping bulge in my pants. Jackie and I still have one thing in common besides our kids: we both like women. That's something to build on, don't you think?

CHAPTER 10

Sarah

Nearly two weeks have passed since Ashley's arrest, and today we find ourselves in a courtroom in downtown Fort Worth, sitting before a judge. Steven, Annabelle, and I are seated on the front row behind Benny and Ashley.

"Ms. Lange, do you take full responsibility for your part in the break-in at Sherman's Pharmacy?"

I watch Ashley's hands shake as she faces the judge. At this moment, she again seems like a little girl—not quite tall enough to see over the counter to where Mr. Sherman keeps the jar of lollipops—rather than the seventeen-year-old version of herself, who is in trouble for committing a crime.

"Yes, sir. I do. And I'm very sorry." The words *very sorry* hang in the air like one of those soap bubbles.

When the kids were little, they used to beg me to drive them to the dollar store to buy them each a bottle of bubbles. After I did so, I would say, "No blowing bubbles in the car. Wait until we get home." But invariably Ashley would ignore my instructions and blow bubbles in the backseat. AB would laugh and try to pop them before they made their way up to the front seat. I did my best not to laugh and even tried to sound irritated at them. But the laughter was so genuine and innocent. It feels like a lifetime ago that we did that.

What I wouldn't give to go back there now. I wouldn't bother telling them not to blow bubbles in my car. I would just let them do it. It's certainly not the worst thing your kids will do—so I'm learning. I reach over and pat Annabelle's knee. She wanted to be here to support Ashley. At first I wasn't keen on the idea of her missing school, but she reminded me that "being absent one day won't kill me." Of course she was right.

Benny stands next to Ashley and urges the judge to grant her leniency. He points out that Ashley comes from a respected family and nothing in her history suggests this kind of behavior is normal for her. He argues that she makes good grades, is a member of the volleyball and track teams, and even volunteers at a homeless shelter every month.

Ashley has me to thank for that last part. I've been on the board of St. Agatha's Night Shelter for going on three years. My main job is to spread awareness through our community about the need for volunteers. After I'd been there a year, I thought it a good idea to introduce the girls to community service, so I had them volunteer to serve dinner two nights a month. (This also helped them appreciate everything they enjoy in their lives.) Annabelle loves working there. She spends more than the two required days, mostly playing with the young children in the women's building. Ashley hates going, but probably not for the reasons you think. It makes her incredibly sad; her heart visibly aches for the people she finds there. You can see the anguish in her eyes. Still, it's important work, no matter how much it breaks your heart. She finds my reaction to her feelings rather harsh.

I bet she's thanking me for making her go now.

With her hands still shaking, Ashley seems to be staring into the judge's face while he makes notes in a file. It's so quiet I almost think I hear her heart beating in her chest. Or maybe that's the sound of mine. Steven is sitting to the left of me, holding my hand. It feels normal, having him so close to me that our knees are touching. To the judge it probably appears that we're a couple, man and wife, partners in life. It's so familiar I almost fool myself. Unfortunately, the feeling doesn't last long.

Reality kicks in, in the form of a certain someone clearing her throat. It's Monica, the homewrecker, seated directly behind Steven. I haven't the slightest idea why she's here. I quickly pull my hand from his and flash him a stern look. He knows exactly what I'm saying.

He seems to apologize with his eyes. I don't forgive him. This whole thing with Ashley has me wondering, would we be going through this if Steven and I hadn't split up? Is this some kind of by-product of divorce? It's hard on kids; I know that. It's hard on adults too. Would we still be navigating across this treacherous terrain if our family hadn't splintered? I reach over and grab Annabelle's hand. She squeezes mine in hers, the warmth spreading over my entire body. We look at each other and try to smile.

The judge puts down his pen and clasps his hands together. "Ms. Lange, it is this court's finding that you be sentenced to two years' probation, one hundred and fifty hours of community service, and drug and alcohol counseling. We will reconvene in one hundred and twenty days. Should you fail to adhere to any of the court's orders, you will be sent to county jail for a period of six months. You will need to have completed your service hours and drug counseling before we meet again in one hundred and twenty days. Am I making myself clear?"

Ashley nods. "Yes, sir. Thank you." She seems to go weak in the knees and practically collapses back in the chair before turning around to face me. Tears well up in her eyes as she looks from me to Steven. Then she says something I wasn't expecting. "I want to live with you, Dad."

Her words cut me to the quick. I am suddenly out of my mind with sadness. I wish my mom were still alive. I've just gone from feeling fear, to elation, to relief, and now agony. I'm not sure, but I think your mom is the only person who can help you digest all of those feelings, help you make sense of them, put them in their proper place.

I know my mom wasn't exactly that kind of mother to me and Benny. But in my fantasy, if my mother were here, she would drive me home, help me into sweatpants and a T-shirt, tuck me into bed, and ask me if I wanted her to make soup. Of course I would say yes, and after an hour she would deliver a tray with homemade tomato basil soup, buttery garlic toast, and a giant bowl of mint chocolate chip ice cream. She would put the tray on my lap and then hurry back to the kitchen to make me a steaming cup of tea. She would hold the mug in her hands, blowing on the hot liquid until she was sure it wouldn't burn my mouth. Then she would tell me how to fix everything in my life that's gone wrong.

She would call Steven just to tell him what a gigantic fool he's making of himself, carrying on with that silly twit of a girlfriend. She would sit Ashley down and shake her finger in her face and scold, "You should be ashamed of yourself, breaking your mother's heart like you're doing." She would take AB to the mall and let her buy the jeans she's been talking about for weeks now. And then she would come back to me, sit on the edge of the bed, and tell me to forget about Steven and move on. It would happen exactly like this; I just know it.

But the reality is Ashley wants to live with Steven, which means she doesn't want to live with me. Steven wants Monica, which means he doesn't want me. And my mom is dead, which means life is unbelievably cruel.

CHAPTER 11

Steven

Two days after Ashley's court appearance, the trunk slams with a thud. "I think that's the last of it," I announce.

Jesus, how much stuff can one seventeen-year-old own? I didn't have this many clothes when I was Ashley's age. Hell, I don't have this many clothes *now*.

I slide into the driver's seat. Ashley is already seated next to me, her eyes fixed on something out the front windshield. "Are you sure you don't want to tell her goodbye?" I ask her. "She's pretty upset. You should at least run back in the house and say goodbye."

"Can we just leave already? Please?" Ashley never looks at me. She's still staring straight ahead.

"Okay, but just so you know, I don't approve of the way you're behaving. I'm not even sure why you're so upset with your mother. From where I'm sitting, you screwed up. Your mom and I stood by you and supported you through a very scary, tense time, and—"

"Dad, please just...stop...okay? I know all of this already. Why do we have to keep rehashing all this crap? I messed up, big time, and now I'm paying for it. You won't understand what I'm feeling because you can't. Please just let me stay with you, and I won't be any more trouble. And I'm begging you...*please* stop talking to me about Mom. I can't deal with her any more. And I know she's happy I'm not her problem now."

I know that isn't true. I've never seen Sarah this upset. She wasn't even this devastated when I admitted to having an affair. She was pissed as hell, and probably wanted to chop off my penis, but she wasn't like she is right now. Today she let me hold her for a brief moment. It was like she forgot she hated me. For those few seconds we were on the same team again. She cried into my shoulder while I stroked her hair. We had come to an agreement about Ashley.

I know it was hard for Sarah to concede to letting Ashley move in with me, even temporarily, but we decided it might be a change for the better. Maybe a part of her is relieved to see Ashley leave. But it's a tiny part—microscopic. She hasn't said as much, and she would never admit it, but I know her pretty well. We only live a few miles apart, so Ashley won't really be all that distanced from her. I bought a place close by so the girls wouldn't feel like I'd totally abandoned them. I guess we'll see how this plan goes.

I was still holding Sarah when Ashley walked in the room.

"You have got to be kidding me right now. What, are you guys getting back together?"

Her words had cut through the air like ninja swords. If her intention was to rip Sarah and me apart, it worked. Sarah shoved me away and ran after Ashley. I heard Ashley screaming down the hall: "Don't touch me. Get away from me. *I hate you!*"

Sarah ran back in the room, flew past me, and slammed the bathroom door shut. She hadn't come out when we left the house.

After another moment, I finally back the car down the driveway. As we turn left down Main Street, headed for my condo, Ashley turns to me and says, "And for the record, I don't approve of the way you're behaving either."

My right eye begins twitching, and I feel a hurricane of hot lava rush over me. I jerk the steering wheel into a hard right and drive into the parking lot of the Quick Lube, tires screeching to a halt. I throw the car in Park and grab Ashley by the shoulder. "You listen here, you ungrateful little brat. I don't know who the fuck you think you're talking to, but I'll tell you this: If you *ever* speak to me *or your mother* this way again, your ass will be on the street. *Mark my words.*"

I'm not going to lie. The way her eyes are boring into mine is scaring me a little. She is hollow, distant, and suddenly I feel as if this girl sitting next to me is a stranger. She isn't my Ashley. I don't know who this person is, but she's not my daughter.

"I'm sorry."

Those turned out to be the only words she said to me for the next two days.

I've called Sarah with updates, but I have almost nothing to report. Ashley has stayed in her room with the door closed most of the time. I really just wanted an excuse to talk to Sarah anyway, to hear her voice. I know it's killing her, this distance, this…whatever is going on between her and Ashley, and I just want her to be okay.

Monica is trying to be helpful. She keeps telling me, "*Girls need space. They need separation from their mothers sometimes. This is pretty normal for a girl Ash's age.*"

I want to believe her. I want what she's saying to be true. But I don't know. This feels like more than just "needing space." This feels like some real, life-changing damage is being done. I have never felt so helpless.

By the third day, Sarah sounds better on the phone. She's even laughing, telling me a story about how she scared herself half to death and then was almost arrested for murder.

"What the hell are you talking about?"

She explains that yesterday she went to the back of the garage to look for the plastic bin that contains her old cheerleading uniforms. Something about someone wanting to borrow one for some costume party, I don't know. She forgot the six-foot-tall mummy she puts on the front porch at Halloween was back there, and when she saw him, she screamed bloody murder. The old man next door, Mr. Winton, heard her screams and called the police, assuming the worst. In the meantime Sarah decided to prank Annabelle and dragged the mummy down the driveway. The police showed up right about then and pulled their guns on Sarah, yelling at her to drop to her knees because they thought she was dragging a body.

At this point in the story I really begin to laugh, picturing Sarah on her knees with her arms above her head while the police check on the guy, only to discover it isn't a body at all, but a Halloween decoration.

We laughed for a full five minutes. It was glorious.

CHAPTER 12

Daniel

I haven't been this nervous in a long time. I've had other dates come to my house, but none of them was Sarah. I look over the room and do a mental check. There are no shoes lying around. The pillows are placed neatly on the sofa. The furniture is dusted, and I even lit a candle and put it on the coffee table. It feels a bit chilly in the house. I think about lighting a fire in the fireplace. Will that seem too intimate? Too romantic? I don't know what to do, so I decide to forget the idea for now. I wish there was an 800 number I could call to get advice for this kind of shit.

I'm pacing back and forth, looking out the front window every few seconds like a girl waiting for her prom date. Pathetic. I've known Sarah for what now, a couple of weeks? Why am I getting so worked up about her coming over?

This takes me right back to high school. I wasn't the most popular guy, but I wasn't a pariah either. I was somewhere right in the middle, which can be worse. If you're popular, there's a place for you at the top. If you're a lowlife, your rightful place is at the bottom. But if you're somewhere in the middle? You don't really fit anywhere.

I'm making it sound like high school was bad. It wasn't. Parts of it were even great.

There was this girl, Kelly Finch, who was the most beautiful thing I'd seen in my seventeen years on Earth. She transferred from some small town in Oklahoma and was a junior like me. It took exactly three minutes after enrolling for her to rise to the top of the Most Popular list. The girls fought over who was going to be her new best friend. She didn't seem to notice the locker room wars being waged between the cliques. Who Kelly would be going to Homecoming with quickly became the entire student body's favorite topic.

I didn't give two shits about all that. I just thought she was a goddess sent directly from heaven. She had the greenest eyes and the prettiest long, flowing hair. It was the color of butterscotch. Her smile was crazy infectious too. I'd never seen teeth so white or so straight. Every guy had the hots for Kelly, and some girls too. You can't imagine how many closet lesbians came out of hiding when Kelly made her way down the upperclassmen hall that first morning. She just had that effect on people.

On top of being gorgeous and gifted with the body of a swimsuit model, Kelly was the sweetest girl in school. I heard through the grapevine that after being at our school a few weeks, she went to Mr. Avery (the principal, a real ballbuster) with some new ideas. Apparently he was not immune to Kelly either, because very shortly after their meeting, something changed. From then on, every morning after the announcements over the school's loudspeaker, Kelly would deliver a Thought for the Day. This was totally unexpected, and nice.

You could hear the sincerity in her voice as she quoted Eleanor Roosevelt: "You gain strength, courage, and confidence by every experience in which…you really stop to look fear in the face…You must do the thing you think you cannot do." It seemed like she really wanted us to be the best we could be. Or I could've had such a hard-on for her that I let myself believe that. Nevertheless, Kelly Finch was, in my book, the girl to measure every other girl against.

She knew who I was, and she may have even considered me a friend. I sat next to her in anatomy class our senior year. When it was time to pick lab partners, she turned to me and said, "You have to be my partner, Danny."

I nearly choked on my own spit. The thought of dissecting a sheep's heart had never been so appealing. And the way my name came out of her mouth—it was almost too much. So, yes, of course I agreed to be her lab partner. Anatomy quickly became my favorite class, even though I was squeamish when it came to blood and guts and shit like that. Being close enough to smell her shampoo and her bubblegum-scented lip gloss was enough to get me an A in anatomy. On top of acing the course, I never once skipped class. The same cannot be said for my other subjects.

After graduation, Kelly went to school somewhere in the southeast—Auburn University, I think. I went to college in Denton and didn't keep up with anyone from high school. After some time passed, though, I started to look forward to seeing Kelly at our ten-year reunion. I wondered if she was still as beautiful and sweet as she'd been all those years ago. I wanted to meet the lucky guy who got to call her his wife, the man who would forever get to smell her and touch her.

But when I arrived, I found out Kelly wouldn't be attending the reunion. She wouldn't be doing anything anymore. Kelly Finch and her unborn baby had died in a terrible car accident six months before the reunion. I cried actual tears. That was the last time I remember crying, aside from the days my daughters were born.

I don't know why I'm thinking about Kelly now, other than to say Sarah is the only woman since Kelly who's stirred up these kinds of feelings. I can't even say that about Jackie.

I look at my watch. It reads 6:30 on the dot.

Just then I hear the sound of a car door, and when I look out the window this time, Sarah sees me and waves. I take a deep breath and walk to the front door.

"You look beautiful," I tell her as I open it. And she does. God, she's prettier every time I see her.

"Thank you." She smiles. "You're not too bad yourself." She walks straight into my arms and wraps herself around me. I'm doomed.

We stand there like that, holding each other, for a solid minute. Again my mind is busy studying her, memorizing the firmness of her body, the smell of her hair, her perfume, feeling her breath on my neck. It's all I can do not to rip off her clothes and take her right here in the entryway.

She finally pulls away and says, "So are you giving me a tour or what?"

We spend the next twenty minutes walking through my condo as I point out the bedroom, bathroom, kitchen—you get it. The tour should have taken exactly thirty seconds. But Sarah stops and studies every photo in every frame, asking questions about where they were taken and making comments like, "You look really happy." or "You have enormous biceps." I especially like when she says that. She definitely knows how to build a guy's confidence, that's for sure.

We end up in the kitchen, standing on opposite sides of the so-called island (it's really an extension of the counter, but the realtor insisted it was an island) while I struggle to open a bottle of wine. My hands are shaking, literally. I haven't been this nervous about a woman since…ever. I can look around the room and point to the different places I've kissed women over the past year or so, but none of those times felt like this. This scares me a little.

"Here, let me help you with that." Sarah reaches across to grab the bottle. Our hands touch, and electricity courses through my veins. The hairs on my arms stand at attention. She pops the cork with ease and pours the fragrant red liquid into two glasses. I watch her face while she does this, wishing I could read her mind.

"You want to know what I'm thinking?" she says as she lifts her glass to her mouth.

Well, that's a little spooky. "Very much so." I take too big a gulp of wine, and now my throat burns.

She doesn't seem to notice that I'm struggling to keep it all together. If she does, she's not running for the door, so that's a good sign.

"I think we should light the fireplace and rent a movie and order a pizza and…make out like teenagers. Is that too forward of me? Please say no."

I'm left speechless. I'm just standing there, holding my wine glass, staring at this beautiful, quirky woman.

"Oh God, too much?" Sarah puts her glass on the counter and covers her face with her hands. "I shouldn't have said that part about making out. Now you think I'm crazy. Or slutty. Or both."

I realize my silence is making her feel this way, which isn't my intention at all. Do I want to make out with her? Well, that's a big *fuck yes*. I just can't believe she's the one suggesting it.

I hurry to her side of the "island," pull her to me, and dive my mouth into hers. It's rough at first, tongues thrashing, lips and teeth in the wrong place at the wrong time, but after a few seconds, we get into a rhythm. And it rocks. We stand there, wrapped up in each other, kissing like we're in it to win, for God only knows how long.

During a pause to catch my breath, I pull back, grab her by the hand, and steer her into my bedroom. I only hesitate for a split second. I wonder if this will freak her out and leave her to assume I'm going to try to get her naked. It is definitely my intention to take off her clothes; I just don't know yet if that's what she wants.

Turns out she wants it.

It hasn't been that long since I last had sex. It has, however, been a long time since sex was this good. My God, this woman is incredible in bed. And quite knowledgeable too. People assume a single man will automatically go for a much younger woman. And I admit, there are perks to being with someone younger. But there are a lot of negatives too, which, in my experience, outweigh the good. The thing about a woman in her forties is this: she knows what she wants and what she doesn't want. She knows her body and knows what makes her feel good. She doesn't mind telling a man or showing a man how to get her off, because she doesn't have time to waste on bad sex. I find that extremely erotic. I generally come way too fast under these circumstances. I'm already thinking about the next time I get to be inside her.

Hours later, I'm standing in the middle of the driveway wearing nothing but blue jeans and a giant smile. Sarah looks at me one more time, blows me a kiss, and waves before driving off. I feel a tugging in my chest. It's not an unfamiliar feeling, but one I've experienced only a few times in my life. It's exciting and terrifying all at once. I must be crazy to have these kinds of feelings for someone I just met and hardly know.

I can try to deny it all I want, but it won't change the outcome. I'm falling hard and fast for this one.

CHAPTER 13

Sarah

My vagina has never been this sore. Seriously, I can barely walk.

I keep going over it in my mind. His hands, his lips, his tongue…*oh God, his tongue.* It was the most intense sexual experience of my life. Not that sex with Steven wasn't great. It was great. Okay, it wasn't great. It was good…really good. And to be honest, I wouldn't have known the difference between good sex and great sex had I not just had *amazing* sex with Daniel. Are you kidding me with his body and his, you know, penis? Jesus Christ on a cracker, I'm going to need more of that, please.

I don't even care if what just happened makes me a little whoreish. My good name is worth scandalizing if I can keep doing that with him. I don't know how to explain how or what went on back there, but it almost makes me want to post it on Facebook.

Status: *Sarah Lange just tried the reverse cowboy for the first time and* is loving life. *Sorry, not sorry.*

I probably should hold off posting my sex life on social media, if for no other reason than people don't generally like braggers.

By the way, I had seven orgasms. *Seven.*

I really need to get control of myself and my emotions. I feel drunk even though I had only a few sips of wine before the whole making-out thing happened. It surprised me a little when I was forward in the kitchen, but I just couldn't stand it one more minute. We've been flirting for a couple of weeks, the stress of my real life has taken its toll on my mental state, and I just had to put it out there. I'm grateful he took charge of the situation (and of me) and...well, let's just say I'm a pretty satisfied customer.

He wanted me to stay. It was hard to leave, but AB is home alone, and I can't forget I still have people who need me and count on me to be there. Ashley may hate me right now, but I still have one child who wants her mom. Being a responsible adult sucks sometimes—it really does.

My phone beeps. At a stop sign I reach in my handbag to find it. It's a text message from Annabelle:

Spending the night at Kelsey's. Love you.

I look around for any oncoming traffic and make an illegal U-turn in the middle of the intersection.

CHAPTER 14

Ashley

"Are you sure they're not coming home?"

God, sometimes Russell is so lame. "Yes, I'm sure. My dad and his girlfriend went to Houston for the weekend. They won't be home until late Sunday. How many times do I have to tell you this? You're annoying the shit out of me."

Russell suddenly looks like a pouty little two-year-old. "Okay! Sorry. I just don't want to get caught. You should worry too, you know? I mean, it wasn't that long ago that we got in trouble."

I am now regretting inviting him over to my dad's house. But he's the only person I know who has pot. And Xanax. And he will have sex with me without expecting a blowjob. I hate giving blowjobs. I mean, seriously, pee comes out of that thing. I don't want pee in my mouth.

"Do you want a beer? My dad keeps some in the garage."

Russell grabs his T-shirt off the back of the sofa, pulls it over his head, and walks down the hallway to the garage. I reach under the table and locate my panties.

Russell and I don't have sex very often, but I like him (except on days like today when he's being lame), and I know he wouldn't hang out with me if I didn't put out, so I mostly just lay there and wait for it to be over. I don't really get what the big deal is with sex. It seems pretty primitive to me. The groaning sounds he makes when he's coming are the same sounds I imagine cave people made when they were trying to communicate with each other a bazillion years ago.

I go to his backpack and dig through the front pocket until I find the familiar plastic pill bottle. I just want to chill, you know? One Xanax, a couple of hits off a joint, and a beer or two is not a big deal. It's not like I'm shooting heroin or something crazy like that. Everyone I know does this same thing. It's just everyone else's parents don't get all freaked out about it like mine.

My mom really pissed me off. The way she was crying in court last week, her eyes told me everything. She's disappointed in me and embarrassed to have me as a daughter, and I don't give a shit anymore. I tried to be the person she'd envisioned, but it was too much. Even her own brother barely talks to her. What does that say about her? She's not as great a person as she thinks she is. Her own brother dislikes her. So she and Annabelle can just be best friends and go through life all mother-daughter-like, and I'll do my own thing. And right now doing my own thing means just chilling on a Saturday with Russell.

I still can't believe Dad left me here by myself. Like, I seriously don't know how it even happened. But I promised I wouldn't have people over (a tiny white lie) and I would stay home and work on my research paper. Fuck that. My teacher is whack. You know she actually assigned a five-page research paper to be due the Friday before spring break? Who does that? Our topic choices are: *The impact of consumerism on society and government; Should recycling plastic be mandatory?; Should cloning be legalized and practiced on a large scale?; Nuclear weapons and their use, impact, and future.*

I'm falling asleep just thinking about those topics. Nobody cares about any of that stuff. Trust me.

Russell hands me a beer, and I put the cold aluminum can to my lips and take a swig. The fizzy liquid is exactly what I need. I pop a tablet in my mouth and wash it down with another sip. Russell plugs his iPhone into the iHome and puts on his favorite playlist, which I just so happened to make for him. I lay my head back on the sofa and slowly feel my body doing what it does on days like this. I'm fading away.

I wake up. There are two people having sex on the couch next to me. I turn onto my side and close my eyes again.

The next time I open them, I see Russell and some kid I don't know taking bong hits. My eyes are so heavy I can't manage to keep them open.

The last time I remember waking up, I see Russell and Amanda making out. Fucking asshole.

CHAPTER 15

Steven

It's Sunday afternoon, and I know something is wrong as soon as we pull up in the driveway. Through the front windows I can see that every light is on in the house. When I get to it, the front door is unlocked, and music washes over me as I step inside. Ashley is lying on the sofa, and my first thought is that she's dead. Her skin is pale, her body limp and lifeless. I almost don't recognize her at first—the way her eyes sink into her face and her lips curl under. I feel like I'm looking at a stranger.

I rush to her and try to rouse her, but she is out of it, obviously fucked up on something. What was she trying to do, commit suicide?

I can tell other people have been here too.

"Ashley, wake up. *Wake up!*" She's breathing. She has a pulse. She's alive—she's definitely alive. She's just really out of it.

I shake her a couple more times, and she finally groans and slurs a few words together. "What do you want?"

I sigh and look around the room, surveying the damage. I count roughly seventeen beer bottles, two pizza boxes, an empty prescription pill bottle, and someone's underwear.

"Steven, come in the kitchen!" Monica sounds frantic.

I rush in there to find the refrigerator door standing wide open and an entire gallon of milk poured on the hardwood floor. The wood under the milk is already beginning to swell, indicating it's been like this for quite a long time. This will cost a fortune to repair.

Monica gets busy cleaning the floor while I walk from room to room, wondering what other horrors await me.

That's when I notice things are missing. There's an empty spot on the bookshelf where my signed Troy Aikman helmet used to be. I paid five thousand dollars for it two years ago at a charity auction. Gone. I hurry into my closet where I keep my gold watch. It's not there. Fury and anger are quickly rising to the surface, and I suddenly have the urge to punch something (or someone). I notice then that both of my hands are clenched so tightly my knuckles are turning white.

"Steven!"

I follow the sound of Monica's voice to the bathroom in the hall. I nearly vomit when I see the overflowing shit and piss all over the floor. Again, the hardwood is beginning to buckle. I cannot believe this is happening.

I know what I have to do. I call Sarah.

The phone rings seven or eight times and then goes to voicemail. I'm unsure what to say. *"Hey, it's Steven. Our daughter is fucked up on drugs and trashed my house—no big deal. Anyhoo, give me a call. Toodles!"*

I hang up. I'll just try again in a few minutes.

I find Monica in our room, crying. "Steven, look what they did to my things."

It's bad. Whoever was here tossed several pairs of Monica's panties up onto the ceiling fan. Her makeup (which I can only assume is expensive) is broken and smashed on the vanity table in the bathroom. Monica is one of these sentimental types who saves everything. She has a box where she keeps every note, card, and even some of the flower petals from bouquets I've given her. The box has been dumped on our bed, the memories scattered and crumbled and ruined. I have never seen her cry like this before. And I am the angriest I have ever been in my life.

I charge back to the living room and find Ashley sitting upright. I have to really hold back so I don't physically harm her. "*What the fuck have you done!?*"

She flinches, like she's expecting me to hit her or something. "What? Why are you yelling at me?"

"Why am I yelling at you? Are you kidding me right now? *My house is trashed. My stuff has been stolen. What the hell did you do?"*

"Dad, chill out. I don't even know what you're talking about. I've been asleep."

"Look at this place, Ash. People were here. You had people over. Whoever was here poured milk on the kitchen floor. It's ruined. The toilet in the hall is overflowing. Shit is *everywhere*. My watch, my helmet...*gone*. No telling what else is missing. I haven't even looked through everything because everywhere I turn, it's a fucking nightmare."

"Oh my God, Dad, you think I did this? Why would I trash my own house?"

"I don't know, Ashley. Why would you? And for the record, this isn't your house. This is *my house*, and you don't get to stay here anymore." I didn't plan to say that last part. I'm not sure I even meant it. It just came out.

My phone rings, and I pull it out of my back pocket. It's Sarah. Suddenly I think I'm going to puke.

CHAPTER 16

Sarah

It's crazy how fast a person can go from feeling like her life is wonderful to *oh my God this is the end of the world.*

As soon as Steven answers the phone, I can tell he's frantic and something is terribly wrong—just by the way he says *hello*.

He begins telling me what has happened, and all I can do is say "Oh my God" over and over again. Minutes before calling Steven, I was sitting at the table in Daniel's kitchen, sipping coffee and talking and laughing. This started out to be one of my favorite days. After taking in the information Steven has thrown at me, I hang up the phone and begin to cry.

"What's wrong? What happened?" Daniel stands next to me now, rubbing my back. I hadn't noticed him getting up and coming over.

"It's Ashley. She's done something horrible again. Apparently drugs are involved. I'm sorry, I have to go."

As if my body is operating on autopilot, I get up from the table, pour my coffee down the sink, rinse the mug, dry it, set it on the counter, and hurry to the bedroom to gather my things. I think Daniel is talking to me, but I can't be sure. I keep hearing what I think are words coming from him, but they're muffled. It reminds of the Charlie Brown cartoons when the parents speak. I don't have time to stay and figure out what he's saying; I have to get to Steven's house.

I have the sudden urge to run away from home.

It's funny, I've never had this feeling before. Even when I was a kid and my dad was drunk and my mom weak and detached, I never wanted to leave. I wanted to have a different *family*, or I wanted my family to *be* different, but I never once thought of running away. Maybe it was so unrealistic a desire that my brain pushed it away before the idea had time to fully develop. But now, in this moment, I can easily see myself driving onto the freeway and leaving town, never to return.

I don't remember driving to Steven's, but somehow I'm here, parked out front, my hands gripping the steering wheel as if my life depends on it. If I let go, I will plummet over a cliff to my death or trigger a bomb that will cause the car to explode. I take a couple of deep breaths and turn off the ignition. I pick up my phone and text Annabelle:

Can you stay at Kelsey's a little while longer?
Something has come up. I can pick you up later.
Let me know.

She quickly replies *OK*, and I shove my phone back in my purse.

As I step out of the car, I see Steven standing on the front porch, hands on his hips, looking much older than his forty-five years.

"What happened?" I throw my purse over my shoulder, shut the car door, and head toward the house.

"You won't believe it, Sar. It's an absolute fucking nightmare." Steven holds the door for me as I walk past him.

Once inside, it starts to sink in what's taken place. First, it smells like a port-a-potty. I pinch my nose with my fingers and suggest we open some windows. I turn to the living room, and there's Ashley, sitting. She sees me and leaps off the sofa. She runs to me and throws her arms around me.

"Mom, I'm so glad you're here. Can I please go home? I want to go home."

I push her away from me and hold her by the elbows, looking into her bloodshot eyes. She seems flat, almost hollow. Her eye makeup is smeared, and her hair is a mess—matted and sticky. She reeks of body odor and cigarettes.

Steven sighs loudly and says, "I'm going to see what all is missing and check on Monica. You deal with her." He leaves the two of us standing there.

"How could you do this, Ashley? What's wrong with you? Tell me right now: what drugs are you on?"

"Jesus, Mother. You and Dad need to stop. I'm not on drugs! How many times do I have to tell you this? Yes, I fucked up. *Again*. I'm sorry. God, how many times do I have to say it? I made a mistake. I lied to Dad and had a few people over. We drank some beers, and I took a Xanax, which I *know* for a fact you take sometimes too. I must have passed out and some of the kids did some stuff…I don't know, Mom. I'm sorry. I was *asleep*. I wouldn't have ever let this happen if I'd been *awake*."

This is where my head feels like it's going to spin in circles and launch itself right off my shoulders. "You think you can get out of this because you were *asleep?* No, that's not how this works. First, you disobeyed your dad and had people over without permission. How you were even allowed to be alone is another matter altogether. It doesn't even matter at this point.

"Second, you took *drugs* and had people over and let things get out of hand. Who are these people who were here anyway—friends of yours? Was Russell Berry involved? Because the two of you are banned from spending time together. These friends of yours *stole* your dad's things. They vandalized his property. And you think you can catch a break because you were *asleep?* I don't even know what to say to you right now. I have no idea who you are. You look like somebody I know, but I don't know *you*. *You* are out of control."

Ashley throws her arms back so forcefully and suddenly that I lose my balance and land on my butt.

Just as I hit the floor, Steven reappears and runs to me, screaming at Ashley. "Did you hit your mother? Sarah, did she hit you?"

He pulls me up, and I set my purse on the chair next to the door. "No, I just lost my balance. I'm okay."

I can see Ashley seething. It's as if there's a wild animal inside her, clawing its way to the surface beneath her skin.

"I'm not going to stay here while you two gang up on me and blame me for everything." She moves past us and goes to open the door.

Steven stops her by grabbing her arm. "If you take one more step for that door, I'll call the police."

"You'd call the cops on your own daughter? What kind of parents *are* you, anyway?"

Steven calmly replies, "The kind that will press charges if you don't shut your fucking mouth."

I'm sitting on the sofa in Steven's wrecked living room trying to figure out what to do. What does a person do at a time like this? The worst part of this whole situation is that not one of us saw it coming. There was no gradual decline in Ashley's behavior, nothing that would trigger some warning of things to come. Yes, she's moody and hormonal and unpleasant to be around a lot of the time, but that's normal for a girl her age. I remember acting exactly the same way when I was seventeen. There's been no trouble in school that I'm aware of, and she's always maintained a B average. It must sound cliché, but honestly, all the destructive shit she's doing lately happened overnight. We didn't have time to prepare ourselves to deal with it. How does a parent even go about preparing for something like this?

After some yelling and pleading, we are able to drag out a list of names of people who were here the night of the party. The whole time Ashley seems more concerned about how her "friends" will feel having her dad call them to see if he can get back his stolen items than how having them stolen affected him. It's hard, as a parent, to fully understand why and when a child's loyalty shifts from her family to her peers. We would do anything for our kids, and yet for a space in time they turn on us, choosing outsiders over blood. It's hard to describe the aching, empty feeling where your heart used to be. You're left to wonder—will I ever get it back?

While Ashley showers in the hall bathroom, Steven looks up the phone numbers of the boys on the list and hits pay dirt on the very first one. Some boy I've never heard of named Brent admits to stealing the helmet and the gold watch. He apologizes to Steven and says the stuff is in the trunk of his Honda Civic. I am shocked at how calm and reasonable Steven sounds on the phone as he promises to not call the police if his things are returned. His offer does come with a warning: Brent has exactly two hours to bring back his prized helmet and expensive watch. He hangs up the phone and looks at the clock. The doorbell rings forty-seven minutes later.

Ashley reappears (cleaner and less hungover looking) and perks up after Brent returns Steven's things. She seems relieved and even suggests we all go out to eat. This strikes me as extremely odd. It's like she thinks, *Okay, Dad, you got your stuff back. Are you happy now? Who wants sushi?* Steven and I look at each other, and he proceeds to tell her she isn't getting off that easy.

From that point on, it's obvious she's detached herself from her actions the previous night. She honestly seems like two different people. Earlier she was spaced out and moody and mean. A few hours later, now she's over it and ready to move on. She shows little, if any, remorse for trashing her dad's house and disobeying his rules.

The final blow is when she announces, "I don't know if you know this about me or not, but I get over things pretty quickly. Like, what happened yesterday is in the past, and you have to let it go."

I don't even know where to go from here.

Steven and I spend the next week searching the internet and reading articles about teenagers with behavioral/substance abuse issues. These recent episodes with Ashley are the first time we've really had to come together as a team in our post-married life. It's been easy for the most part, except for the times I've wanted to blame him for what happened at his house. I've lost hours of sleep wondering what was going on in his head that made him think it was okay to leave Ashley unsupervised. When I can't stand it any longer, I confront him.

We are sitting at the table in my kitchen. "I want to say this as non-threatening as I can," I start.

Steven takes off his reading glasses and turns to face me. "I know what you're going to say. How could I leave Ashley alone overnight."

I'm a little surprised he hit it on the head. I forget how well he knows me. "Well…yes."

"Honestly, Sarah, I don't know what I was thinking. She looked at me dead in the eyes and swore on her life she would just stay there and order a pizza and work on her research paper. She agreed to no visitors and no going anywhere. I fell for it hook, line, and sinker. I didn't want to bother you with it. I'm pissed at myself."

I pat him on the back. It's obvious he's really torn up. He looks terrible. And old. "It's okay. But if I'd known you needed to leave town, I would have made her come home with me."

He suddenly gets defensive. "Yeah, I get that now, Sarah. Woulda, shoulda, coulda. Jesus. I said I'm sorry. I fucked up. Now can we just agree that we need to figure out what to do going forward?"

The hair on my arms stands up. It's the second time he's snapped at me in recent weeks. And both times have been because of Ashley. "Yes, I'm sorry."

When I met with Dr. K a few days after the nightmare at Steven's house, she was very helpful in letting me work out my need to point the finger in his direction. She helped me redirect my anger at the real problem: Ashley's bad behavior.

Dr. K gave me the name and number of a hospital fifteen minutes away in Arlington that specializes in teenagers with substance abuse and behavioral issues. I made an appointment for Ashley to be assessed, and I wake her up early for it on Wednesday morning. She growls and pulls the blanket over her head. She's spent most of the last couple of days sleeping. I'm keeping her home from school until Steven and I figure out what to do.

We agreed that I would take her home with me after everything that happened over the weekend because Monica was so upset she was threatening to move out. Steven was terrified she would actually go through with it, so basically I saved their relationship by bringing Ashley home.

My life is so fucking weird. It's like an English version of a Spanish *telenovela*. I have never seen Steven so relieved. As for me, I have never felt more like a prison guard than I do this week.

I've spent a lot of time these last few terrible days sitting in my room, talking to Daniel on the phone. He's currently my only source of comfort. I filled him in on everything, and it says a lot about his character that he's still taking my calls. He has teenagers of his own; he doesn't need the burden of more adolescent drama. Yet he's still here, listening to me and offering unwavering support. I ache for him to hold me. I ache for my daughter to be okay.

"Get dressed, Ashley. We have to be in the car in fifteen minutes."

"What? Where are we even going? I'm tired, Mom. I just want to sleep."

"And I want you to behave better than you have recently. We don't always get what we want. Now get dressed, please, and meet me in the car."

I leave the room and hear her stumble out of bed and slam the door. I pour more coffee in my mug and notice my hands are shaking. Swimming in uncharted waters frightens me. Being a parent in this kind of rocky, unknown territory scares me. The thought of the future stirs up fear in my mind and forms a heavy weight in my stomach. I know how to parent a newborn. I know babies cry for every reason and no reason at all. I can manage the sleep schedule, or the lack of sleep schedule. I can fix boo boos with Band-Aids and potty train like a champ. I can teach a child the alphabet and check under the bed for monsters. But I don't have the slightest idea how to do this.

As we pull out of the driveway, Ashley asks, "Where are we going, anyway?"

"I told you. We have an appointment with a child psychologist."

"God, Mother, this *again?* First you and Dad go ape-shit on me, then you keep me practically locked in my room. I mean, you're not even letting me go to school, which is laughable. And now you're dragging me to the doctor because you think I'm crazy? You people are unbelievable. I cannot *wait* until I'm eighteen. August cannot get here soon enough."

That's one thing I'm grateful for right now. She's still a few months from being a legal adult. This week I have researched rehabs and youth ranches. I even called a few of them and spoke with the directors. Pretty much the first question any of them asks is, "Is your daughter eighteen yet? Because you can't force her to go to rehab if she's over eighteen."

We drive the rest of the way in silence. I don't have the strength to keep arguing with Ashley. Every minute of the last several days has been tortuous: We sit together at the table and eat in silence. The only sounds are our forks as we move the food around on our plates. I've tried to talk to her. I brought up fun things we've done—like the time I took her to the American Girl store in Chicago, a surprise trip when she turned ten. I remember her face as she stood outside the massive metal-and-glass building, the way she ran from one corner of the store to another, like she was trying to take it all in as fast as she could. I remember spending a lot more money on doll clothes than I had intended, but I couldn't say no to those big brown eyes.

Now it all feels like a life I didn't actually live—something I watched on some made-for-TV movie. This older version of the girl with the big brown eyes is different, harder to please. I can't seem to reach her anymore. She doesn't want to hear stories about the good times we've had, and I don't understand why. She wants to argue with me about everything. I can't keep having the same conversation over and over and not get anywhere with it. Ashley is not in a place to take responsibility for any of her actions, so we just keep getting bogged down in this never-ending back and forth—and dammit, I just want to have sex with Daniel and pretend like none of this is happening.

I might need to make another appointment with my therapist.

This is the hardest decision I've ever had to make.

After a week of therapy appointments and assessments by psychologists for Ashley, Steven and I make a plan. It hasn't been easy getting here, that's for sure. We have been tested, our parenting skills honed and tweaked and challenged. No one prepares you for this scenario. There's no user guide or how-to manual with step-by-step instructions. And yet, when you find yourself here, you just strap on your boots and head up the hill. It's the scariest place I've ever been. Every day it feels like my heart is being ripped out of my chest.

It has been recommended that we take Ashley out of her current environment and send her to a program in Utah that specializes in teenagers with destructive behavior. Utah. It seems so far away. I know nothing about Utah, having never been. And yet I'm at a place in my life where Utah sounds like an answer to my problem. Weird how things happen you don't expect.

I found the program online and read countless reviews before I spoke at length with the director. He seems knowledgeable enough. And he thinks Ashley would be a good fit for the program. The second conversation we had we did on speakerphone so Steven could be involved too. After we hung up I asked him, "What do you think?"

"I think Ashley is going to Utah," he said. His face seemed to drain of all its color.

Sending Ashley to this program in Utah is drastic—I'm the first to admit that—and we have other options. There's a weekday program she could attend. I could drop her off there every morning at nine and pick her up at five. She would get her classwork done and have one-on-one therapy and group sessions. The downside is that after five o'clock and on the weekends, she's right back in the same place: same people, same friends, same patterns, same routines.

At first, the thought of her being away from home for three or more months terrified me. I couldn't imagine it. The longest I've gone without seeing either of my girls was when Steven and I went to Europe for ten days for our tenth anniversary. I couldn't wait to get home and snuggle with them. I probably hugged and kissed each of them a thousand times when I saw their sweet little faces. It seems like a long time ago that I felt something like that for my girls. I wonder if that makes me a bad mother.

Steven is the only person who really understands what I'm going through, and I'm thankful we're able to be there for each other—although obviously it's different from what I feel with Daniel. Steven is as emotionally invested in the relationship with Ashley as I am because he's her dad. He *has* to stick around and help me sort through this. Or at least he should. And because I know the kind of man he is, I know he will.

However, on the other side of that, Daniel is the much-needed objective, emotionally uninvolved person who also tells me everything will be okay. He seems to have raised great girls. He mostly listens as I share my fears and my worries. It's not like he has any real answers for me; no one knows exactly if this is the right thing to do. We're winging it at this point—throw it against the wall, see if it sticks. Together the two of them are keeping me from losing my mind.

Steven and I spend a lot of time at the coffee house downtown on the square trying to work out all the details. There are seventy forms to fill out before the program will admit Ashley. There's the cost: forty thousand dollars. And then there's trying to figure out how to get her there. Families in this situation have two options: You can take your child to the program yourself and save money. The downside is that your child will most likely beg and plead and make promises to do better if you give her one more chance. The director of the program we chose warned us that while this is the most economical way to get your child to Utah, it's also the most emotionally difficult.

The second option is to hire a transport team. This is the easiest on the parents of the child, but costly. You have to pay for the husband-and-wife transport team's airfare to your city and back, and their fee. It adds another six thousand dollars to the cost of the program, but this is the option we're choosing. Ashley will be taken in the middle of the night, completely unaware any of this is happening.

Every time I start to imagine what that's going to be like, I feel sick to my stomach. She will be caught totally off guard, awakened from sleep. She will most likely fight and yell and scream and resist, but they tell me eventually she'll give up and go with them. I hope we're making the right decision.

I'm lost in thought when there's a knock on my bedroom door. "Mom, are you in there?" I hear Annabelle ask.

"Just a second," I say as I scramble to get the paperwork into a pile and then shove it under my pillow.

"What's taking so long? I need to talk to you." She sounds impatient.

"Come in. Sorry, I was getting dressed."

Annabelle opens the door, looks at me, and makes a face. "You were getting dressed? That's what you were wearing earlier today."

I look down at my Baylor T-shirt and running shorts and suddenly realize I've been wearing an outfit like this for going on two weeks. I should consider dressing better. "Oh. Well...what did you need, sweetie?"

Annabelle plops down on my bed, and I can't help but look over at the pillow I shoved the papers under. I didn't do a very good job of hiding them. More than a few are peeking out the corner. Maybe she won't notice. I'm trying my best to keep this a secret from AB too. She'll find out soon enough.

"Something is going on, and I want you to tell me."

Crap.

"You and Dad are meeting each other at the coffee place."

I put my hands on my hips. "How in the world do you know that?"

"So it's true." Annabelle stiffens and crosses her legs.

Her moving around on the bed helps the forms inch out even more. If she turns around, she'll see them for sure.

"A girl in my homeroom has an older sister who works there. She said she saw you and Dad in there four times in the last week. She kinda has a crush on Dad, which is a little creepy, so she notices him."

The girl at the coffee shop? And Steven? Oh, this explains so much. Every time we've been there, the girl behind the counter gives Steven a blueberry scone for free.

"Mom!"

"Huh?"

"I asked if you and Dad are getting back together."

"Oh, heavens no, AB. We're just talking...you know, parenting stuff. We have to be on the same page when it comes to raising you girls."

Annabelle gets up and walks around the bed to hug me. "Whatever you and Dad decide to do about Ashley, I'm on board."

I pull away from her and look her in the eyes. "What are you talking about?"

"About Ashley and all the doctor appointments. She tells me things, and I have eyes and ears. I live here, you know. I know you and Dad are trying to figure out how to keep from losing Ashley. She's pretty messed up right now, if you haven't noticed."

Annabelle manages a smile and then walks out of my room, leaving me standing there like a giant buffoon.

After another week of filling out forms, countless discussions with Steven, and meetings with Dr. K, the date is set. Ashley is leaving for Utah tomorrow morning.

CHAPTER 17

Sarah

Marcus and Beverly seem like nice people. When they knocked on the door at four in the morning on Saturday, I was already standing in the foyer, pacing back and forth. My hands were shaking, and I'd never felt anything like this before. It was fear times a million. I questioned our decision over and over again. *Are we doing the right thing? Are we overreacting? Is this the right program? Will Ashley hate me?*

Marcus is soft-spoken with kind eyes, and the minute he went over the plan, I started to feel a little better. Beverly patted me on the back and held my hands in hers. They've done this before. They know what they're doing. Everything will be okay. I had no other option but to believe that.

Steven was late. I'm trying desperately not to be angry with him, but honestly, you can't be punctual the one time strangers are going to be taking your child a thousand miles from home? He should've been here before they arrived. I shouldn't have had to do any of this alone.

But the minutes ticked by, and then Marcus was ready. He kept checking his watch. The three of them have a seven o'clock in the morning flight scheduled and needed to be headed to the airport soon. I'd gathered the items for Ashley they requested, and I handed them to Beverly: a change of clothes for the plane ride, a coat, a toothbrush, a few photos, and her medication.

I took a deep breath and led them up the stairs to Ashley's room. I told myself we would do this with or without Steven.

And that made me think about the other times Steven hasn't been there for me. Once when we were dating, he forgot to pick me up from the airport. He was at work, and I was flying back from a friend's wedding in South Carolina. I stood on the curb for over an hour, waiting for him, looking at every car that drove past. When he finally remembered, I was so hurt I seriously considered breaking up with him. He apologized over and over again and told me there was a terrible accident on the freeway causing a huge traffic delay. I knew it was a lie—I could tell when Steven wasn't telling the truth. Years later, after we were married, he admitted he got busy at work and completely forgot about me.

Another time we were coming back from a family vacation in Hawaii. The girls were really small, probably two and four years old. At the airport, the gate agent told Steven he could upgrade to first class if he wanted. I laughed, saying, "Yeah, right. Like he's going to sit in first class while I stay back in coach with our children. Ha."

But he took the seat in first class. I couldn't believe it, couldn't believe Steven actually felt like this was okay. I'm not sure if I was too stunned or too hurt to say anything or put up a fight, but something inside me chose to keep quiet. He did make sure we got settled in our seats before finding his way to the front of the plane—not that it made me feel better. And I know a couple of people (both women) noticed what was happening because their eyes beamed sympathy toward me and bore daggers into Steven when he walked past them.

I remember that as the second time in our relationship that I'd felt completely unimportant to Steven. I sat near the back of the plane with two exhausted, restless toddlers for the eight-hour flight while Steven relaxed in his large, leather, reclining seat. A couple of hours into the flight he had the flight attendant bring back three chocolate chip cookies, as if that would make the whole situation better.

When I think back to that now, I realize I closed off a piece of myself from him after that. I lost some respect for him, and part of me fell out of love. Sometimes I still can't believe it really happened. But it did.

I was kind of having that feeling all over again as I stood with Marcus and Beverly outside Ashley's door. Marcus nodded for me to open it. I turned on the light as we'd planned and walked to Ashley's bedside as I'd been instructed. I placed my hand on her arm and shook her a little. She pulled away from me and groaned. I said her name a couple of times until she finally opened her eyes and looked at me.

The next five or so minutes felt like a slow-moving car crash. Ashley was confused and afraid...I was on the verge of breaking down... Oh yeah, Steven showed up...Ashley fought and screamed for help... Steven escorted me out of the room...There was more yelling...

I'd like to give him a piece of my mind for being late at the worst possible time, for making me feel less than important all over again. He's good at that. But somehow I don't even have the energy to confront him right now. And I suppose without him I might still be standing frozen in Ashley's room.

My anger has evaporated into fear and horror at what we've done, and now we're hiding behind the door in my bedroom just waiting for this to be over...It turns silent...The front door opens and closes...I hear nothing but the sound of my own heart beating...My knees buckle, and I fall into a heap on the floor. Steven stands over me, trying unsuccessfully to hide his emotions. He's bawling like a baby.

It's over. She's gone.

CHAPTER 18

Daniel

Headlights shine through the three windows in my den. I hurry to the front door and open it before Sarah can knock. I'm on my second cup of coffee, so there's a slight buzzing in my head. Too much caffeine on an empty stomach has that effect on me.

Sarah looks pitiful, the poor thing—like she just got the shit kicked out of her in a boxing match. Her tear-stained face and puffy eyes say it all: she's heartbroken.

She throws her arms around my waist, burying her head in the place between my chest and shoulder. The cool early-morning breeze is a reminder winter isn't over yet, and I pull her inside and close the door.

It takes a while for her to start talking. We spend the first half-hour sitting on the sofa. She sobs quietly in my arms while I stroke her hair. Finally she sits up, wipes her eyes with the backs of her hands, and says, "Are you hungry? Because I'm starving."

She follows me to the kitchen and sits down on a stool at the counter while I pull out breakfast essentials from the fridge: bacon, eggs, strawberries, blueberries, milk, butter, and a can of buttermilk biscuits.

I mostly listen (I read an article in last month's *Men's Health* that said that's what women want from men—to just listen and not try to fix) while she recounts the events of the night before, or I guess early this morning, actually. I can't help but feel an aching in my heart. I imagine what it would be like if I had to do something like this with one of my kids.

Bridget and Emma are great girls and were pretty easy as children. The hardest part of raising kids is those pesky teenage years—especially (in my experience) the relationship between mother and daughter. When Jackie and I were still married, I remember countless days when I found her in the bathroom crying because Bridget had been mean to her. I totally didn't get it. "*What do you mean she was mean to you? You're her mom, not her friend. Who cares if she doesn't like you because you won't let her go to a college party when she's only a junior in high school? I would be mad if you let her go!*"

Jackie would shout at me that it wasn't that easy, that things with teenage girls weren't so black and white. I guess I didn't understand because to me, parenting seemed *very* black and white.

I've always been an active and involved father. I made a conscious effort to be present and there for my kids because my own father was completely absent when I was growing up. Dad was an ad guy—picture Don Draper from *Mad Men*, but with less swagger and hair. Richard Griffin (my mom called him Dick) was the lead account executive at a big ad firm in Dallas. I remember so many afternoons with my mom in the kitchen, eyes glued to the *Galloping Gourmet* on the little black-and-white TV, learning a new fancy recipe to try out on Dad's clients. Several nights a week he would phone from his office downtown and say he was bringing this guy from Coca-Cola or that guy from Chevrolet home for dinner. Mom would holler at me from the kitchen, "Danny, make sure you have on clean clothes, your father's bringing home the Coke man again! And for God's sake, don't ask him if he brought you any free samples. It's embarrassing to your father."

The nights Dad brought home the men whose money he desperately wanted (I'm pretty sure I have straight teeth thanks to the Coca-Cola Company) were about the only nights Dad really paid any attention to me. "Danny, show Mr. Glasgow here how you can strum a guitar. He's really very good at playing rock-and-roll music."

I would run off to my room and come back with my guitar, play a few chords from Led Zeppelin, and then be dismissed. I couldn't have been more than eight or nine years old at the time, and I was desperate for my father's approval. This was about as close as I came to getting it.

My older brother, Ray, used to make fun of me and call me monkey boy. "*Look at the monkey boy go. Play your guitar, you little ape. Make the crowd clap their hands.*" I tried to ignore him, to pretend he was just jealous that he wasn't being asked to entertain company. Truth is, Ray and my dad had a much easier time getting along. Ray was a big baseball star in school, and my dad would find any excuse to brag about him. "My boy Raymond pitched a no-hitter against last year's state champs. He's got a good chance to play in the majors if he keeps it up."

Later that year, my mom got really sick. The diagnosis was grim: colon cancer. And by the time the doctors figured out what was wrong with her, it was too late. I remember being asleep when the door to my bedroom opened. It made this horrible creaking sound. My mom had been after my dad forever to get out the WD-40 and fix it. But it was one of the many things my dad never got around to. Ray walked over to the side of my bed, punched me in the arm, and said, "Mom's dead."

After that, Dad began drinking so much that he eventually lost his job. Ray stopped playing baseball and moved in with some friends. I was left to care for myself and my father until one day he got in his car and drove to the store to get more beer. He hit a telephone pole and died on impact. I was sent to live with my grandparents in a small town a few hours from where I grew up. Looking back now, I wouldn't be surprised to learn that my dad ran his car into that pole on purpose.

Because of my personal experience, I worry I won't be an objective listener when it comes to helping Sarah navigate her way down this treacherous path. I worry about her daughter, Ashley. I worry this is may be tougher than Sarah realizes. I worry I won't be the person she needs me to be right now.

I worry I've overcooked these eggs. I guess it's what I get for worrying.

CHAPTER 19

Sarah

I wake up to the sound of buzzing. I look around the room and have no idea where I am. It takes a few minutes for it to register—this is Daniel's house. I've fallen asleep on his sofa. It must be late afternoon by now. I hear the buzzing again and realize it's my phone, vibrating. I see an unfamiliar number with an out of state area code. *Probably a sales call,* my brain tells me. But then I suddenly remember my current reality and slide my finger across the screen. It could be Marcus or Beverly with an update.

"Hello."

"Sarah, it's Marcus. I just wanted to let you know we landed in Salt Lake City. Beverly and Ashley are in the ladies room, so I thought I'd give you a quick call."

I breathe a sigh of relief. They have carried out the plan. "How is Ashley?"

"She's good. She cried on the way to the airport. But once we got through security, I asked if she was hungry. Turns out she was. The girl can put away some food."

I laugh and feel a little better. That definitely sounds like Ashley. Maybe everything will be okay after all. Daniel appears, and I point to the phone. He nods and sits next to me on the sofa. "Yes, she can," I say.

"She talked all through breakfast, wanted to know things about me and Beverly. Then she asked about Utah. She seems better—less afraid, less angry."

"That's great news. I've been dying over here. I'm grateful for the update." I get up and pace back and forth in front of the coffee table in Daniel's living room. I look over at him, and he smiles and gives me a thumbs up. I remind myself to call Steven with the update as soon as I get off the phone with Marcus.

"No problem. We have a four-hour drive ahead of us, so I'll call you later tonight after we arrive at New Horizons. After that, you'll get a call in a day or two from the therapist they assign to Ashley. Get used to being in the dark for a while. That's how this works. Just remember she's okay and well taken care of. The not knowing what's going on day-to-day will be the hardest part for you."

I breathe in deeply. Daniel places his hand on my knee and squeezes. "Thank you again, Marcus. You have no idea how much better I feel. Please tell Ashley I love her very much."

"Will do. Goodbye for now."

"Bye."

I look at my phone and see that Annabelle has left a message. "*Mom, it's me. Just wanted to check in with you. A bunch of kids are going to play miniature golf, and they asked me to go along. Kelsey's dad is taking us. I'll be home after, probably eight or nine tonight. Love you. Bye.*"

I once again feel like the worst mom ever. I completely forgot about Annabelle.

CHAPTER 20

Ashley

After driving for hours, we finally turn down a long, winding driveway and stop in front of a building that looks a lot like a log cabin. Everywhere I look there's snow. I've never seen so much of it. We hardly get any in Texas. In front of me there's a big front porch with wooden posts and smoke coming from a chimney. It seems harmless enough—nothing to be afraid of. And still, I'm so scared I feel like I might throw up. I've never been away from my parents like this before. I don't know what to expect, and I'm not sure when I'm going home. I really want my mom right now. Even though I hate her.

Marcus parks the car in the space marked "arrivals" and turns off the engine. Beverly opens her door, steps out, and puts on a coat, zipping it all the way up. Marcus turns to me in the backseat and says, "This is us, kiddo."

I like Marcus. If he lived near me or was a teacher at my school or something, I think we'd be friends. I can see why they hired him for this job. Snatching kids up from their homes in the middle of night can't be easy work, and at first I wanted to hate him, but he has this way of making you feel safe and like everything will be okay.

I grab my inhaler and bag of photos off the seat next to me and get out the car. It's freezing here, much colder than Fort Worth. At home there are signs of spring. The grass is starting to turn green, and the birds chirp a lot. I know that because they're so loud outside my bedroom window I find it hard to sleep past eight in the morning. Here the cold air is biting at my nose. I can see smoke coming out of my mouth when I breathe. I can't help but shiver. I'm going to need something heavier than the jacket I have with me.

Marcus closes the car door and walks with me toward the log cabin-looking building. As soon as we step on the front porch, the door opens. It appears they're expecting me.

"Come in. You must be Ashley."

The woman who greets me (she introduces herself as Maggie) is a little older than my mom. Okay, maybe a lot older; it's hard to tell someone's age if they're over twenty-five, in my opinion. She's wearing a faded blue sweatshirt with a wolf on the front, jeans, and old tennis shoes. Her hair is reddish-brown with lots of grey streaks. She smiles at me with kind eyes, and I notice then she's wearing two pair of glasses—one on her face and one on top of her head. I don't know why, but I like her.

"Come over here with me, and let's get you settled." Maggie puts her arm around my waist, escorts me to a room, and points to a chair where I am to sit. She closes the door, and I am totally alone. Marcus is nowhere to be seen, and I close my eyes and listen hard for the sound of his voice. Surely he wouldn't leave without saying goodbye. He's the only person I know here! Now he's gone, and Beverly's gone, and I'm in a strange place with some woman wearing ugly clothes and two sets of glasses.

I stand up and try to decide what to do. If I can find a phone, I can call my mom. No. I'm not doing that. She won't help me. She's the one who put me here. I look all around the room. It looks like a doctor's office. There's a desk and an examining table, a laptop and some medical equipment—but no phone. There's a knock on the door, and when it opens, Marcus peeks his head around.

"You okay, chief?" he asks me. "You look a little green."

I suddenly begin to cry.

Marcus comes in and puts his arms around me.

"Please don't leave me here by myself," I cry to him. "I'm scared."

"Hey now, you remember this morning when you hated me and didn't know who I was? And now you're okay with me."

"Yeah."

"It'll be like that here too. Maggie is awesome, I promise. She's getting your paperwork finished, then a nurse will give you a little physical and make sure you're healthy—Oh, don't worry, I already told them you eat *a ton*."

This makes me laugh.

"—And then you'll catch a ride up to the mountain. It's scary because it's new. In a couple of days, you'll feel right at home. You just need to adjust, that's all."

"And where will you be?" I ask as Marcus hands me a tissue. I wipe my eyes and blow my nose.

"Bev and I will go home for a couple of days and then, you know, I have another case."

"You mean child snatching."

Marcus rolls his eyes and pats me on the back one last time. "Ha ha, very funny." Then he looks at me and says, all serious like, "Listen, Ashley, do yourself a favor and learn from this experience. I know it's hard for someone your age to understand everything that's happening in her life, but your family worries about you and wants the best for you. And for you to be here now means you're not there yet. Take advantage of the program, and talk to your therapist. They're all great here. You'll learn some really valuable tools to take back home with you that will help you make better decisions. Okay?"

I nod and look away from him.

"Okay, lecture's over. I'm going to leave now. Try not to eat all the food."

And with that, Marcus walks out of the room, and once again, I am alone.

The ride up to the mountain is long and bumpy. It's pitch black outside—so dark you can only see the few feet in front of the truck where the headlights shine. I'm with some guy named Clay, who can't be that much older than me. I think. I'm not sure I can tell how old anyone is anymore. I'm feeling kinda out of it. He doesn't talk much, this Clay person, so I'm bored and lonely. Not that I want him to talk to me, because really I don't. It's just that if he talked to me at least I'd have some proof that I'm really here—that I'm not imagining all of this.

I look at my arm where the nurse took blood. There's a cotton ball and three pieces of white tape over the spot where the needle went in. Three pieces of tape for one teeny tiny pinprick seems a little excessive to me. The nurse was totally inexperienced—like, it wouldn't surprise me if it was her first day on the job. She might not even be a real nurse, now that I think about it. She had to take my blood pressure twice before she was satisfied with the numbers. She couldn't get the digital scale to turn on, so I had to tell her how much I weigh. I shaved off five pounds. She had me pee in a cup but couldn't find the strip-thingies they use to test the pee. She had to call Maggie in. So when she came at me with an alcohol swab and a needle, I closed my eyes and prayed.

"You say you're from Texas?"

The sudden sound of Clay's voice makes me jump a little.

"Yes, Fort Worth."

"Fort Worth. Is that near Dallas?"

"Uh-huh."

"So you have a horse?"

"A horse? No. Why would you ask me if I have a horse?"

"Because you're from Texas. When I think of Texas, I think of horses and cowboys and boots. You know, western stuff."

Clay is an idiot.

"Nope. No horse. No cowboys. No boots. It's just a regular place."

"Huh. Well, whaddya know. I guess I need to check out Texas someday for myself."

"Okay."

I changed my mind. I liked it better when Clay wasn't talking to me. If I close my eyes, maybe he'll think I've gone to sleep. I've just done that, close my eyes, when Clay turns the truck sharply to the right and comes to a stop. I open my eyes and find him staring at me.

He smiles and shrugs. "We're here."

Here? Where's here? I see nothing out the window but total blackness. I'm in the middle of nowhere with a stranger. I don't know

Clay. He could be a rapist. Or a murderer. Or a rapist *and* a murderer. I've seen those crime shows on TV. In fact, I watch them all the time. This could easily be an episode of *Crime Scene Investigators*.

Ashley Lange was just seventeen years old when her parents sent her to a Utah youth program for troubled teens. That's where she met up with a fellow named Clay, who worked for the camp. Little did anyone know that Clay wasn't really Clay, but David Walker, an escaped rapist-murderer, who preyed on teenage girls. David Walker was known to drive his victims to a remote spot somewhere in the mountains of Utah. He would befriend the girls and make them feel at ease with idiotic small talk before raping and killing them and cutting them into small pieces.

My door opens, and I scream.

"Damn, girl, you scared me." There's a large woman standing between me and the door of the truck, holding her hand over her chest. "What are you trying to do, give me a heart attack?"

Clay is still sitting in the driver's seat, now laughing his ass off.

The woman I mistook for a second murderer-rapist is named Gail. She is the leader of D1, my assigned group. There are seven of us in the group, I'm told. I haven't met any of them yet because it's the middle of the night, and everyone is asleep in tents. I make the mistake of asking, "Oh, we're camping?"

Clay and Gail look at each other and then back at me. "We're not camping, newbie," Gail says. Apparently when you're new you get called this. "We live on the mountain, in tents—girls in one, boys in the other. What'd you think, there was some five-star hotel up here in the middle of nowhere? You're not on vacation; you're in rehab."

Clay shakes his head. "The new ones, they always make me laugh. You should see your face right now, newbie."

Clay and Gail start unloading supplies from the back of the truck. I stand there trying to figure out what the hell is going on. I can't see anything except the ground right outside the truck. I wonder if there are bears—or mountain lions.

"Newbie, come back here and grab a bag or two. Clay's gotta get over to the other campsite before dawn." Gail is barking orders at me already.

I do as I'm told.

After carrying a bag of bananas and another bag of oatmeal over to the spot where Gail points, I suddenly feel as if my body's hit a wall. I've been up since four in the morning the day before. I have no idea what time it is, but I figure it has be two or three in the morning. Gail comes over, hands me a blanket, and says, "Go find a spot and get some sleep. The tent's right there next to the fire." She points to what I can only assume she means when she says "tent." It's less like a tent and more like a canvas tarp. My fears about bears and mountain lions race back to the front of my mind. Suddenly the thoughts I had earlier about Clay being a rapist-murderer don't seem nearly as scary as the idea of being mauled by a mountain lion.

I make my way to the girls tent in boots I'm not accustomed to wearing. Back at the log cabin (which now seems like a mansion compared to these accommodations) I was outfitted with official New Horizons camp gear: a long-sleeve yellow T-shirt, khaki pants, ugly green socks, hiking boots, and a red all-weather jacket. The jacket does not seem like it's thick enough to keep me from freezing to death. Anyway, my clothes are hideous. I look like one of those men who works road construction. Although now I totally get the reason behind the wool socks—it's freezing up here, and I can't feel my toes.

I find a spot next to some sleeping girl and wrap the blanket around me. I lie down and close my eyes, no longer able to fight off sleep.

"She looks dead."

"She's not dead; she's snoring. And her mouth is open. Dead people's mouths are closed when they're, you know, dead."

"You don't know what the fuck you're talking about, you know that, Crystal? I think you just talk to hear the sound of your own voice."

"You said a curse word, Avery. That's your first mark for the day."

"Only if you tell Gail. I hate that you're like the hall monitor. Why can't you take a day off from being *you* for once?"

I open my eyes and find two girls about my age standing over me, arguing. They're wearing the exact same outfit as me. These must be my people.

"Oh look, it's Sleeping Beauty," the taller one says. I don't know why she hates me already, but it's clear we're not going to be friends. I can tell just by the way she's glaring.

I sit up and try to stretch my back. It feels like I slept on a rock or a stick. I feel around on the ground and find the reason my muscles are aching—a rock the size of my fist. I throw it a few feet away and try to stand up. It's a lot harder than it sounds. The girl named Crystal extends her hand, and I take it. When I'm on my feet I smile and thank her.

"No problem," she says. "I'm Crystal, and this ray of sunshine next to me is Avery."

"Hi," I say.

"Hey," says Avery. She's studying me like there's going to be test later.

The sun is up, and it's my first opportunity to look around—to know the place where I'm going to be living for a while. There are trees are far as you can see—and mountains covered in snow—and sticks and rocks and more snow and probably bugs and snakes and maybe bears and mountain lions. I try not to think about that last part.

The campsite is exactly what you might imagine a campsite to look like. There are makeshift tents and a fire and backpacks and gear. I got my backpack last night, but I haven't looked inside it yet. I assume I'll know when I need something out of it. I have no idea what to do. This is completely foreign to me. I'm not sure what is expected. Also, I've never been this cold in my life.

"What'd you do?" Avery asks.

"What do you mean?"

"I mean, what'd you do to get sent here? Drugs? Stealing? Premarital sex?"

She laughs when she says premarital sex. Crystal flips Avery the bird and says, "You're such an a-hole."

Avery shrugs and says, "What? It's true, isn't it? Your parents busted you and your boyfriend doing the nasty, freaked out, and shipped you off to this place."

This is shocking. Even my overreacting parents wouldn't freak out if they caught me having sex. "Really? Is that true?"

Crystal sighs. "It's only half true. My parents walked in on Brandon and me having sex. And they went ballistic like I killed somebody and grounded me and forbid me to see him anymore. So…I thought I'd show them, and I took a whole bunch of pills."

"You tried to kill yourself?" This is obviously the first time Avery has heard this part of the story.

"I guess, technically, yes. But I don't think I really wanted to die. I just wanted to get back at them, you know?"

"Well done. And now you're here in paradise with me and—" Avery stops mid-sentence and points to me.

"Ashley."

"With me and Ashley." She turns her attention to me again. "You never said why you're here."

"Why are *you* here?" I admit, I am being a little aggressive, but I'm beginning to feel ganged-up on.

Avery's face suddenly changes. "I killed one of my classmates in the locker room after school. It was self-defense; she attacked me first. My dad is super rich and hired this big-time attorney who was able to keep me out of jail by offering to send me here for an extended period of time. I've been here almost two years."

My mouth is agape. Seriously, birds could nest in the giant hole in my face. I can't believe what I'm hearing.

"Hey, newbie, close your mouth. I'm only kidding. Drugs. I'm here because of drugs."

The two of them start laughing, and I'm not sure whether to laugh too, or punch them both in the face.

Before I can decide, Gail shouts, "Girls, knock it off. Eat your breakfast and then get to the fire for Circle Time."

I learn quickly that Circle Time is lame. The seven of us in the group sit on the ground around the campfire and listen to Gail read from a book of daily devotionals. Our lesson today: gratitude. After she closes the book, she instructs each of us to take a turn sharing something we're grateful for. Crystal volunteers to go first.

As she starts talking, I study the other girls in the group. There's a girl who can't be more than twelve years old. She's holding a stick and using it to draw pictures in the snow in front of her. She hasn't made eye contact with anyone since we've been sitting here. Next to her is a really attractive girl who looks like she would be the Homecoming queen at school. She smiles and nods her enthusiasm as, one by one, we take turns talking. Sitting beside the Homecoming queen is a girl with facial piercings. She has two in her eyebrow, one in her nose, one in her lip, and one in her cheek. She reminds me of a human pincushion. And rounding out the group is a girl named T-Bone, who won't stop talking over the other girls. I know her name because Gail keeps saying, "That's enough, T-Bone. You've had your turn." And then she delivers a warning. "If you don't stop interrupting the group, you'll be asked to leave."

T-Bone stands up then and yells, "Bitch, what do you think I'm trying to do? I wanna leave this stupid-ass group. You think anyone gives a shit about gratitude? Look at these punk-ass girls. Every damn one of them wishes they could be anywhere but here. You think we like living on this damn mountain day in and day out? Gratitude. I'll give you gratitude. *Fuck you.* There...happy?"

Gail marches over to T-Bone, grabs her by the elbow, and says, "That's about enough. You're done. I'm calling the director and asking him to send someone up to get you. This isn't working anymore. You're out."

T-Bone pulls away from Gail and very calmly says to her, "Good. It's about time you let me out of this prison."

Gail smirks. "Too bad you'll be going to actual prison now. That was the deal. You're here or you're there. Have fun."

"At least I won't be sleeping on no damn mountain out in the freezing cold, getting snowed on and worrying about mountain lions and frostbite and shit."

Gail points to T-Bone's tent and says, "Get your backpack together and wait there."

Then, as if nothing has happened, Gail turns her attention back to the group and says, "Everyone, let's all say hello to Ashley."

CHAPTER 21

Sarah

I just got off the phone with Daniel; he's coming over later to cook me dinner. Annabelle is babysitting the Witt kids. I've recently become friends with Kate Witt, which has opened up quite the moneymaking opportunity for AB. She'll be down the street until eleven, so Daniel and I will have the house to ourselves.

I've been spending a lot of time with Daniel. He's a distraction from everything that's going on in my "real" life. I swear, being with him is like being on vacation. We talk a lot about our childhoods, our failed marriages, our likes and dislikes, our jobs—you know, all the things you talk about when you're getting to know someone. Only every time we circle back to sharing stories about our kids, I start to cry. It takes me right back to the moment I said goodbye to Ashley.

It's hard not knowing what's going on with her. I wonder constantly if she's okay…if she's hungry…if she's cold…if she hates me.

One thing I can say about Daniel, he's a great guy. I'm not sure I know anyone quite like him. I've never met a man who would put up with this kind of misery when he doesn't have to. I mean, it would be safe to say I'm a hysterical woman most days—my emotions jumping all over the place. Sometimes I can't stand to be with me, and yet here's this guy who seems to really like me and doesn't mind the fact that one minute I'll be laughing at his joke and the next minute bawling into his T-shirt. Every morning I wake up and think, *Okay, yesterday's sobbing fit was probably enough to scare him away. He doesn't need this. He's not going to call.* And then, lo and behold, the phone rings, and it's him—checking in, asking when he can see me.

I'm beginning to wonder if there's something wrong with *him*.

Daniel has shared some of his childhood stories with me. When he told me he lost his mother when he was just a little boy, my heart shattered in a million tiny pieces. It was so achingly similar to my story of losing my mom. We're not that different, Daniel and me. We both bear tragic battle scars.

But despite that, it hasn't been all sad and depressing. Like a vacation, remember? There's also the part where we continue to have amazing sex. Maybe that's why he keeps calling.

The phone rings again, and I look at the caller ID. It's a Utah area code. I've learned quite a bit about Utah in the last few weeks. The capital and largest city is Salt Lake City. It's made up of mostly white people. The majority there are Republicans, and Mormons make up half the population. But most importantly, Utah is currently where my older daughter resides.

"Hello."

"Hi, Sarah. It's Brent."

Brent is Ashley's therapist and my only connection to her these days.

"Hi there, Brent. How are you? How's Ashley?"

"I'm doing well, thank you. Ashley seems to really be making some good progress in her first week. You know, when you and I first chatted she was still showing some signs of anger. She wanted to blame others for her predicament. She wasn't willing to accept much of the responsibility for being here, and she was a real challenge." He pauses.

I feel sick to my stomach.

"But now I've focused on getting her to open up with me. It's really important for her to feel like she can trust me—that I don't work for you or her dad, that I'm a true ally and friend. Make sense?"

"Yes. Very much."

"So once I was able to gain her trust as a friend and not as her therapist, she let down her guard and really started sharing things with me." He laughs. "I gotta tell you, Sarah, she's a great kid."

Tears begin to fall down my cheeks, and relief washes over me.

"She wrote you a letter, and I'm going to stick it in the mail in the morning."

"Do I want to read it?" Nervous energy fills my veins like I've had one too many cups of coffee.

Brent laughs again. "Yes. You want to read it. She wrote one to her dad and Annabelle too. It's all good. It's part of the process. So listen, next time we speak she'll be on the phone call with me. You'll have thirty minutes to talk to her. She's looking forward to it."

"Oh God, I'm so nervous. I'm not sure what to say."

"She's nervous too, trust me. It will get easier; the first call is always the toughest. But she loves you very much. She talks about you a lot."

"Really? She's not mad at me?"

"She understands why you sent her here. I'm telling you, we've made some progress. This is a good day. You should hang up feeling happy. We're getting somewhere, and that's the plan, remember? We're spending these next couple of months breaking down barriers and getting to the root of the pain."

"Yes. I remember. Thank you, Brent. I don't know what we'd do without you there, helping our little girl. I'm truly grateful."

"No worries, Sarah. It's my job. Talk to you next week. Goodbye."

"Tell her I love her," I shout into the phone. But he's already hung up.

Surely she knows I love her, right?

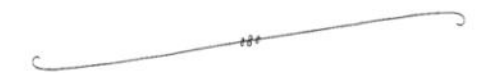

Three days later I'm sitting on my bed staring at an envelope. I run my finger over my handwritten name. It's Ashley's handwriting. I'd know it anywhere. She makes a beautiful swooping S in Sarah and always adds a tiny heart after the E in Lange. I want desperately to rip it open and devour her words, but the fear of not knowing exactly what the letter says paralyzes me. Annabelle knocks on my door and peeks her head around, holding a white envelope in her hands too. I pat the bed with my free hand.

She comes to sit next to me, and we count to three and open our letters from Ashley.

Dear Mom,

I saw my first deer this morning, although I don't know if it was technically a deer or some animal that looks like a deer. It seemed like a deer to me. For a minute we just stared at each other. I didn't move—or breathe. I didn't want to scare him off. I wanted to take a picture, but I didn't have my camera with me. Did you send that camera to me? Or did the camp provide it? I don't know where it came from, but I found it in my backpack. If you sent it, thank you. I've taken a few cool pictures. Maybe you can send me another camera if they say it's OK. I'm kinda into the whole taking pictures thing. I didn't know I liked photography until I started exploring the mountains around us. Don't worry, I won't fall off the side of the cliff or anything. Haha.

I want you to know I'm not mad at you. I was for, like, five minutes, but I'm not anymore. OK, that's not exactly true either. Sometimes I am mad, but I'm trying hard not to be. I know you and Dad did what you think was best for me. Don't get me wrong, it's pretty hard being here, but mostly only at night. The darkness scares me, and that's when I miss you the most. Do you remember that song you used to sing to me when I was little? Raindrops keep falling on my head? I sing that to myself every night, although I'm not sure I know all the words. I just make up the parts I'm not sure of. It helps a lot. I miss my room and my bed so much. It is not comfortable sleeping outside on the ground. I will never complain about my bed being too mushy ever, ever again. Ha!

I think about you and Dad and AB. I wonder what y'all are doing and if you're happy again. I know I made you unhappy. I know I was a pain in your ass. I know I was wrong. I'm sorry, Mom. I'm not going to say I like it here, because I don't. But I also get why I'm here. I like my counselor, and I like Brent. He's super cool and easy to talk to. I know we get to talk on the phone soon. I can't promise I won't cry when I hear your voice.

I love you, Mom. Tell AB I miss her.

From Utah,

Ashley

After we read our letters, Annabelle and I sit in silence for a few moments. She reads hers again, and I run my fingers over Ashley's handwriting, willing my body to feel her in the room with me. Annabelle folds the letter and slides it back in the envelope. She looks at me and asks, "Do you think Ashley is okay?"

I'm not sure what she means. "Like, in Utah? Or in general?"

"I don't know. Maybe that's not the right question. What I meant to say is Ashley's not a bad person, Mom. But I let her believe she is. I made things worse by yelling at her and then ignoring her. And I haven't done much in the way of defending her at school. People are talking, you know. Her letter to me is so nice, and I feel kind of bad." Annabelle starts to cry.

I wrap my arms around her and hold her to me. "It's okay, sweetheart. This is not an easy situation for any of us—Ashley, you, me, Dad. Who knows what's the right way to respond? How does anyone do this and not feel completely lost?" I stroke her hair. It was once so white, like cotton. Now it's a honey gold color and so long, almost to her waist. It's one thing the girls have in common. Good hair.

Annabelle pulls away from me and gets up off the bed. "I'm going to write Ashley back and tell her I'm sorry, and that I can't wait to see her."

"Sounds good, love."

CHAPTER 22

Ashley

I've been on this mountain for three weeks. I've learned all kinds of skills, none of which will do me any good when I get back home to Texas. Like, I know how to start a fire three different ways, using different kinds of wood. I know how to make dough out of flour and water and use it to cook ash cakes over a campfire. I can build (and have built) a latrine.

This "camp" is nothing like I imagined it to be—although I didn't give much thought to "camps" or rehabs before I was sent to one. When I first got here, I figured we'd be hiking through the mountains for a couple of days and then go to some dorm or motel-like building, with beds and running water. That's not at all what's happening. You see, we live on the mountain every single day. We sleep in tents, and we cook our own food and build our own toilets. It's pretty disgusting, actually, if I think about it too much—the idea of peeing and pooping in a hole in the ground. But it's true: when you gotta go, you'll go just about anywhere.

I've gotten pretty good at making (somewhat) edible food. We're not given much choice in the matter of groceries. Every week Gail (or one of the other leaders) passes out supplies: one can of SPAM, several packages of Ramen noodles, a few potatoes, an onion, a couple of carrots, a small bag of flour, some sugar, a small container of oatmeal, a block of cheese, and macaroni noodles. Once a week we get fruit—mostly bananas, oranges, or apples.

Avery taught me how to make ash cakes. You mix the flour and water until it forms a dough. Then you roll it out as best you can (there are no counter tops or rolling pins, in case you're wondering) and then you pinch off pieces of the dough and place them in a hot pan over the fire. Sometimes I add cheese or bits of SPAM. It makes a kind of meat-and-cheese Hot Pocket. When I want something sweet, I cut up an apple, sprinkle it with sugar, and make a turnover. It's not bad. But it's not my mom's cooking either.

It has snowed a few times lately. It's not as bad as I thought it would be. Gail told me the first day I was here that I'd get used to the cold and the snow. She's right. I only really freeze to death at night. We kind of all huddle together in the tent. I've never slept so close to another human being in my life. Not even with my mom or my sister. You do it to stay warm; you don't think about how weird it feels.

When I think of home, I think about all the little things I miss. I miss the smell of coffee in the mornings, even though I don't drink coffee. I can always tell when Mom is up because she makes coffee first thing. It sounds corny, but her making coffee in the mornings makes me feel…I don't know…safe. I miss the way she says, "We're off like a herd of turtles!" every time we get in the car together to go somewhere. Next time she says it, I won't roll my eyes or sigh because I'm annoyed. I miss AB and the sucky music she listens to. She's into boy bands and Taylor Swift, and I give her such a hard time about what crap it is. She usually ignores me and turns it up louder. What I wouldn't give for some dumb One Direction song right about now.

I miss Dad, and I worry he'll never forgive me for what happened at his house. I know it's only been a month since all that went down, but being alone with yourself and your thoughts twenty-four hours a day for three weeks straight gives you plenty of time to think about your life and the mistakes you've made. I can't wait to tell him I'm sorry. I wish I had never started partying with those losers. I wish I'd never smoked pot or taken those pills. Kids in my high school steal prescription meds from their parents all the time, and for some reason it didn't seem like a big deal. I just wanted them to like me. I liked all the attention I was getting. People wanted to hang out with me. I didn't care that they were super douchey.

I wanna go home.

I'm just finishing up eating mac-n-cheese when Gail yells over to me, "Ashley, you're on cleanup duty. Don't forget."

Cleanup duty is the second-worst job to digging a latrine. You have to gather everyone's leftover food and burn it so the smell doesn't attract bears or other animals. Apparently my fears about there being bears and mountain lions around us are not off base. The rest of the food, what we haven't used yet, has to be stored in bear boxes. We also don't have deodorant or hair conditioner because, again, the bears. The shampoo we use has zero smell to it, so I wonder what's the point. I miss my shampoo at home. I love how my hair smells after I get out of the shower. Oh God, the thought of using a real bathroom and a real shower is almost too much to take. I can't get the smell of burning wood and ash off me soon enough.

Every few days, we change camps. We never stay in one place for too long, and it takes several hours of hiking up the sides of cliffs and through fields to get to the next site. Once there, it takes another couple of hours to pitch our tents, build the latrine, and start the fire.

Each morning we get up at six, dress, and eat breakfast. After that it's Circle Time and then schoolwork. I have math and English and history lessons. My teacher is pretty nice, although I only met with her one time. She's in touch with my school at home, and they put together the curriculum I need to stay up with my classmates. I can't let myself think too much about what's going on back at school. I can only imagine what they think happened to me. I'm probably, like, some urban legend now—or infamous.

I don't have any real friends anymore. I hadn't realized that until Brent made me list the names of my friends on a piece of paper. I couldn't think of one person. I used to have friends in middle school. I was always spending the night at someone's house on the weekends. Mom would let me have sleepovers, and she would cook us an extravagant breakfast in the morning. I'm not sure what happened in high school. I don't spend time with any of the friends I used to have. It's weird. I'd never given it much thought before Brent made me talk about it. I suddenly feel very alone in the world.

Also, I miss school cafeteria food. Okay, now I must be going crazy.

I'm a few points away from making Ranch Level. Right now I'm at Camp Level, which means I have no flashlight, no chair, and no hotplate; I'm simply a peon. Every day that I complete my chores and my schoolwork, write in my journal, and meet with my therapist, I get points. The most points you can get in a day is twenty-five. I need less than half that to move up to Ranch Level. It probably sounds lame, but when you haven't sat in a chair for more than three weeks, you kinda miss it. I'll never look at a chair the same way. And having a flashlight with me at night when I get up to pee would be a luxury I never knew I'd taken for granted. And the hotplate? Well, that just makes life that much better. I'm learning life is all about the little things.

"Ashley! Get moving faster! What are you, daydreaming? You're moving at a snail's pace. You'll never finish packing the gear at the rate you're going."

It's Gail, and she's on my case today.

"Sorry. I'm almost finished."

I snap back into reality and scrape the leftover food into a hole in the ground. Then I start a fire using the stick I found on my walk this morning. It's not quite nine o'clock in the morning, and we're getting ready to move camps. The days we pack up and leave are the hardest. There are fifteen extra things to do. And I'm in charge this time, which means I'm the one with the most responsibilities.

Reminding myself that I'm so close to Ranch Level is the only thing that keeps me going.

CHAPTER 23

Daniel

Driving home from work in heavy traffic leaves a lot of time for reflection. I am currently reflecting while going zero miles an hour on the freeway.

How do you know when you love someone? I have loved three women during my lifetime: Debbie Clarkson, my very first serious relationship back in high school; Jackie, my now-lesbian ex-wife; and Sarah.

It's true; I love her. There's just something so incredible about her…I'm not even sure there's a name for it—or if there is, it's not a word in my vocabulary. I feel like I met her at just the right time, for me. I worry the same cannot be said on her end. She has so much on her plate right now that I'm afraid if I tell her how I feel she'll freak out and bail. I've come so close to telling her, but I haven't been able to pull the trigger just yet. But I can't hold out much longer. When I think something, I say it. When I feel something, I show it. When I love a woman, I'll do anything to make her happy. The stuff Sarah's going through with her daughter makes me love her that much more. It takes a strong person to be able to endure something like that with the amount of grace she has. It may sound crazy, but stress makes her sexy.

Women I've dated in the past have always said the same things about me: I'm a great boyfriend. I'm thoughtful, I'm attentive, and

I'm interested in what they have to say. There's a flipside to that too. I'm also jealous and maybe even a little possessive.

Sarah has seen glimpses of my jealous side. One night last week I took her to this fancy seafood restaurant for a quiet, romantic dinner. After we were seated, I noticed a man sitting a few tables over staring at her. And it wasn't a quick glance, something that shows appreciation for her looks—because there's no question, she's an unbelievably beautiful woman. You'd be an idiot not to notice her. But this guy kept looking over, obviously trying to get her attention. And she was talking to me, but she knew someone was watching her. So finally she looked his way, and he lifted his wine glass and toasted her—like I wasn't even sitting there. Of course she didn't respond, and she quickly focused her attention back on me, but I turned bright red. I know I did. I could feel all the blood rushing to my face.

Sarah stopped mid-sentence (I have no idea what she was saying; I was too busy fuming) and asked, "Are you okay, Daniel?"

I held my breath and let it out. "Yes, I'm sorry. I'm fine. I just hate guys like that. I mean, you're obviously with me, and he thinks what? You might decide you'd rather be with him?"

Sarah didn't say anything for a second. She just stared at me. I was worried I'd blown it by letting her see this side of me.

She reached over the table, grabbed my hand, and held it in hers. "You're the best thing that's ever happened to me, and I mean that. Seriously. I don't know what I'd do without you."

I smiled, relieved by her words, and opened my mouth to do it. I was going to tell her I loved her, right in the middle of Waters Edge or Water Town or whatever the fuck that restaurant was called. I was just about to—and the waiter came to the table and asked, "Any questions about the menu?"

Suddenly, I chickened out. The moment was lost. I'll try again some other time. Fucking waiter.

The girls know about Sarah, although I'm not sure Sarah's girls know about me. Ashley is difficult to communicate with for obvious reasons, and also, Sarah's approach to this may be a little different from mine…I try to be as upfront as I can with my girls. They want me to be happy, and they know it's not my fault their mother and I aren't together anymore.

Before I met Sarah, I was just casually dating a few women here and there, and I never considered introducing any of them to my kids. None of them were serious relationships—or even relationships, for that matter. A couple of women I only went out with a handful of times. So the question of when to introduce my girls to someone never entered my mind...until now.

Sarah is coming over tomorrow to meet Bridget and Emma. It felt awkward leading up to telling them about her. I don't know why, but I was nervous. Hell, I *do* know why. This is making things with Sarah public. It's no longer just something she and I share alone. My palms are sweating like crazy.

The girls and I are sitting at the kitchen table, working a thousand-piece puzzle. We do this a lot on the weekends. Emma is always asking me to go with her to the toy store downtown on the square because "they have the best puzzles." Hey, I will gladly take my sixteen-year-old to the toy store. Hell, I'll buy her a Barbie Dreamhouse if it will keep her from growing up too fast. I'm just putting the last piece on a house I've been working on for over an hour when the doorbell rings. Suddenly, knots form in my stomach. My hands continue to sweat.

"I'll get it," Bridge says as she heads to the front door. A second later she opens it and greets Sarah for the first time.

I watch Bridget's face when she sees Sarah. I'm waiting for a reaction from her—good *or* bad. She smiles and says, "It's so nice to meet you. Dad hasn't been able to stop talking about you."

Is this true?

Sarah and Bridget shake hands, and Emma and I get up and go to where the others are standing. Emma introduces herself, and Sarah proceeds to win the girls over with her charm and wit, just as I suspected she would. She compliments Bridget's eyes, going on about how she's "never seen that color green before." Emma, the more introverted of my two girls, stands so close to me the hairs on her arms are tickling mine.

Sarah pulls a book out of her handbag and hands it to Emma. "Your dad tells me you love to read. Have you read any Jane Austen?"

Emma takes the book from Sarah and shakes her head. "No. But I think I'd like to."

Sarah's eyes light up as she points to the cover. "*Pride and Prejudice* will become your favorite book. Mark my words. And there's even a movie based on it starring Colin Firth." Emma thanks her and immediately flips to the first page.

Suddenly Sarah looks over to the table where the puzzle is laid out and proclaims, "I love puzzles! Can I help put it together?"

This is going to be too easy.

It's after eleven in the evening before I realize we've been working on the puzzle for hours. It turned out to be a great night—way better than I anticipated—which is a relief. The girls were very nice to Sarah, and I sat back and watched as they bonded over retelling their favorite scenes from Will Ferrell movies. We ordered pizza, and Emma made cookies—the slice and bake kind. I saw Bridget yawn, and that's when I looked at the time.

After this realization, I urge the girls to go on to bed, offering to clean up the kitchen even though that's usually their job. They stand up from the table, and Sarah joins them. They take turns hugging and exchanging kind words, and I feel the happiest I have in a very long time.

The evening has been a total success. There were no weird moments or lulls in the conversation. They all got along as if they'd known each other forever. Sarah even talked about Annabelle—and Ashley. She went into great detail about the program in Utah, and I was so proud of my girls. They listened and asked questions and wished the best for Ashley. They also told Sarah she should have brought Annabelle with her. They said they couldn't wait to meet her.

After the girls disappear upstairs, Sarah scrubs the cookie sheet and wipes down the counters while I gather the empty pizza boxes and carry them to the garage. When I return to the kitchen, I spot the bottle of wine I'd bought for tonight sitting on the counter. I hold it out for Sarah to see. She raises her eyebrows, smiles, and says, "Yes, please."

The two of us sit on the sofa in the living room and talk for two more hours. She picks my brain about my how I've raised my girls. She's desperate to find out if she could have done things differently.

She's jealous, she says, that I seem to have the parenting thing down while she's bobbing up the down in the water like a fish with no fins.

I assure her my kids are far from perfect. We've had our share of issues and bumps in the road. Bridget is dyslexic, which is like learning a new language. We had no idea the struggles she would face in school. And it took forever to figure out exactly what was going on. For months Jackie and I agonized and lost sleep over it. But then when she was diagnosed with dyslexia it was like a light bulb went on. Of course! Dyslexia!

I tell Sarah how in middle school, Emma became friends with a mischievous girl, Lacie, who got Emma to do things she normally wouldn't do. They got caught making copies of a science test in the teachers' lounge and both received zeros on it. Another time they wrote the word SLUT on some girl's locker. I don't know what was going on in Emma's head her eighth grade year, but I was never more glad than when I learned Lacie was moving to Florida. As we drove past her house on the last day of school I said (to myself of course), "Don't let the door hit ya where the good Lord split ya!" Since then, Emma hasn't gotten in trouble again. Yet.

I hate seeing Sarah blame herself for Ashley's stumbles, but I guess any parent in her position would do the same thing. Who knows why Ashley is acting out the way she is. Sarah worries it's because of her divorce, but I think that's BS. Lots of kids watch their parents split up—more than half, according to statistics. I don't think it's anything Sarah (or even Steven) has done. I think it's just how Ashley is wired. Do I think she'll grow out of it and become a reasonable adult? I do. Will it be easy? Maybe not. I wish I could magically fix all this for her. And for Sarah too. I'd do it in a heartbeat.

By now it's well after one in the morning, and I know Sarah's tired and probably needs to get home and go to sleep, but I have a hard time letting her go. I wish she never had to leave. Suddenly I can't hold back any longer.

I brush my hand across her forehead and smooth back her hair. "I love you, Sarah."

Without a pause or a hint of hesitation she replies, "I love you too, Daniel."

It is the perfect night.

CHAPTER 24

Ashley

The last session I had with Brent was a real breakthrough—those are his words, not mine. All I did was finally tell the truth.

We were sitting on the ground, away from the campsite. We've been camped at this particular spot on the mountain for the past three days. I think that's the longest we've been in one place. We have to stay one step ahead of the mountain lions. (At least that's what I think.)

"Why do you think you're here, Ashley? In the program. No BS. The *real* reason." Brent peered over the top of his glasses at me. Some of his curls were covering his right eye, and he kept blowing them out of the way. It was both hilarious and distracting. I looked over his shoulder and out into the trees to keep from laughing.

"I'm here because I messed up," I told him. "And my parents didn't know what to do. I get that. But part of me feels like they gave up too easily. Like, I became a problem and they didn't want to deal with me, so they shipped me off and made me someone else's problem. When I think about them that way, I get mad. And they did it so quickly. I mean, it's not like I hit rock bottom."

Brent picked up a small rock and began playing with it, rolling it around in his hand. "Have you considered that maybe your parents were afraid they were losing you? And that maybe by taking you away from the things in your life that scared them, they were saving you? I find it interesting that you use the term *rock bottom*. Do you suspect things could have gotten worse for you? Were you aiming for some kind of self-destruction?"

The thing that scared them was Russell. And no, I'm not into self-sabotage. "I know kids who've done way worse things than me whose parents didn't send them away. I'm not a bad person."

"Of course you're not a bad person. No one says that or believes that. Try this, Ashley. Instead of holding on to the anger and frustration you feel toward your parents for 'sending you away'—" He uses air quotes when he says this. "—use this opportunity to really think about the person you want to be. Be selfish. Focus on you—your hopes, your dreams, your life. It's not often a person gets to disconnect from her 'normal life'—" Again, air quotes. "—to really figure out who she is and what she wants. This is your parents' gift to you. You may not recognize it now, but I think in time you will."

I didn't say anything. I just sat there and let the words bounce from shoulder to shoulder. I watched Brent as he placed the rock on the ground and reached into his backpack. He pulled out a notebook and opened it to a new page. "Any thoughts on what I just said?"

I closed my eyes tight and hugged my knees. My butt had fallen asleep.

No matter how long I sit on the ground, day in and day out, my butt will never get used to how hard the ground is. It's true I have a chair now, but we have our sessions off the campsite, usually under a tree somewhere. Brent says kids usually open up more if they don't have to worry about anyone hearing what they're saying. He's probably right about this.

I opened my eyes and looked at him. He seriously has the curliest hair of any human I have ever seen.

"I get what you're saying. And you're probably right. I know my parents love me and were afraid for me. They didn't know what to do. They're doing the best they can, and I made their lives harder than they already were."

Brent wrote something in the notebook. "Talk about that. What was hard?"

I haven't talked about my parents' divorce with anyone. Not even AB. I never wanted to. But something about being stuck on a mountain in the middle of Utah makes it easier.

"I am pissed at my dad for blowing up our family and for making my mom turn into a zombie. It really killed her—his affair, his moving out. It changed my mom's whole personality. She isn't funny anymore. She stopped writing, stopped caring about anything, really, including AB and me. She used to drive me bonkers, always in my room, asking 'How was your day? How are classes going?' and saying 'Tell me about school. Any juicy gossip?' She would plop on my bed and start randomly picking up things and looking at them, and folding my clothes. I didn't feel like talking to her. I just wanted to listen to my music and Snapchat my friends. She was so annoying. But after Dad moved out, she didn't come in my room anymore. She hardly noticed me, or my sister. She seemed really depressed, which made me start to hate her. She had always been so strong and so… there. And then she was gone, just like that. I couldn't believe Dad did what he did to her, but I also couldn't believe she let him affect her like that."

Brent was really scribbling now. I wished I could see what he was writing.

I kept going. I couldn't stop. "My mom doesn't have a lot of friends outside her writing friends, and most of them live somewhere else. She doesn't have that friend she talks to on the phone, or goes to lunch or the movies with. My dad was her friend. They did everything together for as long as I can remember. But then as I got older, I started noticing they weren't that close anymore. And then Dad tells us he's moving out? It was crap what he did. But I also thought my mom was stronger than that. They both pissed me off."

It felt so—what's the word?—*amazing*…to say all that out loud.

Brent's hand was moving so fast I worried it might fly off his wrist. He was nodding, and then he looked at me and said, "Ashley, I'm really proud of you right now. This is the most you've opened up with me. I mean it. Good work. In our previous sessions, you've sometimes told me what you think I wanted to hear, but not today. Today is a good day." He smiled and kept nodding.

It's only then that I realized I was crying. I'm not even sure how long it had been happening. Something else was happening too. I felt better—like I was buried in sand up to my neck, and somehow I managed to get free. No one else had to help me get out. I saved myself.

Brent got up and offered me a hand. I reached for it, and he pulled me up and wrapped his arms around my neck. I hugged him back, closed my eyes, and exhaled. It's like I'd been holding my breath for months.

I am glad I'm here. (I really mean that, which is surprising.) And I will be really glad to see my parents. This weekend is Parents' Weekend.

CHAPTER 25

Sarah

It's been thirty-seven days since Ashley left for the mountain. A lot has happened since then. Annabelle is busy with school and has a semi-regular babysitting job with the Witt family down the street. The mom, Katherine (or Kate as she told me to call her), and I have become friends. We met a few weeks ago when I was jogging through the neighborhood and noticed a woman struggling to get a box out of her car. I ran over to help, and we managed (not too easily, I might add) to carry the box from the back of her SUV to the front porch. After we set it down, I joked about it being so heavy there must be a dead body inside.

With a deadpan expression she replied, "It's my mother-in-law. It couldn't be helped. The woman is pure evil. Well…she *was* pure evil. Now she resembles a tossed salad."

That's when I knew I liked her. It turns out she's a writer, too, so we have a lot in common. Even though her children are much younger than mine, she's been really supportive and a good listener on days I need to vent. I find myself jogging more and more these days just so I can pop over to her house and chat for a few minutes. Sometimes a few minutes turns into many cups of coffee and much needed laughter. I've cried to her on occasion, too. It's nice having Kate in my life.

And when she found out I had a fifteen-year-old she yelled, "Oh God, does she babysit? Please say yes. I'm desperate to find a new babysitter!"

That's how Annabelle got her first babysitting job.

This morning I've just finished running, and I'm sitting in Kate's kitchen.

"How are things going with your new man?" she asks, holding a box of donuts in front of me. I take one and place it on a napkin. It's hard to say no to donuts. It's a good thing I exercise.

"Good. Great, actually. I'm afraid I've got it bad for him. He's kind of perfect. It's scary and awesome at the same time. Oh, and I finally told Annabelle about him. I just sat her down last week and said, 'AB, I need to say something. I'm seeing a man. His name is Daniel. He's a few years older than me, and he has two teenage daughters, and I really like him.'"

Kate sits across from me and bites into a cream-filled donut. She wipes the corner of her mouth. "And? What was her reaction?"

"Get this. She said, 'It's about time you said something. I knew you were dating someone. I could tell by the way you've been practically dancing through the house, and how you hum all the time again, and how you regularly look like you've been making out. It's totally gross. But given the fact that your life has been shit lately, I'm happy for you.' Or something like that. That's pretty close to verbatim."

"I'm so glad the cat's out of the bag. With everything you have going on, you deserve to be happy. And I knew Annabelle would be okay with it. She gets it. She's a smart girl."

"Too smart," I say and take a big bite of donut.

Then she adds, "But I gotta be honest. You're making me look bad with all the exercising. You're constantly running! I mean, it kind of pisses me off, so knock it off, okay?"

We share a laugh and finish our donuts. Then we each have another.

"How are things with Ashley?" she asks after a few minutes. "Annabelle doesn't say much about her when she's here babysitting, and I don't ask."

I shift in my chair and stretch out my legs. Running isn't as easy in my forties as it was in my thirties. My muscles tighten often and quickly. "I've talked to her on the phone a couple of times."

"How's that going?" Kate sits a little straighter in her seat.

"The first time it went how I thought it would go, I think. It was pretty emotional. I was so nervous. My hands were shaking. But after I heard her voice, I went from nervous to incredibly sad. She sounded like she was ten years old again."

Kate nods and puts her hand on top of mine.

"She was upset with me in the beginning. She felt like I betrayed her trust by planning all this stuff behind her back. I listened and explained that I felt like she left me and her dad with no other option. And then something changed in her voice, and she said she understood why we did what we did. Then the conversation shifted and we talked about life on the mountain and her feelings and then she asked about Annabelle…and then the time was up. It went by so fast. Each time we speak it feels like five minutes instead of twenty-five. The last ten minutes or so I talk to Brent about her progress."

"So it's all productive, yes?"

I nod as Kate gets up and grabs the coffee pot. I wave her off. "No more for me. I need to get going. I've got to pack for Utah. I'm going to see Ashley this weekend. Steven is going too. This should make for an interesting trip—for lots of reasons."

We hug, and Kate walks me to the door.

"Yes, it should," she says. "I can't wait to hear all about it. Safe travels, and keep me posted. Does Annabelle need a place to stay? She's welcome to stay with us."

We step out onto the porch. "You know, that's not a bad idea. I'll run it past her. I'm sure her friend's parents are tired of hosting her. It's happened a lot lately."

Kate laughs and says, "Send her over here. The kids would love it. And I would too."

I hug her neck one more time. "Thanks, friend. I'm so glad I helped you carry the box of dead mother-in-law parts. Otherwise, you wouldn't be in my life."

"Ditto. Now get going, you."

Three days later, I'm on a plane on my way to Salt Lake City to spend the weekend with Ashley. She's been gone more than a month. Steven is a few rows in front of me in first class. I find this hilarious. As you know, it's not the first time this scenario has played out—although this time I'm not wishing he would be would magically and swiftly ejected from his seat to plummet thirty thousand feet to his death. No, this time I'm in a much better place: in the comfort of my cramped middle seat in row twenty-seven, sandwiched between a large, sweaty man in a business suit and an elderly woman who talks too loud.

Annabelle is spending the weekend at Kate's house. I thought for sure there was no way she'd want to do that. I assumed she'd prefer Kelsey's. But no. She told me it would be a nice change of pace to stay at the Witts'. She says they have better food. Also, she likes Kate as much as I do. She's told me so.

I have all kinds of feelings and emotions driving me right now. I'm excited to see Ashley, to get to hold her and talk to her and spend time with her. I'm also scared shitless. This is a new chapter in our lives, and hopefully the story has a happy ending. I'm optimistic that the changes Ashley's making are real and permanent, but I'm also cautious. It takes a lot of work and persistence to change a behavior—that's what I'm learning in my weekly phone calls with Brent. Three times now I've been able to talk to Ashley, and she sounds great. It's all been positive, for the most part.

The way Brent approaches her is completely different from the way I was raised, and the way I've raised the girls. He tends to listen more and talk less, while I spew out dos and don'ts as a way of "controlling" my kids' behavior. He says they need to feel like they have a voice—that they can talk to you about anything, good or bad, and you'll help them. It's hard for me to understand this, because my childhood was less than ideal.

I've always lived a play-it-by-ear approach. I'm learning now this wasn't the best course of action. If kids don't feel like they can get the answers or guidance they so desperately need from their parents, they start to look elsewhere. And they don't always pick the best person or people to follow. When I think about it, I have applied the play-it-by-ear thing to other relationships as well: first with my brother Benny after our mom died, then with my college roommate, and of course with Steven.

One thing is for sure. Steven and I have a lot to learn as parents, and possibly as human beings. We haven't exactly compared notes after our separate conversations with Ashley and with Brent, but I would guess we share most of the same feelings.

As we descend over the snowcapped mountains in Utah, I turn to look out the window and think, *she's out there somewhere*. Butterflies swim laps in my stomach as the plane lands on the tarmac. The large, sweaty man to my right suddenly coughs in my face, then goes on about his business without so much as an "excuse me" or a "here, let me help you wipe my germs off your face." I need to get off this plane as soon as possible.

Steven is waiting for me when I get to baggage claim. He holds his duffle bag in one hand and reads something on his phone with the other while I struggle to pull my bag off the carousel. It takes more than one try and most of my strength to retrieve it. He never looks up or offers to lend me a hand: Number 245 on my list of things I don't miss about being married to Steven, in case you're keeping score.

I glare at him as I wheel my bag over. He looks up then, smiles, and says, "Ah, you got your bag finally. Shall we head over to the car rental desk?"

"Sure."

While Steven signs the rental agreement (he suggested we share a car, which he also offered to pay for), I check my phone for messages. I have one voicemail from Daniel. He misses me already and wishes me luck. I can't help but smile. I'm not a religious person, but lately I have thanked God for sending him to me. I'm not sure I believe Daniel came to me through spiritual intervention—it could have just been dumb luck (being in the right place at the right time), but I'm not going to question it. All I can do now is hope he sticks around. I may even consider praying about it. I don't know who I am anymore.

The drive to New Horizons is four hours, but when you're riding in the car with your ex-husband, it feels longer. We chit chat and make small talk for the first hour or so, reminiscing about memories of the girls or funny things from college. It gets quiet after we run out of things to say, so I stare out the passenger window and get lost in my own thoughts. I think about Daniel, a lot. I wonder what he's doing, what he's having for lunch. I even think about what shirt he might be wearing today. He looks incredible in everything he puts on. He may be nearing fifty years old, but he has the body of a man in his thirties. I close my eyes, and I must even moan a little because Steven suddenly asks, "Did you say something?"

I just got busted (by my ex-husband) for thinking about my boyfriend's body. There's a country song about this very thing. I'm sure of it.

"No. I do need to stop soon, though." I feel like my face is three shades of red. Steven doesn't seem to notice. He keeps his eyes on the road and says, "Okay, there's a bunch of places coming up."

After doing my business (peeing) and grabbing a bottle of water and a package of Cheez-Its, I'm back in the car. Steven is on the phone as I reach over to secure my seat belt.

"It hasn't come up," he says. "I gotta go. I'll call you later."

He ends the call and pulls the car onto the highway. I open the package of crackers. I offer the bag to Steven, but he declines.

"You're still addicted to Cheez-Its, I see."

"If eating Cheez-Its is wrong, I don't want to be right," I tell him.

He laughs and shakes his head.

After licking the last of the crumbs from the inside of the cracker bag, I dust my hands off on my jeans (a terrible habit of mine, not to mention messy) and scroll through the dial on the radio. I land on a classic rock station playing "Blinded By the Light," lay my head back on the seat, and quietly sing along.

"Blinded by the light…wrapped up like a douche, another runner in the night."

Steven shouts, "Oh my God, those aren't the words! I've told you a million times, it's *deuce,* not *douche*. Who would put the word *douche* in a song?"

"Those weirdo rock stars, that's who."

Steve looks over at me then, all crazy-like, which makes me snort. We both laugh so hard I think I might throw up the entire bag of Cheez-Its.

After a few minutes of giggling and arguing over the words, Steven turns down the radio. "Um, hey, I need to talk to you about something."

I have no idea where this is going, but knowing Steven like I do, I'm probably not going to like it.

"Okay."

"Well, first off, Annabelle tells me you're seeing someone. I'm really happy for you."

"Steven—"

"Sar, please let me talk," he says as he cuts me off. "I mean it when I say I'm happy for you. You deserve a guy who'll treat you, well...a lot better than I did. I know I fucked up, and I'm sorry. I don't know how serious it is, but AB seems to think it is—serious, I mean."

He takes a deep breath and grips the steering wheel before continuing. "Monica and I are getting married. I know how you feel about her—"

He really has no idea since we've never talked about it, ever.

"—and I know how we met was shitty and sneaky and how I failed you and all that business. I know. But despite how it happened, the truth is, I love her, and I want a life with her. I hope we can continue to work together as parents and maybe even one day become friends again. I just wanted you to hear it from me and not from anyone else."

"Okay." I look down at my hands. My fingernails are misshapen. I make a mental note to file them when we get to the hotel.

"Okay? That's all you have to say?" His voice is louder than necessary, which irritates me.

"What do you want me to say, Steven? That I'm happy for you? That I wish you and Monica all the happiness life has to offer? Give me a fucking break. *We* had a life together. If I remember correctly, you said these exact words about us—how you loved *me* and wanted a life with *me*. I loved you. And yes, you drove me crazy; you still do, if I'm being completely honest. Maybe if you'd come to me and told me how you felt—that you didn't love me anymore or that you had feelings for someone else, this wouldn't hurt so badly. But the way you went about it was disgusting. And while no, I'm not still holding on to hope that we'll get back together—nor would I want that—what you did just crushed me. It made me feel unlovable."

An uncomfortable silence settles in the car. I hadn't planned on going off on him like that. I said *okay*, which was all I'd planned on saying (in the one second I had to plan my response) because I felt like *okay* was the least hostile way to reply.

"You're anything but unlovable. But you know and I know that our marriage had issues. Did I handle things badly? Absolutely. And I'll keep apologizing to you for as long as I need to."

"Don't patronize me, Steven," I snap.

"I'm sorry. That came out wrong. Look, Sarah, there will always be a part of me that loves you. I have thousands of wonderful memories with you, and you're the person who gave me the best gift anyone could ever give: two beautiful children. We're connected forever through them."

He's starting to sound like a cheesy Hallmark card. I wish he would just stop talking already. I try to channel therapist Brent and reroute the conversation. "Where will you get married?"

He clears his throat. "On a beach in Puerto Vallarta."

"Sounds amazing. What's the attire? Beachwear? Sundress?"

Steven turns his head toward me with this kind of blank stare on his face.

"I'm invited to the wedding, right? I'll bring my boyfriend. It won't be awkward at all."

The awkwardness in the car, however, can be felt for miles and miles. And on the inside I'm laughing my ass off and high-fiving myself for my snarky attitude. That'll teach Steven to talk to me about his love life and his new fiancée.

Kate would find all of this hilarious. I can't wait to tell her about it.

The last hour of the car ride is mostly silent. I can tell Steven is relieved to have unburdened himself by announcing his news. Don't ask me how I can tell, I just can. I've known him a long time.

He turns off the main highway onto a dirt road and drives a few more miles. It's covered in snow and ice, and I adjust my seat belt tighter. Steven is not accustomed to driving in these wintery conditions, and I worry we might crash into a tree—or off the side of a cliff. On the left we see a sign over a massive front gate that reads *New Horizons*. It has icicles hanging off the bottom of it. Jesus, it's freezing here. My poor girl is living outside in the freezing cold.

Suddenly I feel panic and possibly terror setting in. I'm so freaked out about seeing Ashley. My brain keeps telling my heart, *Calm down. She's your daughter. Everything will be fine.* But my heart's not buying it. It's the same feeling I had a few weeks ago when I was jogging off my regular route and a dog came out of nowhere and chased after me, barking. You've never seen a person run as fast as I ran those two blocks before Cujo got tired or bored and gave up trying to catch me. My heart was pounding so fast I thought it might fly out of my chest and land in the middle of the street.

It took me a couple of days to get over the fear that it might happen again. But I reasoned that as long as I stay in my neighborhood, where the dogs are familiar with me, I shouldn't have to worry about being attacked. That first day back I must have checked behind me a thousand times. It's a wonder I didn't give myself whiplash.

Steven parks the car next to a building that looks a lot like a ski lodge. At first impression, this seems like a pretty nice place. I look around in every direction, and the view almost takes my breath away. Everything is white with snow. It's quite peaceful.

"You ready to go inside?" Steven's voice startles me. I realize then I had completely zoned out there for a second. I wrap a scarf around my neck and pull on my coat.

"Okay."

Steven makes a face. He clearly now opposes the word *okay.*

As we make our way up the steps to the front door, it opens, and standing before us is a nice-enough-looking woman wearing a Charlie Brown sweatshirt. The second thing I notice about her are the two pair of glasses sitting atop her head. She smiles with her eyes—always a good sign—and introduces herself.

"So nice to meet you; I'm Maggie." We shake hands and exchange pleasantries. She invites us in and offers us something to drink. I decline, but Steven asks for water.

There are other people there—probably parents like us, visiting their kids, too. We all share the same expression: we have no idea what to expect. I find two chairs next to a woman busy knitting. She smiles and stops working the needles long enough to move her bag over so I can sit down. Then she goes right back to work. Steven sits in the chair next to mine and immediately gets on his phone. He's checking text messages or reading emails or looking at porn—who knows.

Maggie is still smiling at us (I'm guessing there are about fourteen people in all) as she comes to stand at the front of the room with a clipboard.

"Okay," she begins. "I think everyone is here. That's great. First off, welcome, parents and loved ones. We're so glad you could be here for this very special weekend in your child's recovery. This marks the halfway point in the program for a lot of you, and it means your child is doing well and participating and making great progress toward success. Now, with all that said, there are still challenges ahead. We don't perform magic or place any kind of voodoo hex on your kids—" Laughter breaks out. "—that miraculously changes them into perfect people. Don't I wish."

She pauses for more laughter before continuing. "But, what I can offer you is this: Take this weekend to enjoy your child and really talk to him or her. Just let the dialogue flow. We ask that you do a lot of listening. The kids are working with their therapists to learn how to open up and share their thoughts and fears and also how to talk to their parents, you guys, in a productive way. You see, a lot of issues kids have these days are because they don't feel like they have a voice. We're trying to help them realize they do, but to also use it in a way that works—in a non-destructive way. Does this sound agreeable to all of you so far?"

We collectively nod and answer yes.

"Great. Here's the plan: The kids know you're here and are very excited, but they're also nervous, just as I know you are. It's okay. It's normal to feel like this. The last time most of you saw your kids was a pretty traumatic event."

The memory of that morning invades my mind now—just as it often fills my dreams and wakes me up crying.

"The campsite where you'll join your kids is about forty-five minutes up the mountain. We'll caravan up there, and you'll be reunited and get to spend a few minutes hugging and visiting. Then the counselors will have the kids rejoin their groups to show you some of the wilderness-living skills they've learned and use on a daily basis. Then lunch will be served: sandwiches, chips, soda or water, and a cookie. This is the part where the kids get really excited. I know most of you know this because you've had the opportunity to talk to your kids on the phone, but they normally eat SPAM, oatmeal, lentils—things like that. A sandwich will seem like a porterhouse steak to them today."

Again, laughter among the parents.

"After lunch I'll go over the guidelines for the weekend, including rules the kids are to continue to follow and so on and so forth. They already know what's expected of them, but we'll revisit the conversation so they know you're on board too. Then the fun begins. You get to take your child for the next seventy-two hours. We only ask that you stay in Utah—no jetting off to Hawaii, unless you're going to take me with you—and keep the social media to a minimum. We discourage the use of Facebook, Twitter, Snapchat, et cetera. This tends to be challenging, but social media can be very confusing for the kids. Using it, they're able to reach out to people who may not be good for them at this point in their lives, so avoiding those platforms helps keep them moving in the right direction. We can't force the issue, but we encourage it. That's all I have to say about all that. Now...let's head up to the campsite!"

During the car ride up the mountain, I realize I can't get to Ashley fast enough. We're moving so slowly—this line of eight cars is traveling at a snail's pace. The road we're on has obviously been traveled a lot, so the ice and snow are mostly gone. Seeing this helps ease my fears of sliding off the side and crashing to my death below. It feels like we've been driving for days by the time we reach the top and find a parking space. Lawn chairs are set up in a circle around a campfire, and I wonder how much longer before I see my girl. I start to shiver.

"Are you nervous?" Steven asks as we grab bottles of water off a plastic table and find our seats.

"A little. You?"

"My hands are shaking." He holds them out to show me.

Before I can say anything more, someone starts singing. It's a tall man with a beard and beer gut. He looks like some kind of wilderness man with his canvas hat and walking stick. We sit quietly and listen as he sings a song about a bird. Or maybe it's about a car. I have no idea what he's saying, but it's...soothing.

In the distance we see them—a group of seven or eight kids, all wearing matching clothes, making their way to the campsite. As they get closer my eyes race across their faces. I'm trying desperately to find Ashley.

There she is, the fourth person back. She looks taller, but much younger than her seventeen years. She's wearing a hat similar to the singing wilderness man's, and her clothes are so dirty she reminds of the homeless guy who's always standing on the corner near the post office. His sign reads: *Not on drugs, just hungry.* If Ashley held a sign right now it would read: *Not homeless, just need a shower.*

She looks over, appearing to scan the crowd for a familiar face. As soon as she sees me her eyes widen, and she smiles so big I can almost see all of her teeth. The relief I feel is so great I'm afraid I might melt into a giant puddle. I wonder if my legs will be able to hold me up when it's time to stand. Once the group of kids has reached the circle area, the counselor—a stocky woman who looks to be about my age—dismisses them. Kids scatter in every direction, and I wipe my sweaty palms against the sides of my legs in anticipation of holding Ashley in my arms.

She runs to me. I take a few steps forward (legs still work!) and she's there, in my arms, sobbing into my shoulder. It's a good cry, a happy, joyful release. I know this because I'm crying too, and it feels good to be holding her again. She pulls back from me, still smiling and crying, and reaches for Steven. I watch as she wraps herself around him, his body dwarfing hers. She seems so small in his hold, like she's seven years old again.

I see tears streaming down Steven's face as he says to her over and over again, "I love you so much."

After a few minutes of hugging and talking and crying and hugging some more, the counselor (Ashley said her name is Gail) calls the kids back together near the fire. I hold on to Ashley's hand, not wanting to let her go so soon. She promises she'll be right back, and as I watch her walk away from me, I am overcome with emotion. The next thing I know, Steven wraps his arm around my waist, and the two of us stand there and sway back and forth. Tears continue to fill my eyes—Steven's too.

The kids put on quite a little show for us. We watch them make fires from sticks and rocks, which is pretty cool. Ashley is really skilled at wilderness life. Who would've known? She seems to be a leader among the group, which surprises me but also doesn't. Now that I've spent some time thinking about it, I've realized that over the last couple of years, Ashley has lost all of her childhood friends. Could this be true? I wrack my brain trying to picture a girlfriend in Ashley's life and have come up completely blank.

As a little girl, she was always the one who would start a game and get everyone to play along. Friends looked up to her and wanted to be around her all the time. I can't tell you how many sleepovers we had with her friends. She was happy. I always said to anybody who would listen that she was a born leader. And then something happened right after middle school. It was like she lost her confidence and doubted her self-worth. I asked around — the teacher, the nurse, some of the other moms — if anyone knew whether something had happened. Every person said the same thing: Nothing had happened. Nothing had changed. And yet, I could see something was different.

I brought up my concerns with Steven one time a few years ago and suggested Ashley maybe see a counselor. He thought I was being overdramatic.

"School is hard," he told me. "Kids are mean to each other. Ashley's fine. She's just a teenager. You worry too much."

I listened to him because he tends to be the more levelheaded, rational one between us.

I know the divorce didn't help things either. I became depressed. I was lonely. I was unhappy. I was emotionally unavailable. This probably exacerbated an already difficult time in Ashley's life. I see that now. If I could get a do-over, I'd try to react to things differently.

I watch as Ashley helps a much younger girl get her fire started, and I can't help but swell with pride. It's like watching your daughter score the winning goal. If I had pom-poms, I would be cheering, "Goooooo, Ashley, go, go, go!" That would most definitely embarrass her.

Lunch is served. To me (and probably Steven), it's just a substandard sub sandwich made with turkey and processed cheese and wilted lettuce on a hoagie. To Ashley, it's clearly a gourmet meal. She finishes off her sandwich in no more than four bites. Which is something to see. The kids are allowed an extra sandwich if they're still hungry after the first one, so Ashley eats a second, plus part of mine. The poor baby is practically starving. She shoves Steven's cookie in her pocket for later.

After listening to Maggie and Gail speak to the kids one last time, Steven, Ashley, and I head to the rental car to begin our weekend together.

Ashley is quiet for the drive down the mountain. I don't ask questions or try to force a conversation. I just let her be. Music from the radio plays softly, the volume so low I have to listen hard to hear what song is playing. Steven's phone buzzes in his pants pocket every few minutes. He keeps ignoring it, but someone clearly needs to get in touch with him.

"Dad, answer your phone. That sound is annoying me."

Ashley's first words since we got in the car sound like Ashley from home. At least we know she hasn't had a personality transplant.

Steven pulls the phone from his pocket and looks at the screen. "It's just work. I'll call them later."

It takes about an hour to get to the hotel I've booked for us. It's a local place, not one of the major chains. Trip Advisor reviewed it as the top hotel in the area. However, there are only four hotels, total, in a twenty-mile radius. So really, "luxury accommodations" could mean "better than a cardboard box." We shall see.

I booked two rooms next to each other. Ashley will stay in my room tonight and in Steven's room tomorrow night—if that's what she wants. We lug our things up to the second floor and enter the rooms. The first thing Ashley does is collapse facedown on the king-size bed. She's still wearing her dirty yellow T-shirt, khaki pants, and hiking boots. Her backpack smells like fire and burned things. Her hair is stringy and matted, like she's one week away from dreadlocks. A minute after lying down, she's dead asleep.

I slip quietly out of the room and walk toward the lobby, choosing this time to call Daniel and check in with Annabelle. I call, but she doesn't answer. I send her a quick text. And Kate too.

Daniel answers the phone on the first ring. The sound of his voice propels me to a peaceful place. Even the way he says "hello" calms me. We talk for fifteen minutes or so, and I try my best to fill him in on everything that's happened. I even jokingly mention that we're invited to Steven and Monica's wedding. He doesn't seem to think it's as funny as I do. Damn, I should've just saved the joke for Kate instead.

Daniel says he loves me before hanging up, and I say it back. We end the call, and when I turn around to go back up to the room, I nearly crash into Steven.

"So it is serious," he says.

"What are you talking about?" I know exactly what he's talking about.

"I heard you, just now, on the phone. You said I love you."

"I could have been talking to Annabelle."

"But you weren't. Because I was." *Damn.* That's why she didn't answer the phone when I called.

"How is she? Okay?"

"She's fine. She's the last person you should worry about."

"You've said that before...about Ashley. Remember?"

"Yes, but this time I'm right."

He has this way about him, the way he finishes sentences—like he believes the words coming out of his mouth should be scribed on stone tablets. I used to find it sexy and powerful. Now he just seems like an arrogant dick.

"So this guy you're seeing, will I like him?" Steven hasn't blinked once since we nearly ran into each other. It's a little creepy.

I might as well just get this out in the open. "I think so. He's nothing like you, but you'll get why I like him. He's really good to me. He makes me happy."

"That's great, Sarah. I look forward to meeting him. Do you think you'll marry him?" Steven shoves his hands in his front pockets and starts rocking back and forth on his heels. He finally blinks, thank God.

"I don't know. It's too soon to know. We haven't dated that long."

"But you love him."

"Yes."

"Would you have more children?"

"What? Are you serious? Steven, how old do you think I am? I'm peri-menopausal, for cryin' out loud. Plus, I've had a *hysterectomy*, remember? I can't physically birth children anymore."

"Oh, I forgot about that."

Of course he did.

"What is going on with you? You seem...odd." It's true. He's been acting strange since we left Texas. This isn't about Ashley either. This is something else. This guy is not in his right mind.

Steven looks down at the ground, not making eye contact with me. "Monica's pregnant."

A baby. At his age—it's laughable. But I did feel bad for the guy. You should've seen his face as he talked about becoming a father again.

I mean, honestly, though, what did he expect? Monica is practically a teenager—no, a toddler. Her boobs haven't begun to sag, and she probably thinks cellulite is some kind of protein drink. It's ridiculous, actually. And I say, better him than me. Not that I could have any more children even if I wanted them. And I don't. Of course I don't. I haven't the strength or the patience to go through all that again. So why is there an aching feeling in my chest? It feels a lot like loss. It's the same feeling I experienced after having a hysterectomy four years ago.

I'd been having issues with my parts down there. It felt like my uterus was falling out of my vagina. And so I made an appointment with Laura, my friend and OB/Gyn. After an examination she said to me, "Sarah, your uterus is falling out of your vagina."

See? I told you that's what it felt like.

That was pretty much the end of the road for my reproductive organs. Laura took out everything except my left ovary. She said it was still perfectly pink and viable and would allow me to live free of hormone replacement therapy, hopefully until menopause. I considered writing a book about the whole experience and titling it *My Left Ovary*, but Rachel, my editor at the time, said it was a stupid idea, and no one would read it. I didn't have the heart to tell her I was only half kidding. She was in her early twenties, so of course it seemed stupid to her. I'm sure *all* of her parts were pink and viable, not just one sad little ovary.

Having your organs (the very ones that distinguish you from a man) taken from you messes with your head—or at least it messed with mine. It made me sad to think I would no longer be able to create a life, to birth a human being. Not that I wanted more children. I didn't. But that was on my terms. *I* made the decision to not have more kids—not someone else.

But after the surgery, this was no longer the case. I had lost control of my own body. Not that I could ever control what my organs do or don't do, but seriously? My body revolted against me and started making decisions for itself. I found this infuriating, depressing, and totally unfair. Laura even put me on an antidepressant for a year. It was that bad.

As it was happening, I tried to find the humor in it—thus the idea for *My Left Ovary*. I even bought a glass jar and brought it to the hospital on the day of my surgery. I joked with Laura about saving my uterus so I could keep it on the nightstand next to my bed. I think that was about the time she encouraged me to take medication. She refused to put my failing body parts in the jar.

Steven tried to be supportive during that time, although not one part of him understood what I was going through. He didn't know what to say or how to act around me—like I'd suddenly grown another head, and he wasn't sure where to look. And I didn't push it. How could he possibly relate to what was happening to me? He's a man. Men don't understand what it's like to grow a human being inside you—and what it would mean if you couldn't anymore. Just like I don't have the slightest clue what having a penis is like. I imagine it's heavy (depending on length and girth, of course), and I'm pretty sure getting a boner would throw me off balance to the point where I'd be running into walls and stuff…

What I'm trying to say is I'm a little envious of Steven right now.

CHAPTER 26

Steven

My ex-wife thinks I'm acting odd. She just said as much before she went off to find an ATM. For the record, I'm more than a little odd these days. I'm going to be a fucking father again.

When Monica first told me we were going to have a baby, I busted out laughing. This had to be some kind of joke, right? I mean, we were sitting on the sofa watching the Mavs play the Heat in a pivotal game in the NBA playoff picture. The Dallas Mavericks had been hovering over the eighth seed spot (the last spot) for the last two weeks, and a few more losses would doom their chances of making the playoffs. A win over the Heat would hopefully help them turn the corner and get on a winning streak. Monica had been quiet during the game, not really paying attention to the action on the TV, but I didn't think anything of it. She's not really a basketball fan.

Then as soon as the buzzer whistled the end of the first half, she turned to me and said, "By the way, I know it's terrible timing, but I'm pregnant."

After the words registered in my brain, I decided she was fucking with me, so I started laughing. But then I looked at her face, and she was doing the exact opposite—she was crying. I reached for her hand, but she jerked it away and stormed out of the room. She slammed our bedroom door so hard it felt like the whole house was shaking.

I went to her and tried to open the door, but it was locked. "Monica, please open the door. I'm sorry. I thought you were kidding. I know now—obviously—that you aren't. Please come out so we can talk about this."

The door opened, and she stood there with black streaks under her eyes. I put my hand up to her face and used my thumb to wipe the tears away. "I'm sorry, baby. So…pregnant, huh?"

She didn't say anything. She just smiled and nodded. This was good news to her.

I knew this was a possibility when I signed up for the relationship. Monica is just thirty-one years old. Of course she wants kids of her own. I thought maybe it wouldn't come up—that if I kept her happy and entertained and showered her with gifts and nice trips, well, maybe that would be enough. I guess I bet on the wrong horse.

"Let's go sit down and make a plan, okay?" I led her into the kitchen, and we sat opposite each other at the table and mapped out the next twenty years of our lives. I'll be sixty-three when this kid graduates from high school. The realization of all this—the starting over from zero, the newborn stage, the terrible twos, the Little League games, the homework, the sleepovers, the trips to Disney World, the worrying all the time—I was almost done. We're going to beat this thing with Ashley. I could see the finish line.

I have two girls. That's always been enough for me. I've raised kids with Sarah. I've already done this. And now it appears I'm going to do it all again.

"Steven, are you feeling okay? You look pale." Sarah is standing in front of me again with her hand on my shoulder. She seems to have found the ATM.

"I'm fine," I lie. "Shall we go?"

Already this weekend, Ashley, Sarah, and I have spent hours talking, and it's only the second day. As I stare into the hotel bathroom mirror and give my face a quick shave, I know there's more to come. We haven't talked this way in years. Maybe ever. I've learned so much from our daughter. Through her therapy sessions with Brent, she's beginning to understand why she's made all the wrong choices lately.

We sat and listened to her explain how the divorce and her lack of self-esteem caused her to self-sabotage.

When she brought up the divorce, I was immediately overcome with guilt. I am partly responsible for her pain. I was not aware until now that she doubted her self-worth. I would never in my wildest dreams imagine that she could think of herself as anything other than smart, funny, vivacious, and beautiful. She's like Sarah in so many ways, and yet she told us she thought of herself as a failure.

She said Brent has been able to help her see the error in that belief system. She's starting to see the things in herself that everyone else who knows her sees. And it's giving her confidence and a new reality. These are *her* words. It's funny, this girl in front of me is so much older and so much more mature than the one who lived with me just a couple of months ago. She's bright-eyed and optimistic and, dare I say, happy?

So far, Utah is beautiful. There's a river about an hour's drive from where we're staying, so we go there to rent a raft. "River rafting" was printed on the sheet of Things To Do that Maggie handed out. Sarah, being Sarah, buys a Styrofoam cooler and packs it with sandwiches (that she makes on the hood of the car) and bottled water. A kid in a van drives us (and our raft) another hour away and drops us off in a designated spot. None of us is an experienced water person (or particularly adventurous), but the man at the rental place assures us the river is safe.

The views are spectacular. The sounds of water and nature drown out the dialogue constantly playing in my head. I stare at every angle of my surroundings, taking mental pictures to refer to later. Looking at the vastness around me, I am quickly reminded just how insignificant I am. This moment is important. And it isn't at all about me.

There's an easy lilt in Ashley's voice. I'm not sure I've seen her this way since the time we took her to Magic Kingdom to meet Cinderella when she was six. Sarah is happy too. And I know I have nothing to do with it. She's met someone, and he's filling my old shoes.

The thought of another man touching her or loving her shoots a fiery shockwave through my body. She's not mine anymore, and I'm responsible for that. I screwed it up, but not when I had an affair. I destroyed our marriage a long time before Monica came into the picture. I pushed Sarah away. I'm not even sure she realizes that. She was changing, evolving into a confident, clever woman. She's incredibly witty and good with words. People all over the world read what she writes. She was bigger than life. It threatened me in some way. Like maybe she would outgrow me. That she might find me ridiculous. So I pushed her out of reach before any of those outcomes could materialize.

The raft moves lazily across the cold water. We have paddles, but so far we've been able to let the currents drive us down the river. Sarah uses her phone to take pictures of the views and then a few of Ashley and me. I realize this weekend is a good thing happening in our lives. Maybe even the whole Ashley situation is a good thing. It sure didn't feel like it a few months ago. It felt scary and out of control and dangerous—like watching a hurricane make landfall when you can't get out in time. But we're surviving the rising water and mass destruction and utter devastation, and I can see the sun just up ahead, signaling a new beginning. Just maybe.

We guide the raft to land and pull it up on shore. Sarah grabs the cooler and struggles to get a good grasp on it. Lord knows it's loaded to capacity. I reach over and take it from her, to help her. She looks at me like she's seeing me for the very first time. It's strange. She points to a tree a few feet away.

The three of us sit down under a tree and huddle together to keep warm and eat sandwiches.

"I can't believe you can make a fire by rubbing sticks together," Sarah says. "I thought that only happened in cartoons."

Ashley laughs. "I know. I wouldn't believe it either. At first I was like, there's no way this is going to work. But it does."

Sarah puts down her sandwich and grabs Ashley's hand. "I admire you, Ash. You're so smart. I mean, when you're not being dumb." We all laugh. "Seriously though, I'm proud of you. This can't be easy, and it's a lot of work."

"Me too," I say. "You're doing great, kid."

Ashley stands up and wipes dirt off her behind. "Well, it's not like I had a choice. I'm here, so I guess I should make the best of it."

"That's the spirit," Sarah says. "Now help me get up."

We finish our lunch and take turns peeing behind bushes. Both girls laugh and say this is the only time they wish they had a penis. I tease them and say, "Want a tip? Never eat yellow snow." It makes them laugh. After that, we're off again down the river. It's been quite a pleasant day. Cold, but pleasant. At least the sun is shining brightly. There isn't a cloud in the sky.

There have been difficult moments too, of course—filled with sadness and anger and tears. It was gut-wrenching sitting on the bed in the hotel room, all three of us, listening to Ashley tell her version of things. As she spoke, I wondered if I would have been willing to do this—to let her share her side of the story—before she went away. I'm not sure I would. I'm stubborn and, at times, unwilling to accept the fact that I'm not always right.

After dinner that night we sit in front of the fire in the hotel lobby. There's no one around but the three of us.

Ashley turns to me. "Dad, why'd you leave us? I mean, what's the real reason? Not the reason you think we want to hear."

Her words cut through me like a Samurai sword. Sarah is quiet, listening. She must want to know too. She's certainly not jumping in to help me.

"First off, baby, I didn't leave you. I left your mother."

"Ouch," Sarah says.

Ashley moves next to Sarah and puts her arm around her, and I suddenly feel like a giant asshole. "That came out wrong. Look, Ashley, I love your mother. She knows that. Sarah, you know that."

They say nothing. They're just sitting there, staring at me like I'm some kind of monster.

"Sweetheart, it wasn't an easy decision, or something I planned. Your mom and I started moving in different directions. We were growing apart. She had her writing, and I was working insane hours. The only thing keeping us together, in my mind, was you girls."

I don't know what's happening, but suddenly I'm sobbing. The tears started flowing before I had time to fight them back. I think this is what my therapist would call a breakthrough.

Yes, you heard that right. Therapist.

After Ashley left for Utah, Monica encouraged me to see one. I fought her on it for a few days, but ended up making an appointment with a man one of my colleagues recommended. Of course I didn't tell him it was for me. I said it was for a friend. Can you believe that tired old lie still works on people? Or maybe he knew I was bullshitting, but he didn't call me out.

Either way, I've never been in therapy before. I believed it meant admitting weakness or that I somehow lacked control. People need to see that I'm in control. I need to know I'm in control. Control is what separates successful people from average people. People in control are the rulers of the world, the decision makers, the caretakers, and the wealthy.

After a month in therapy I've learned to stop worrying about controlling everything and start realizing I'm not God. Yes, the comparison to God has come up once or twice. I've since been knocked off my throne.

Therapy is not fun for me. I get defensive; I lash out. But my therapist just keeps hammering back. After every session, I feel like I've boxed six rounds—and lost. But the good news is, I'm learning to let God be God. I just need to be the best version of me. There's no way I would've come to this conclusion without intensive counseling. It sucks. You know how I know it sucks? This is one of the few times I've ever cried in front of anyone. It doesn't happen often or easily. I think therapy works. I will never admit this out loud.

The girls embrace me then and the three of us stand in a sort of awkward huddle. I wonder what Sarah must think of me. Does she believe I'm different, that I've changed? God knows I never had any sort of emotional outburst when we were together—except for breaking down when Ashley left with those people that early morning to come here. And why do I even give a shit what Sarah thinks of me? I wish I could get the fuck out of my own head.

After another few seconds, Sarah pulls away first. Ashley holds on to me a little longer, and we sit quietly for a few minutes. The only sounds are the crackling from the burning wood. Eventually we say goodnight, and Sarah and Ashley disappear into their room. I'm left standing in the hallway, unsure what to do next. So I ride the elevator back down to the lobby, walk into the sorry excuse for a bar, and get completely shitfaced on cheap scotch.

CHAPTER 27

Ashley

Spending the weekend with my parents has been really great. I'm sad that it's over. It wasn't long enough, and more than that, I wish I could fit inside my mom's suitcase and fly home with her.

Instead I'm back at New Horizons, once again wearing my camp-issued gear: yellow T-shirt, khaki pants, hiking boots, winter coat. Mom washed all my clothes in the hotel laundry room, and she did her best to get the campfire smell out of them. I'm afraid it's a lost cause. Maybe I'll forever smell like burning wood. My hair has grown so much in the last month and a half. My mom couldn't get over it. She braided it for me. I'll keep it this way as long as I can. It will feel like she's still here.

We're saying the last of our goodbyes now. Dad keeps hugging me over and over, and then it's Mom's turn. Finally Gail yells my name, and I know it's time to leave. I smile, fight back tears, and strap on my too-heavy backpack. One more hug each and then I walk over to meet the group.

As we begin hiking through a clump of snow-covered trees, I turn around to look at my parents one last time (for the next forty-five days or so). My dad is standing next to my mom and has his arm around her. She blows me a kiss, and I pretend to catch it. That makes her smile. I keep checking back until I can no longer see them. They're probably getting in the rental car right about now. Ahead of me, it's a long day of hiking to the next campsite. Another latrine to build. More group meetings. Another pitch-black night, sleeping on the ground in a tent in the freezing cold. But hey, at least now I have a flashlight and a chair. So I guess it could be worse.

Being here is not the worst thing in the world, but it's no picnic.

I do like my sessions with Brent. I'll admit that. He's the first person who's ever really listened to me. My mom is a good mom, but she's not the best listener. I mean, she listens, but she doesn't really hear me. She's one of those people who just wants everything to be okay, no matter what. If I'm feeling sad? *Think good thoughts*, she says. Girls are being mean at school? *Find new friends. You don't need those girls.* That's the kind of advice she gives. It's not terrible; it's just not helpful. She was different than normal this weekend, I'll give her that. She nodded her head a lot and seemed to press her lips together, like she was fighting back saying something.

I've never talked to my dad about anything that's going on with me because he always seems too busy. And I've been afraid he would think my feelings are stupid. Once I was in the kitchen making a sandwich while Mom and Dad sat at the table, obviously in the middle of a conversation. She had written a story for some parenting website (I didn't read it), and she'd printed off a copy for my dad to read. She often did this, to get his feedback—although now that I think about it, she did it less and less toward the end of their marriage.

Anyway, while Dad was reading, my mom had her elbow on the table and her chin propped up on her hand. She was smiling at Dad, waiting for him to finish. His expression was blank, never once cracking a smile. When he finished reading, he handed the pages back to Mom and said, "I don't really find the merit in humor. It seems silly."

The look on Mom's face was horrific. It was like he'd punched her in the gut. I wanted to punch *him* in the gut. I was only sixteen at the time, and even I knew what he said was awful. My mom's writing career is everything to her, and he'd just dealt her the lowest blow.

She didn't say anything, and he just got up from the table and walked away like nothing happened. That's kind of when I knew I shouldn't talk to him about anything. If he thought Mom was ridiculous, what would he think of me?

So he doesn't really know anything about my life—well, I guess he knows some things now. But until all this happened we stuck with the obvious: I'm a girl. I'm a senior in high school. I like sports. And perhaps he knows my birthday. Although maybe my mom just reminds him about it.

CHAPTER 28

Sarah

I got home from Utah late last night. It was after eleven when I parked my car in the garage, so I slipped off my shoes and tiptoed into Annabelle's room to check on her. She was asleep with a book laying on top of her chest. I picked it up, careful not to lose her place, and as I went to lay it on her nightstand, I noticed the title: *The Encyclopedia of Serial Killers*. Interesting. But I was too exhausted to worry about AB's choice of bedtime reading at that moment. I kissed her forehead, turned off the lamp, and closed her door behind me.

I went to my room and changed into sweatpants and a T-shirt. I told myself I could skip washing my face for just one night, but I drew the line at not brushing my teeth. As I slid between the sheets, I found my thoughts drifting toward Daniel. It had been four days since I'd seen him, and I realized I ached for him. We'd talked some throughout the weekend—when I could steal a moment or two—but I really wanted to see him, feel him next to me. I willed my mind to hurry and go to sleep, so I could have just that. He's coming over tomorrow night.

Next thing I knew, it was morning.

I woke up a little after six thirty, and I feel as though I aged ten years overnight. Every muscle in my body is sore, and my head is foggy, like I've taken a sedative. I will myself out of bed and into the bathroom.

Standing at the sink, I splash water on my face. After brushing my teeth and putting on workout clothes (which doesn't necessarily mean I'll exercise, but wearing the right clothes puts me one step closer), I go to the kitchen to make coffee. I hear Annabelle moving in her room and decide to make her favorite breakfast: vanilla french toast and bacon. It's nice not having to worry about AB on school mornings. Ever since she was a little girl, she jumps out of bed without having to be told. Her body clock seems to be set at six AM.

A little while later Annabelle appears in the kitchen as I'm pouring syrup on her french toast. She smiles and sits on a stool at the island.

"How was your trip?" she asks between bites.

I pour another cup of coffee and sit down next to her. "It was good. Really good. Ashley seems to be doing well. She smells bad, though—like charred firewood and canned meat. If you tell her I said that, I will deny it."

Annabelle laughs and bites into a piece of bacon. I consider bringing up her late-night reading selection, and she opens her mouth to say something, but a car horn blasts, and we both jump.

"Oh! Gotta go; that's my ride."

I stand up quickly and protest. "What? Why am I not taking you to school? Who is that?" I walk over to the front window and peer out.

Annabelle grabs her backpack and heads for the door. "It's Kelsey's mom. I wasn't sure you'd feel like taking me since you got home so late. It's fine, Mom. I'll see you later. Remember, I have my study group tonight."

She opens the door and waves to me. "Bye! Glad you're home."

And she's off to school just like that.

I walk over to the plate of leftover french toast and slather it with butter and syrup. There's no sense in wasting all this food.

As the morning rolls on, I find myself in a particularly good (and productive) mood. I wash and fold and put away the dirty clothes that had piled up over the last two weeks. I clean the old food out the fridge and even wipe down the shelves. I make a mental note to go to the grocery store. There is seriously nothing in there but condiments and a jar of pickles. When I'm finished in the kitchen, I give the bathrooms a good scrubbing and vacuum the entire house. I put clean sheets on the beds.

The whole time I'm working, I notice I'm feeling happy again. I even catch myself humming an annoyingly catchy song. It's been a long time since I felt this light. I have a daughter in rehab a thousand miles away, an ex-husband who constantly gets under my skin, and another daughter who may or may not be grooming herself to become a serial killer. But for some reason, none of that matters. Today I'm happy. As I'm pulling the last chunk of hair out of the bathtub drain, it hits me: I feel like writing something!

I put away the cleaning supplies and make a cup of tea. I set it on the kitchen table and grab my laptop and charger from my bedroom. All plugged in and sitting in front of the blank screen, my hands hover above the keyboard, and as if I'm not even present, they begin to move. One paragraph, two paragraphs, six paragraphs, then nine. The old me comes bounding back with a vengeance.

I write about everything that's happened: the affair, the divorce, my near-breakdown, Ashley's downfall and recovery, the effects of all of it on the family, and lastly, about Daniel.

After two hours, I've churned out nearly five thousand words. I reread each line, and afterward I'm overcome with emotion. I close the laptop and push it out of the way. I lean over, rest my head on my arms, and cry. It's magnificent. Such a release. I just let it go, right then and there. I'm no longer angry or sad. I don't even wish Steven was dead anymore.

Yes. I will now admit that I've spent too much time over the last year wishing death upon my children's father. And had Monica been so unfortunate as to be with him when it happened, so be it. But all that has changed, suddenly and so unexpectedly. Writing it all down and seeing it in black and white did something to me. I am no longer willing to let the events of the past control me. I am taking back my power.

I sit up straight, stretch my arms over my head, and look at the clock above the pantry. It's just after five. Holy shit! I need to shower and put my best undies. Daniel will be here in an hour.

When I hear Daniel's car on the driveway just after six in the afternoon, a wave of nervous energy engulfs me. We have the house to ourselves for a few hours while Annabelle's study group meets at Kelsey's. Daniel doesn't knock or ring the doorbell. He opens the door, marches straight for me in the kitchen, and lifts me off my feet in such a deliberate embrace that I gasp. God, he's sexy.

Our lips touch, softly at first. But then he pushes them open wider and thrusts his tongue in my mouth. I've never been kissed this way—the way Daniel kisses me. I wish we could stay like this forever. I am powerless, almost limp. He has total control. His arms are wrapped around my body, his hands rubbing up and down my back and stopping sometimes just under my butt cheeks. He squeezes my ass and pulls me closer. I feel his hardness, which excites the hell out of me. He continues to move his lips around mine and then moves his mouth farther down my chin and neck. A fire ignites in my belly, and I have the urge to be made love to. Immediately.

He pulls away from me, breathing heavy. "Are we alone?"

I nod, and he takes my hand and leads me down the hall. I'm giddy and horny as hell.

After an hour of hot, sweaty lovemaking (okay, let's just call this what it was: fucking. He fucked me like crazy.), we lay in the dark—naked, arms and legs everywhere. I suddenly realize I'm starving. I look at the clock next to the bed and see that it's way past dinnertime. In fact, so much time has passed I worry that AB might be home soon.

Just then I hear the front door open and close and then the sound of Annabelle's voice coming down the hall. "Mom? Are you home?"

I nearly fall out of bed trying to get to my feet before AB has a chance to open my door and find Daniel and me in our birthday suits. Daniel tiptoes over and turns the button on the knob at the same moment AB knocks. We both jump.

"Mom, are you in there?"

I've got one leg in my jeans, but I'm fighting with the other one. Apparently I can't get dressed under such immense pressure. Daniel, however, is fully clothed and currently hiding in the closet. "Yes, honey. Just a second."

"Is Daniel here? I saw his car in the driveway."

Shit. "Uh, yes. He's…in here…with me. We were just…"

"Ew, Mom. I don't need to hear any more."

Finally dressed, I open the door. "Hi. Want some dinner?"

She looks at me funny and rolls her eyes before turning around and walking away. "You might want to fix your hair. You look like you just rolled out of bed, which is disgusting. And no. I'm going back to Kelsey's. I just came to get my book."

Shit.

"Oh, okay. The one about serial killers? Are you reading it for school?" I run my fingers through my hair and refasten my ponytail holder. "Do you need some money?"

When your teenager busts you having sex, you should always offer money. It's the right thing to do.

"No, I'm fine."

I follow her to the front door and reach out and touch her shoulder. "AB, look at me."

She turns around, stone-faced. "What, Mom?"

"Honey, is everything okay? How's school?"

"Seriously? I have to go. I have a paper due on Tuesday, plus Kelsey's dad is waiting outside in the car."

I'm so humiliated. I'm not sure if I should laugh or cry, or dig a giant hole in the front yard and bury myself in it. I've never talked to my girls about *my* sexuality. We've had "the talk," but it was in regards to *them* having sex, not me. God, I can't even imagine how that would work. "Well, you see, girls, sometimes Mommy is really horny and wants to be fucked like there's no tomorrow, but I always use protection!" And then I could pull a wad of multi-colored condom packs from my bra. I almost crack up at the visual.

With Steven it wasn't an issue—or at least it hadn't been one yet. We usually had sex after the girls went to bed or in the early morning while they were still sleeping. And it was happening less and less toward the end of our marriage, so really this is all new territory.

Teenagers and parental sex is a horribly awkward topic no one (the parents *or* the teenagers) wants to broach. But I think I feel so weird because she busted me with someone other than her dad. And yes, I'm aware it sounds fucked up. Try being the one standing in front of a horrified fifteen-year-old girl.

She softens then and relaxes her shoulders. "Look, Mom, everything is fine. I'm happy you met Daniel. He seems really nice, and you're beginning to be your old self again."

She sees it too?

"I'm just a little embarrassed right now because I'm pretty sure I came home to you guys doing *that*, and I don't want to think about *that* because it's gross. Can I just go back to Kelsey's and you pick me up later?"

I am beyond mortified. "Of course. Nine o'clock?"

Annabelle nods and opens the door. I step out on the porch and wave to Jim, Kelsey's dad. AB turns around and yells back, "Seriously, Mom, fix your hair."

Daniel and I sit on the sofa and watch *Chopped* on the Food Network while eating bacon and eggs. I hadn't made breakfast for dinner in a long time—not since the kids were young. They always thought it was so cool to have pancakes and scrambled eggs on a school night. Steven never cared for breakfast for dinner; that's probably why I didn't do it often, and why eventually I stopped altogether. I think I'll add it back to the rotation now. Who says you can only eat eggs in the morning? That's dumb.

After the show is over, I turn off the TV, stretch my arms over my head, and yawn. Daniel slides closer to me and lays my head on his shoulder. I tell him more about the trip to the mountains, and he strokes my hand with his fingers while he listens. I start to doze off a little but remember I have to stay awake long enough to get Annabelle. Daniel offers to pick her up for me when I say as much. He worries about me driving when I'm this tired. I don't know what to say.

"Text her and see if it's okay with her. You can give me the address."

I hesitate.

"Look, I'm in your life—hopefully for good. We're all going to have to get used to being around each other. I'm going to help you out as much as I can. Just ask her."

I hesitate again. But then I pick up my phone off the coffee table and send her a message.

I keep falling asleep. Too tired to drive.
Daniel is offering to pick you up. That OK?

There's a long pause.

Then:

Sure. Can he come now?
I'm ready to leave.

I turn the screen so Daniel can read the message. He leans over and kisses me on the cheek, then gets up and pulls his keys out of his front pocket. "Text me the address."

And just like that, my boyfriend leaves to pick up my daughter from her friend's house. Shit just got real.

CHAPTER 29

Steven

It's been a week since I got back from Utah, and Texas is in full bloom. Spring is by far my favorite season. March, April, and May are the best months here. Things at home with Monica have also been better than usual. She's in a really good mood these days, even though she's still in her first trimester—the beginning of week ten, to be exact. I normally wouldn't know things like this, but Monica installed some pregnancy app on her phone and added my email address as another way to "keep me informed." So now I get weekly updates about the baby.

Week 10: Your baby is now the size of a prune. He or she is starting to take on a more human shape. Isn't that magnificent?

It's definitely something.

I'm in the kitchen getting all the ingredients together to make a protein shake when Monica comes in and fills me in on what's going on with her body this week. She shares really intimate things that I've never considered appropriate topics of conversation. She talks about being constipated and how she used to poop three or four times a day, but since the pregnancy all that has changed.

"Why are you looking at me like that, Steven?"

I'm trying to recover from the poop talk. "What? I'm not looking at you any particular way." The hell I'm not.

"You are." Monica nods.

She's holding a basket of laundry and wearing gray sweatpants, a white tank top, and no bra. Her breasts are bigger now, and her nipples are large and round and currently poking through the shirt so much so that it's hard to focus on anything else. I'm suddenly very aware of my penis and shift my position to try to distract it.

I'm so confused. On one hand, I am turned on by the sight of her breasts, but I'm completely turned off by the thought of her taking a dump three or four times a day. What is she eating? Indian food? She used to text me sexy pics of herself wearing only panties. Good Lord, I would get the biggest hard-on. I couldn't wait until the next time I got to see her naked. Now she texts me pictures of stroller with questions like, "Which one do you think is better?"

When we met, we couldn't keep our hands off each other. Everything about her excited me. Her body was like nothing I had ever seen, and she certainly knew how to use it. We did things I had never done with anyone before. Sarah and I were somewhat adventurous, I suppose. But Monica was on a whole other level of sexual experimentation. I was a goner before I knew what hit me. Now she sometimes worries that my penis will harm her growing fetus. Pleasing me is no longer high up on her to-do list.

"*Steven!*"

The sound of her voice jolts me back to the present. "Sorry, baby, what are you saying?"

Monica puts the basket of laundry on the counter and comes closer to me. I really need to turn on the blender, but I'm afraid if I do it now she might murder me.

She touches my arm, which causes me to flinch a little.

"Steven," she says, her tone lighter. "I know you weren't expecting to be a father again, but we never talked about you *not* being a father again."

Yes, I was too busy trying to unfasten her bra every chance I got.

"But it's happening, and I'm so excited to be someone's mommy. And I'm really glad I'm having a baby with *you*. Nothing else in your life is partly mine, so this means everything to me."

She wraps her arms around my waist and leans her head on my chest. I kiss the top of her head, not sure what to say. What can I say? It seems I'm not in control of this part of my life either. What is happening to me?

Monica pulls back and looks at me, her eyes widening. She's moved over to the other side of the kitchen island. "I almost forgot to tell you! Ha, pregnancy brain. Anyway, my parents want us to come over this Saturday and talk about the wedding and the baby and all that."

She's picking articles of clothing out of the basket, folding them, and laying them in piles on the counter. I'm looking at her and then at the contents of the blender. My usual shake consists of a banana, six strawberries, a handful of spinach leaves, a tablespoon of coconut oil, Greek yogurt, and almond milk. Normally I look forward to having my shake every morning, but suddenly I've lost my appetite.

It's not that I don't want to go to Monica's parents' house (Jerry and Joanna are fine people), it's just that I'm not sure I want to get married again, even though I've agreed to do exactly that in the fall.

Before the pregnancy, I thought perhaps I could put it off and put it off until she grew tired of the subject and we moved on, continuing to live life like it is now. But now that there's a baby involved, Monica talks about getting married non-stop—well, when she's not talking about the baby.

I smile and nod and turn on the blender.

Monica's parents live in a nine-thousand-square-foot mansion in Dallas' Highland Park neighborhood. Like a lot of other Texans, Jerry made his fortune from oil and gas. His wells span from Big Spring, in west Texas, to the Barnett Shale in Fort Worth. Monica is his only child, his princess. He and Joanna moved to Dallas when Monica was in high school so she could attend Southern Methodist University for college. They wanted to stay close to her. He tolerates me because he's a nice guy. Deep down, he probably wants to kick my ass. I know I would want to if one of my girls brought home a man fourteen years her senior. And yet, when we ring the doorbell he welcomes me into his home with a firm handshake.

"Come in, come in," Monica's mom says. She hugs Monica, pats her belly, and then squeezes her cheeks. I can't help but smile. Joanna will be a wonderful grandmother to this baby. It helps that she looks like the sweetest woman alive, too. She's shorter than Monica by a lot, with copper-colored hair in a style that reminds me of a helmet. That's not a good description and would probably not sound like a compliment if I said it out loud, but anyway, it's short. You can tell Joanna was a beautiful woman like Monica when she was her age. She's still lovely. You know how they say you can tell what your wife will look like in the future by judging her mother? Monica will look just fine. Probably better than my old ass.

Joanna turns to me. "Steven, you're looking well. Must be all those protein shakes Monica tells me you're into."

That's probably a conversation I should be thankful I wasn't privy to. Lately Monica has been giving me dirty looks whenever I make my morning shake. She's told me more than once that it looks disgusting and makes her want to vomit. I don't know what to say to her, so I just apologize. Then she sighs and leaves the room.

"Well, yes, if you say so, Joanna."

Jerry slaps me on the back and says, "We've got food. Let's eat."

As we walk toward the kitchen, he grabs me by the arm and says, "Let's take a detour to the den for a drink, shall we?"

Yes, please.

After a quick two-finger glass of Glenlivet (the love of single malt scotch is one of the few things Jerry and I have in common), we join the ladies in the kitchen. It's massive, this kitchen. They even have two dishwashers. I only know this because the first time I was here, I went to put a glass in the one I'd identified, and Joanna waved at me from across the island and said, "No, Steven, that one is full. Put it in the other dishwasher."

I'd never heard of someone having two dishwashers before. They also have a full-time chef, Carlos, and a live-in housekeeper, Beatrice. Joanna is busy speaking to Carlos about the duck entree. That's another thing. Every time I've been here they've served exotic meat, like elk or antelope or bison. It's never chicken or spaghetti or burgers on the grill.

Monica is sitting at the table sipping ice water with lemon. I pull out the chair next to her and sit down, grabbing her hand to hold in mine. She smiles, leans over, and whispers in my ear, "I think I'm horny. Maybe we can fool around when we get home? It's been a while since you've been inside me."

Okay, so maybe marriage won't be so bad.

Shortly thereafter, the four of us enjoy a dinner of braised duck, fingerling potatoes, glazed carrots, and cheddar biscuits. Normally I skip bread because when you're a forty-five-year-old man, bread is not your friend (you should see the fat asses I work with), but god-damn if these aren't the best biscuits I've ever had. In my former life I would have gotten the recipe, shared it with Sarah, and begged her to make them.

When things like this pop in my head, I feel the slightest pang of sadness. So I push the thought out of my mind and remember *this* is where I want to be. Here, with Monica.

Beatrice has cleared our plates and is pouring me a second (or third?) glass of cabernet when the topic of the wedding and baby comes up.

Jerry puts his wine glass on the table, picks up the napkin from his lap, unfolds it, refolds it, then places it back in his lap. "So Steven," he says, "I understand you and Monica plan on making your relationship permanent in the fall."

"Well, Daddy…" Monica intercepts the question. "It was going to be in the fall, but that was before we found out we're having a baby. Now I'm thinking we should get married in June, before I get too fat."

Jerry lifts one eyebrow. "So it is true. You are pregnant."

This is the first I'm hearing of the new plan. A wedding in June? That's less than three months away.

"Oh, seriously, Jerry. I told you she was pregnant weeks ago," scolds Joanna.

Jerry is staring daggers into my face while speaking to his wife. "I know what you told me, JoJo, but I wanted to hear it from Monica and Steven. You know I'm a traditional, God-fearing Republican, and I wish these two had been married before they had a baby. But. It's too late for wishing. Isn't it, Steven?"

"Jerry. Sir, it's as big a shock to me as it is to you." Oh, hey, Monica. See that bus over there? Let's see how you look under it.

"Steven!" Monica shouts. Then she turns to her father. "Daddy, I'm a grown woman, and this isn't the sixties. People are starting families without being married. At least I'm getting married. And you like Steven, right?"

Jerry nods. "He's a scotch drinker, and he's got money and a good job, and he already has kids and is divorced. But he seems stable enough, so yes. I like you, Steven."

It's weird to have someone talk about you right to your face. His biography on me isn't the stuff great American men are built of, so there's another rung out from under my high horse.

I'm not sure what to say so I try, "Thank you, Jerry. I like you too." This has turned into the strangest evening. I gulp the last of my wine. "Is there more of this?"

Beatrice appears out of nowhere and refills my glass. I think I like her the best of all these people.

No one is saying a word. Joanna fiddles with her necklace, and Monica pouts.

After a few more minutes (hours?) of silence, Jerry finally speaks. "Okay, okay. Jesus, I can't take the two of you sulking. I'm happy you're getting married, and I'm happy you're having a baby. Whatever you want, Monica, is fine with me. There. Can we have dessert now? Beatrice, is there any pie?"

CHAPTER 30

Ashley

There's a boy in my group named Seth. He's from California, and he will be eighteen tomorrow. Gail is going to make him a cake over the fire. I can't wait to see how this turns out. Campfire birthday cake sounds lame, but considering I've eaten more SPAM in the last two months than a person should be allowed to, I'll eat it.

Seth arrived on the mountain two weeks after me. He was quiet at first, mostly keeping to himself. During Circle Time he seemed to shrink down as low as possible, perhaps to appear invisible. When Gail or one of the other counselors called his name, he would visibly flinch. I was drawn to Seth from that first day. There's something about him—he looked really sad and seemed so much younger than he was. I kind of decided then to try to be his friend. Seth seemed to really need a friend.

That first day he was leaning against a tree with his hands stuffed in the pockets of his khaki pants. He stared at the ground and his shoes, but I walked over and introduced myself. At first he was standoffish, giving me only one-word answers.

"So you're from California?"

"Yep."

"Huh. I've never been to California. I'd never been anywhere but Florida before I came here."

Head nod.

"I live in Texas."

"Okay."

"Have you been to Texas?"

"No."

He was still staring at the ground. I could have had two heads and he wouldn't have known this about me because he hadn't looked at me once.

"Oh. Well, just so you know, not everyone wears cowboy boots and owns a horse."

"Okay."

This guy is a real wordsmith, I remember thinking. When your mom is a writer, you learn words like *wordsmith*—not on purpose. It just happens, like osmosis.

I needed a new strategy if I was going to get him to talk to me. "So, Seth, have you ever killed anyone?"

He looked up from the ground at me.

A-ha. He had a face! And eyes—green ones! And a nose in the center! You know what else? Seth is kind of a babe.

"What?"

I guessed he needed to hear the question again.

"Have. You. Ever. Killed anyone?"

He furrowed his brow. "No, I've never killed anyone." And then, "Have you?"

"Not in a very long time," I joked.

This made Seth smile. He had teeth! Really, really straight, white teeth. I'd bet he's had braces.

"So is this place as lame as it seems?"

He spoke!

"It's not that bad. I mean, there's probably worse places to be, I suppose. Like prison, or with the Kardashians."

Seth laughed and, pulling his hands from his pockets, reached up and grabbed hold of a tree limb just above his head. His shirt came up and exposed his stomach.

Whoa. Seth has abs.

It's hard to tell what any of us would really look like outside this place, underneath the layers of mustard yellow and khaki. Right now we resemble much taller Minions. I'm guessing none of us would dress like this if we had other options. Well, except for Thomas, the booger eater of the group. He seems like he would wear exactly this outfit every day.

Thomas is from Ohio and was sent here because he tried to kill himself with his father's pistol. He held the gun to his head and pulled the trigger. It slipped just as it fired and grazed him across the forehead, taking a chunk of skin and bone with it. He has a really deep scar, still pink and healing. I can't help but stare at it sometimes when I sit across from him. I only look away when he starts digging his finger in his nose. Makes me want to vomit. Still, I feel bad for the guy. He told us he tried to kill himself because some kids at school bullied him for being smart.

Anyway, I can't speak for anyone else in the group, but after this experience I will never wear yellow or khaki ever again.

After that initial conversation, Seth warmed up to me. He sat next to me during group meetings, and Brent was also his therapist. I showed Seth how to make ash cakes and shared some tips on fire-starting. He'll never be as good as me; I could tell immediately.

A few weeks after Seth got to camp, he received a letter from home that seemed to devastate him. I watched his face go from normal to ghost white. He finished reading it and shoved it in his back pocket. I'd gotten a letter myself that day. It was from my mom, but I don't remember what it said because I was more concerned about Seth's reaction to his letter. He walked toward the edge of the tree line and stared into the forest.

Gail yelled at me, "Ashley, are you listening? I said to get the food bags off the truck and divvy it out to everyone."

I folded my letter back inside the envelope and stuffed it in my bra. Gail seemed irritated with me, so I didn't take the time to put it in my pack. As I got to the truck to retrieve the food bags, I saw Brent walk over to Seth and put his arm around his shoulders. This wasn't good.

Seth didn't talk much for a few days after that. He didn't crack up at my lame attempts at humor or speak out in group like he'd begun to before. He and Brent had more sessions than usual, and

I saw him cry more than once. I ached inside for him. I wondered what was going on.

Today we're all sitting on the ground on the side of the mountain in group when Gail tells us Seth is going to share his story. I instantly feel nauseous. It's quiet for a few seconds, all of us staring at Seth. Gail then reminds us that tomorrow is his birthday and awkwardly hoots and claps. It's a little weird.

Seth shifts from sitting on one hip to the other and begins talking.

"I had a girlfriend back home in Santa Cruz. Her name is Trudy." When he says her name his voice cracks. "Trudy and I dated for two years. She's a year younger than me, and we go to the same school. We were at this party a while back, and there were a lot of kids doing drugs and drinking. This one kid—he's not in school anymore; he's older—came up to us and asked if we wanted to try heroin. Trudy freaked out on the guy and told him no. And then she grabbed me and said she wanted to leave. But I didn't want to leave the party."

Tears start to well in his eyes. He takes in a breath and keeps going. "I told the guy, 'Yeah, sure, I'll try it once.' And then I told Trudy it wasn't that big a deal. This sounds really bad, and I'm an asshole—"

Gail interrupts and says, "Language, Seth."

They are serious about the use of bad words here.

"Sorry," he says as he wipes his eyes. "Anyway, I talked Trudy into doing heroin with me."

He pauses, and I realize I'm holding my breath. I exhale, and he continues. "We follow this guy to a back room, and, well...we shoot heroin."

I can't believe what I'm hearing.

"Next thing I remember is waking up to some girl smacking me across the face and telling me to leave. I didn't know where Trudy was. I tried calling her cell phone, and it went straight to voicemail. I drove home and tried to forget what happened, and I swore to myself I'd never do that again."

Seth lowers his head and sighs. "Trudy finally called me a few hours later. She'd woken up before me and caught a ride home. She was freaked out like I was, but that next weekend we did it again. And then again. And every time was less scary than the time before. But I knew that wasn't the life I wanted for myself, so I told Trudy we shouldn't do it anymore. She laughed and reminded me that I was the one who'd said it was 'no big deal.' The guy who gave us the heroin was a bad dude, and I was pissed at myself that I'd let him into my life—our lives. I was more worried about Trudy because she was liking it and spending more time with that guy than with me. She changed right before my eyes, and it was all my fault. She didn't want to do it in the beginning, and I talked her into it."

He's really crying now. I look around the group. Other kids have agony visible on their faces. Even Gail seems moved by Seth's story. My heart is pounding in my chest so hard I can hear it. I want to get up and run to Seth and hold him, but I would surely get written up for that. The rules are very specific about campers touching each other. Seth composes himself and keeps talking. I can't believe there's more to the story.

"I told my parents what I'd done, and they freaked out on me hard. My mom cried and cried, and my dad paced the room, talking out loud to no one in particular—always the fixer, that guy." Seth kind of laughs when he says this. "My parents were like, 'You're going to rehab, and you're not going to see that girl any more.' I told them over and over again that it was me who started it, but they refused to believe me. While they researched rehab facilities and basically kept me locked me in my room, I tried to get in touch with Trudy. I hadn't realized how much better I would feel after coming clean to my parents, and I wanted to help her do it too. But I never did find her before I got sent here. I had no idea if she was okay or not. Then, I got a letter."

Oh God, the letter was about Trudy. Seth pulls it from his front pants pocket and carefully unfolds it.

"Dear Seth, I hate that you have to find out like this, but your dad and I wanted you to know as soon as we found out. We did what you asked and reached out to Trudy's parents. They were very distraught and worried about her, as you can imagine. They couldn't find her and hadn't seen her in weeks. Her phone stopped working, and she had no access to money that they knew of. They went to the police. They scoured the streets, put urgent messages on her Facebook wall, and called everyone who knew her. Last week the police came to their home and told them the worst news a parent could get. They found the body of someone resembling Trudy in an abandoned building behind the rail station. The girl had overdosed. It was Trudy…"

I'm not sure if the letter ended there, or if Seth just stopped reading because it was too much. But after that it was so quiet. Even the normal sounds we hear every day—the wind in the trees, birds singing, the campfire crackling, an airplane overhead—seemed to fall completely silent.

He folded the letter and put it back in his pocket. Then he looked straight at me when he said, "Trudy is dead because of me. If I hadn't talked her into trying heroin at that party, she wouldn't have died, and I wouldn't be here." He looked at the others in the circle and back at me. "I don't think I'll ever forgive myself."

It's crushing hearing him say this. It takes all my willpower not to jump up and run to him and hold him and tell him everything will be okay.

Besides the obvious—it's against the rules—I'm not even sure I believe it. Maybe everything won't be okay. He didn't just pop some pills and ruin the floor at his dad's house. For a moment I'm actually glad that's why I'm here, rather than something way worse. Because maybe some things stay with you forever.

Happy birthday, Seth.

CHAPTER 31

Daniel

"Can I see the one on the back row?"

The saleslady reaches over and grabs the ring I'm pointing to. "This is an oval diamond, platinum setting, one and a half carat weight, color I, clarity VS1. The price is seventy-five hundred dollars."

The only part I understand is the amount: seventy-five hundred dollars. That's a lot of money to spend on an engagement ring. But it looks like something Sarah would wear. And I'm learning more and more that all I want is to make her happy.

The day after I picked up Annabelle from her friend's house, I realized I wanted to marry Sarah. I don't know what it was about that car ride that convinced me this was the next step, but it did. I haven't given much thought to the *when* or the *where* or the *how* of the proposal. I'll just get the ring and play it by ear.

"Do you take American Express?"

One thing about me: when I see something I like, I go for it. It applies to most things in my life.

I haven't told my girls my plans to marry Sarah, but I will soon. They know I'm head-over-heels for her, and they take every opportunity to tease me about it. I don't mind. They like her too. If they didn't, they wouldn't bring up her name every time I talk to them.

I'm not nervous about how they'll react. I'm just nervous in general. No one likes change. Even if it's a change for the better.

CHAPTER 32

Steven

It's a week before Ashley is due to come home. I think about her a lot, especially if I happen to find myself alone. I think about whether she'll be different. Will she be able to see how flawed I really am? If she does, will she still love me?

My life is crazy these days, but sometimes I'm glad I'm not alone long enough to think about her any more than I do. I have to come to work if I want to steal any me-time right now. And luckily then I'm too swamped with work to think.

Monica is driving me bonkers with planning for both a wedding and a baby. Sometimes I want to scream until my head explodes off my shoulders—I call it violent serenity. Other times I want to pack a bag, slip out the door while she's sleeping, and never look back. I do neither of those things because my life is playing out exactly the way I set it up. Me, the genius who knows everything.

I'm currently standing next to the window in my fourth-floor downtown office, watching people walking up and down the sidewalk. I wonder if their lives are anything like mine. Is that guy having an affair? Is that who he's talking to on his phone? His mistress? Does that woman wish her husband were different? More attentive? Are those women happy or are they plotting revenge on some poor schmuck? Is that man's kid in rehab too?

There's a voice in my ear that distracts me from my daydream. It belongs to a fast-talking hedge fund guy out of New York City named Geno. I've been on the phone with him for a lot longer than I'd planned. A friend of a friend asked me to give the guy a call about a "sure thing" investment, but it's been more than twenty minutes, and the guy won't fucking stop talking. He's young and fairly fresh out of some Ivy League school. He doesn't know shit, but tries to sell it anyway.

That's the problem with the youngsters: they're overly excited about this business. It makes my head hurt. But I listen, mostly, as Geno tells me how his firm is going to change the world and all that crap. I notice my cell phone buzzing and see Monica's name on the screen. Christ, probably more wedding talk. Or baby talk. Or both. Or maybe she's calling to tell me more about the discharge in her panties. It's caused by pregnancy, you know.

God, I may never put my hands (or my penis) anywhere near her pussy again. Why does she think I want to hear about discharge? There is such a thing as too much information. Sarah would…Nope. Do not go there again, Steven. I have got to stop comparing Monica to Sarah. It only tortures me. And it's not fair to either of them.

The buzzing continues, as does the annoying New York accent in my ear. Monica has called me four times so far. I open my top desk drawer, throw my cell phone in, and close it. Maybe that will stop the buzzing. A minute later my assistant, Charlotte, taps on the door and opens it. I interrupt Geno (who is now talking about how good the Giants are going to be next season after their stellar draft picks).

"Yes, Charlotte?"

"I'm sorry, Steven, but Monica is on the line. She says it's an emergency."

"I'm looking for my…uh…fiancée…Monica Parker. She said she's in room two-eleven, but I can't find it. These rooms are not numbered sequentially, it seems."

I'm standing at a nurse's station at Methodist Hospital, just a few blocks from my office. I ran all the way here, and I'm having a hard time catching my breath. The May humidity covers me like a wet blanket. The nurse I'm addressing stops typing on the keyboard and looks up at me. "Room two-eleven is down that hall to the left. I agree with you; the numbering on the rooms makes no sense to me either."

"Thanks," I say as I jog in the direction she pointed.

I'm not exactly sure what I'm about to walk into. Monica was hysterical on the phone, and I could hardly make out what she was saying. But I heard the words *blood* and *miscarriage* very clearly. Room 211 is the last door at the end of the hallway, next to room 218 and across from 220. Whoever numbered these rooms is an idiot.

I knock lightly on the door and open it at the same time. Monica sees me and immediately starts crying. She's sitting up in a hospital bed, wearing a standard-issue gown with the words *Methodist Hospital* stamped all over it. I go to her bedside, pick up her hand, and kiss the top of it. There's a nurse standing opposite me on the other side of the bed, typing something on the computer. She doesn't seem to notice me.

"What's going on? Are you okay? And the baby?"

I didn't realize just how worried I'd become until this very second. I've been less than supportive of the pregnancy. I mean, if I'm honest with myself, I've been a total dick about it. But now the thought of something being wrong with the baby scares the hell out of me.

Monica wipes away a falling tear and nods. "I think everything is going to be okay. The doctor thinks I have something called placenta previa, which is not uncommon. It means I'll probably have to have a C-section, but I can live with that." She begins to cry again.

I lean over and kiss her forehead. "I love you, baby."

"I was so scared, Steven. There was just so much blood. I thought I was losing the baby."

Just then a machine sounds off and causes me to jump. "What's that?"

The nurse looks up from her computer. "It's just the blood pressure monitor. It takes a reading every fifteen minutes."

She says this like she's irritated with me, which seems odd since we haven't properly met. Without missing a beat, she goes back to typing on the keyboard. What is she doing, writing her memoirs?

I hold Monica's hand close to my cheek. "When can you go home?" Only now do I notice all sorts of wires attached to one end of a machine, and the other end to Monica. Then I hear sounds I'm familiar with: the repetitious beating of the baby's heart. Good and strong.

"They want to monitor the baby for a few hours, isn't that right?" Monica turns from me to the nurse (who is still typing, by the way).

"Yep," she says without looking at either of us. Then just like that, she stops typing and walks toward the door. She pauses at the wall near the light switch, places her hand underneath a hand sanitizer dispenser, rubs her hands together, then leaves the room.

I turn back to Monica. "Nice gal. I say we invite her to the wedding."

This makes Monica laugh. And for the first time in an hour, I exhale.

I don't know what possessed me to do it.

After making sure Monica was okay, I told her I needed to make a few phone calls. She said she was tired, laid her head back, and closed her eyes. It was quiet except for the sound of the baby's heartbeat. So I walked out of the room and toward the elevators. I pulled my phone out of my front pants pocket. It was just after four. I opened it up, scrolled through my contacts, and pressed CALL.

"Hello?" came the sound of a familiar voice.

I cleared my throat. "Hi. Are you busy?"

There was a pause. And then, "No. Not really. Just getting ready to pick up Annabelle from school. What's up?"

What *is* up? Why did I even call her? I shouldn't have called Sarah. It was just a kind of reflex. What the fuck is wrong with me? "I'm sorry. I should go. I don't know what I was thinking. Bye."

"*Wait*, Steven. What's going on?" She has that worried sound in her voice I'm all too familiar with.

"It's nothing. Well, it's something, but I shouldn't put it on you. Not this. I'm sorry, Sarah. I just called you out of habit."

"Okay. So…you called me…what is it? You have to tell me now." There's an easiness in her tone.

I relax my shoulders. "I was at work today when Monica called me, hysterical, and said she was bleeding."

Sarah gasps.

"She's here—we're here—at Methodist. The doctor thinks it's placenta something."

"Placenta previa?" Sarah asks.

I sit in a chair near the elevators. "Yes, that's it."

There's noise in the background at Sarah's. She seems to be doing several things at once. She hasn't changed a bit in the year and a half since we split up. Always busy.

"I've known several women who had this condition," she says. "It's usually okay. She will probably need to take it easy for a while, and then I think it requires a C-section."

I nod and move the phone from one ear to the other. A woman in a wheelchair rolls past me. A man (her husband?) is pushing her and humming a song. She's smiling and tapping her fingers on her lap. I can't explain it, but I get the feeling they're happy and very much in love. I find myself envying them. Clearly I'm fucked in the head.

"Steven?" Sarah's voice is louder in my ear.

"Yes. Sorry. I zoned out there for a sec." This makes her laugh.

"Are you okay?" she asks.

How do I answer this question? Have you ever made decisions that affect not only your life but other people's lives as well? Because I'm realizing the consequences of my recent actions. How am I just now seeing it? Fuck.

Somewhere along the way I felt threatened by Sarah, and ignored, and unwanted. She sure as hell didn't seem to need me anymore. She was doing fine on her own. Then I let my dick take over, and I was really fucked. My marriage blew up, and I lost everything I'd worked so hard to acquire. Now I find myself on a path that had you told me about two years ago, I would have called you fucking crazy. *Goddammit.*

"I don't want this, Sarah." The words are out of my mouth before I can stop them.

"You don't want what?"

"This. Everything. Monica. The baby. Oh God—saying it out loud…fuck…I can't breathe."

The phone falls out of my hand, and I reach for it, but the room flips upside down.

CHAPTER 33

Sarah

I pulled into the parking lot of Methodist Hospital, parked near the emergency room entrance, and rushed through the doors.

Minutes earlier I'd pulled up at Annabelle's school, barely coming to a complete stop before rolling down the window and yelling for her to hurry up and get in. As I sped through the school zone, I told her I didn't know much, just that I'd been on the phone with her dad, who was at the hospital, when the line suddenly went dead, and I was unable to reach him after that. I suspected he'd passed out.

Though I didn't share this with AB, it was obvious from listening to him that he'd been on the verge of breaking down. His breathing was loud and forced, and he sounded…well…not good.

Inside the ER, we find Steven lying on a gurney in the hallway. He's holding an icepack to his forehead, and there's blood on the collar of his shirt. As we get closer, I notice a nasty gash peeking out from behind the icepack. That's definitely going to leave a mark.

AB proceeds to throw herself on him and bury her head in his chest. I stop next to the gurney, rearrange my handbag on my shoulder, cross my arms, and try to smile. "I would ask if you're okay, but I have a feeling I already know the answer."

Steven opens his mouth to speak, but before he has the chance, his phone starts ringing. Annabelle stands up so he can pull it out of his back pocket. He looks at the screen, holds it up, and says, "I better answer this."

I nod and turn to Annabelle. "Let's find the vending machine. I'm craving a candy bar. How about you?"

She nods. "Sounds good. I'm starved."

As we follow the signs to the lobby, I hear Steven speaking into the phone. "I'm sorry. I don't know what happened. I'm fine. Just a bump on the head."

Poor Steven. I almost feel sorry for the guy. He's fucked up his life in astronomical proportions. Would it be wrong to high-five myself? How about if I just dance a little? It doesn't make me a horrible person if I suddenly *love* the direction my life is going, right? It's not like Steven's going to die or something dramatic like that. It's just a bump on the head. He said so himself.

After buying junk food and candy out of the hospital vending machine, Annabelle and I return to find Steven in the hallway again. This time he's off the gurney and speaking to a nurse. As we get closer, I see that she's going over some paperwork before handing it to him. The bloody gash on his forehead is swollen, and the whole area is turning shades of blue and black. His right eyebrow is covered with dried blood.

"Good news!" he says to us. "No concussion. Just a bump and a scratch."

Something tells me he has yet to see the *bump* and *scratch*.

"What were you even doing here?" Annabelle asks.

Steven looks from AB to me and back to AB.

Oh shit. I haven't explained to her why her dad was at the hospital. I haven't told her he was here because Monica is here. Monica! *Oh my God.* Do the girls even know about the baby? Of course they don't. He hasn't told them, and I don't think that's my job. *Jesus Christ.* Part of me wants to turn and leave, and the other part wants someone to pass the popcorn.

"Um...Well, you see...Um, Sarah?"

Sarah who? *Sarah me?* I had been staring at a spot on the floor when Steven said my name. I look up and both of them are waiting for me to say something. Steven, the more pathetic-looking of the two, is pleading at me with his eyes. *Asshole.*

I turn to Annabelle and say, "Dad was here to have his prostate checked, which they had a hard time finding—" Steven laughs. "And some blood work—routine stuff because of his advanced age." Steven laughs again.

By the way, I hate him for putting me in this position. I hate him for basically asking me to lie to our daughter.

"I had called him to discuss Ashley's homecoming when he must have gotten light-headed and fainted. Is that about what happened, Steven?"

He nods and says, "Yep. Exactly that."

Annabelle wraps her arms around him again. "Aw, Dad, I didn't know you were afraid of needles."

"Ever since I was a little boy," Steven fibs.

I think I'm going to be sick.

After the hospital theatrics, Annabelle and I drive the ten minutes back home. My phone rings, and I see that it's Daniel.

Annabelle notices too and says, "You can answer it, Mom. It's fine."

I let it go to voicemail. "No. I'll call him back later. I'm enjoying being with you. It hasn't happened much lately. Our lives seem to be charted on a series of maps no one can read or navigate. It's been a little crazy."

Annabelle stares out the window. "It's been a lot crazy. But I think you're doing the best you can, Mom. You don't need to feel bad or apologize for anything. I know I'm only fifteen, but I'm not an idiot. I know you're happy you met Daniel, and I am too. Call him back. Maybe he'll take us to eat Mexican food."

"Oh my God, Mexican food sounds amazing."

At a stop sign I call Daniel. He answers after the first ring. I love the sound of his voice. It's deep with just a hint of raspiness. He's incredibly sexy, this boyfriend of mine.

"Hey there, beautiful," he says.

I'm swooning. Is that still a thing? "Hi yourself. Listen, Annabelle and I are driving home, and we were just thinking..." I look over at Annabelle. She's changing the station on the radio.

"Oh yeah? What were you thinking?" Daniel asks.

"We're thinking we could really go for some Mexican food. Would you like to escort us?"

This makes Annabelle roll her eyes. Then she shakes her head and says, "You're so cheesy. Don't make me regret wanting to go eat with y'all."

"How about if I pick you up in about twenty minutes?"

"Great. See you then." I hang up and grip the steering wheel. I'm happy. Just like that. I was irritated and annoyed with Steven, and then two seconds on the phone with Daniel and it's like—

"Mom. Stop smiling." Annabelle interrupts the conversation I'm having in my head.

"Nope. I can't help it."

"Mom, really. It's totally gross."

"Nope."

"Ugh. I regret everything."

I laugh all the way home.

CHAPTER 34

Ashley

It's my last day on the mountain. Day eighty-seven to be exact. Part of me is so happy to be going home, and another part of me is freaked out. I can't explain exactly why I'm feeling scared—maybe it's the fear of the unknown.

"Up here there's no rope with which to hang yourself," our fearless leader, Gail, always says. On the mountain we're on a schedule. Everything is outlined for us, and there are strict rules...pretty much no room to mess up. I mean, what are you going to do, try to get away? Good luck with that. I hope you know how to defend yourself against bears. And freezing-cold temperatures. And starvation. Those things sound scary, right? I mean, most people would avoid situations like that.

Well...to me, going home kind of feels like running off into the wilderness without a plan for survival. I have to learn how to handle myself out there in the "wild," which was once my natural habitat. "Navigate accordingly," Gail reminds us.

Being back in school again and around the people I used to hang out with scares me more than you can imagine. I still wonder what the kids at school think of me. Do they know where I've been the last three months? Will they whisper when I pass them in the hall? Do the teachers think I'm a troublemaker or a bad kid? These are the things that keep me up at night. While everyone else in my group is sleeping, I lie in my tent in the pitch-blackness and think about home.

I've received lots of letters—some from my dad and Annabelle, but mostly from my mom. Sometimes she tells me funny stories about things that are going on with her and with my sister. Other times her letters are more emotional. I imagine she's crying as she writes them. In one letter she wrote about meeting a man named Daniel and how he's made her happy. And then in that same letter was a note from Daniel. I thought it was pretty cool that he wrote to me. It wasn't anything too deep. Just a *Hi, how ya doing?…I can't wait to meet you* kind of note.

Then a week later I received another letter from Daniel. And then another one the next week. In each one he told me a little more about himself and his daughters. He seems nice, and his letters are kinda funny. He ends each one with a joke. I think I understand why Mom likes him.

But as much as I liked getting the letters, they've make me feel like I'm missing so much. My mom has met someone in the time I've been gone? How long have I been away?

Things are happening with my dad too. I'm not sure exactly what's going on. His letters have been a little cryptic. I'm sure it has something to do with Monica, though. If I had to guess, I'd say they're probably getting married.

I clean out the tin cup I eat and drink from for the very last time. Different people in my group have handed me notes and trinkets so I'll remember them. Crystal made me a bracelet from leather and beads. We all know how to make jewelry now, and we spend a lot of our free time doing it. Avery gave me her favorite dream catcher—we make those too.

Gail comes to my tent while I'm finishing packing and sits opposite me on the ground. It's just me and one other kid named Ryan leaving today. We both finished our weeks with enough points to "graduate." I didn't know a person could graduate from rehab, but apparently that's what you do.

"How do you feel?" she asks.

I roll up my raincoat and tie it onto my pack with rope. "I'm okay. I'm nervous about being home. I think it's going to feel different—like I don't belong there. Like I'm just visiting. Does that make sense?"

Gail nods, picks up a rock she's been eyeing and squeezes it. "Makes perfect sense. It's going to be different because *you're* going to be different. You're going to be fine. I have no doubt about it. And I really hope you'll think about what we talked about."

Gail and a couple of the other leaders talked to me about coming back and working as a counselor. At first I blew it off—no way I was coming back here on purpose. But when I mentioned it to Brent, he thought it was a great idea and told me not to brush it off too quickly.

So I practiced what I've been taught. I just let the idea marinate in my brain for a while. And now I can see myself coming back to work here. Maybe. It's totally different working on the mountain than being part of the program, Gail assures me. Most counselors spend three weeks on the mountain and then one week off. New Horizons offers housing to employees: an efficiency apartment with all bills paid and some money to live on.

I haven't mentioned any of this to my mom and dad. I don't want them freaking out before they absolutely have to. Because that's exactly what I imagine my mom doing: flipping the fuck out. I'll have to bring it up at just the right time. I can't imagine when that will be. She won't want me to live so far from home, permanently. But I think it's a legitimate option for me.

"I'm going to seriously consider it."

"Good," Gail says as she struggles to her feet. "I think you'll be a great asset for us up here on the mountain. Now, give me a hug and get on over to the truck. Clay is going to take you down in a minute." She points at him.

He's leaning against the truck, obviously waiting for me. I think back to the night he first brought me up the mountain, when I thought he was creepy and possibly even a rapist and murderer. And he was super stupid about Texas. Since then we've had several conversations about what life is really like down south. He still seems shocked to hear that I don't own a horse. It's almost like he doesn't believe me. Poor Clay. I suppose he'll remain clueless forever.

I say goodbye to Gail one last time, and she squeezes me a little harder than I'm used to being hugged. Before leaving my tent, she offers one last sentiment: "Remember what you learned up here. Remember where you came from. Remember where you're going."

And then she heads back over to where the rest of the group is getting ready to hike to another campsite. "Get this mess cleaned up and the food burned. And, Avery, stop yapping your trap already unless you want to build the latrine all by your lonesome."

There are definitely things I won't miss about being here.

Time to go home.

My mom hasn't stopped talking since I met her at the New Horizons office. She was standing at the desk, whispering to someone I don't know (maybe she's new?) when I saw her for the first time in over a month. She looked happy—really happy. And then my sister came out of the bathroom. I had no idea she would be here! What a total surprise.

I put down my backpack and hurried over to her. She smiled at me, and we hugged for what seemed like forever. I let her go and looked at her face. I couldn't believe how much she'd changed in just three months. She looks like a grown-up. Her hair is longer—way longer than mine now. Her braces have changed her smile dramatically, and her freckles are less noticeable. Maybe she's wearing more makeup?

Speaking of makeup, she has on a thick layer of mascara. This is new. Is Mom letting up on her strict "no mascara until you're sixteen" rule? Whatever the changes with my sister, she looks beautiful. And mature.

"It's so great to see you, AB. I've missed you like crazy."

Annabelle's smile widens. "I know. I've missed you too." She grabs a wad of my hair and makes a face. "What in the world is going on with this mess?"

"What? You don't like dreadlocks?" I flip my tangled hair from side to side.

Annabelle puts up her hands to shield her eyes. "God, stop it. It's like it's alive or something."

Mom comes up behind me and wraps her arms around me so tightly I let out a sound. This is twice today I'm being squeezed to death.

"You girls have no idea how happy it makes me to see you together again. Let's get a picture."

In unison, AB and I protest. "No pictures!"

Annabelle looks me up and down and shakes her head. "You know, Mom told me what you wore every day, but I had no idea it would be this hideous. You look and smell like a hobo."

"On the mountain, we call it campfire chic. It's all the rage in Paris."

"Maybe Paris, Texas," Annabelle says.

We laugh. In all seriousness, though, I'm ready to leave. The new girl behind the counter shows me to a room where I shower and change into "street clothes." That's what she calls them.

Mom brought a bag with jeans, a pullover top, and a cardigan sweater. She put in two pair of flats—so I would have options. It was thoughtful, but totally unnecessary. I would wear tissue boxes on my feet as long as it means I can take off these clunky hiking boots. It will be a long time before I wear any kind of boots again. Seriously.

I scrub as much of the dirt and grime off my face and out from under my fingernails as I can. This is not an easy task. A fireman's hose would be useful about now. When I'm finished showering, I towel off (a towel is a luxury item these days) and spritz my hair with the detangling spray Mom brought. It doesn't help much in the way of releasing the rat's nest on my head, but it smells good.

I dig around in the smaller bag to find moisturizer. Then I apply lip gloss and mascara for the first time in a long time. I look in the mirror and think, *this will have to do*. I try to hurry—I want to get out of here quickly before someone (my mom? Gail? The director?) decides I need to stay.

The drive to the airport is a good one, mostly because we're driving away from the mountain range. We spend most of the time talking. Well, Mom is pelting questions at me left and right: What are the other girls in the group like? What was my favorite thing to eat? Will I show them how to build a fire? Am I ready to go back to school?

I'm answering as efficiently as I know how, but it doesn't take long for all of this to give me a gigantic headache. I ask if we can take a break for a while.

When it's quiet, I stare out the window, thinking about what my group is probably doing. My guess is they're still hiking to the new campsite. Clay will already be there, unloading the supplies. Gail will have doled out bad marks to Avery, most likely for cussing. At the rate Avery's going, she's never going home. The thought of that sends a shiver up my spine.

I guess my mom can't stand the quiet because she reaches over and puts her hand on my arm. "You okay, Ash?"

"Yes, I'm fine. I'm just tired."

She pats me. "We'll be home before you know it."

That's what I'm afraid of. I find myself in a weird place: I don't want to go back to the mountain, but I'm afraid to go home. The possibility of landing somewhere in the middle sounds good. But I know that's not really an option. "*Remember where you're going,*" Gail said to me.

One airplane ride later, we pull up in the driveway of our house. I notice there are more cars than normal. One is Dad's, but I don't recognize the other two. I get out the car and feel the warm sunshine on my skin. I love this weather so much more than the weather in Utah. I won't miss the snow, that's for sure.

"We're here!" Mom practically sings the words.

She opens the front door and holds it for me. I'm surprised to see a handful of people standing around and a banner with the words *Welcome Home* hanging overhead. It might as well have been a blinking neon sign: *You're out of rehab. Let's celebrate!*

Dad greets me first, holding me in his arms and kissing the top of my head. He apologizes for not coming with my mom to Utah to help bring me home—something about "too many cooks in the kitchen."

I have no idea what this means, but I nod anyway and say, "I totally understand. It's no big deal." He has a bruise on his forehead and—what is that, a scar? Monica is right behind him, and she steps in between us.

She hugs me and asks, "Are you so happy to be home? I bet you are. Was it cool being in the mountains?"

Before I have a chance to say, "Actually, no, but thank you for asking, dipshit," my dad grabs her by the hand and pulls her off to the side.

Is she fat? She's definitely gained weight. What is she doing here, anyway? And in my mom's house? I can't even believe Mom would be okay with this. I worry about how this is affecting her, but when I look over, I see she's talking with her brother, Benny, and a man I don't recognize, and she's smiling and laughing. The man is handsome, rugged looking. He reminds me of Mel Gibson. Yes, that's exactly who he looks like! That must be Daniel.

I'm feeling a little overwhelmed. There aren't a ton of people here, but way more than I had expected. I was hoping to get home, shower again, eat a giant, greasy cheeseburger and fries, and then go to sleep. Having people hug me and ask me the same questions over and over again wasn't on my list.

Mom comes over with Mel Gibson and says, "Honey, I want you to meet Daniel Griffith."

Daniel puts out his hand and shakes mine. "This is probably not the way you imagined spending your first few minutes at home, huh?"

It seems Daniel is perceptive. I like him already. "Yes. I mean, I appreciate it and everything, but I'm exhausted and mostly just craving junk food and sleep."

My mom suddenly looks horrified. "Oh gosh, Ashley, I'm so sorry. I wasn't thinking. Here, let me scoot everyone out the door so you can decompress and go to bed."

Daniel winks at me. I raise my eyebrows as a gesture of thanks. "By the way, thanks for writing to me. I told the jokes to some of the other kids in my group."

He pats me on the back. "You bet, kid."

Mom did start shooing everyone out, but in the process the most hilarious thing happened when she introduced Daniel to Dad and Monica. I'd assumed they'd already met, but it seems they saved the momentous occasion for me to witness.

Mom marched Daniel over to Dad and Monica and introduced him as her boyfriend. Daniel stuck out his hand first while Dad kind of looked him up and down. They finally shook hands, and Monica made a weird face and pointed at Daniel.

"You know you look just like Mel Gibson in *Lethal Weapon*."

"Wow, you've seen *Lethal Weapon*?" Daniel said. "That movie *had* to have come out before you were born."

You should have seen my mom's face. And Monica's face. And Dad's face! I almost forgot how exhausted I was. It was pretty awesome.

After that everyone started leaving, so I decided it's okay to walk back to my room and put my backpack on my bed. Then I look at it again and think it's probably better if it goes in the garage. On the mountain it didn't seem dirty because I was surrounded by dirt. But on my white comforter, it reveals its truth: it's covered in filth.

I quickly move it to the floor and slap the dirt off the top of my bed. I worry my mom will come in and see I've already made a mess. But then there's no way she's going to yell at me or get mad on my first day home. Still, I'm not going to take any chances. I lug the bag to the garage and drop it in the corner near the garbage cans.

On my way back to my room, I look into the living room and see that everyone is gone now. I'm relieved. I go grab clean clothes from my chest of drawers and head across the hall to the bathroom. The familiarity of my house and my things is more comforting than I had imagined. The hot water nozzle sticks; you have to put some muscle in it to get it to turn. The door to my room squeaks when I open and close it. There's a creak in the hardwood floor in the hallway outside AB's room.

These little things used to bug the crap out of me. Now they just feel like home. *Grateful* is a word that comes to mind. And all of the sudden, just like that, the mountains seem like a place I might have visited one time a long time ago. Or perhaps it was a movie I saw when I was a kid.

CHAPTER 35

Sarah

I don't think it's possible for me to be happier. The last couple of weeks have been a dream. Ashley is home and seems like a completely different person from the girl who left almost three months ago. She's making her bed and offering to do things around the house—unloading the dishwasher and doing the laundry.

Sometimes at night I wake up in a panic, like her being home isn't real. I tiptoe down the hall and open her door (it squeaks, which sort of negates the tiptoeing part) to see with my own eyes that she's really there. Last night she finally sat up in bed and, in a sleepy voice, asked, "Are you going to keep checking on me much longer? Because we need to fix the squeaky door if that's the case."

I'll try to remember to pick up some WD-40 the next time I go to Home Depot.

Things seem better between Ashley and Annabelle too. They've been hanging out together and aren't arguing over stupid stuff like they used to. One night when Ashley first got home, I overheard them talking as they sat on the sofa, watching one of those ridiculous reality TV shows.

"Were you scared?" Annabelle asked.

"At first I was totally freaked out. I had no idea what was happening to me. I couldn't believe Mom and Dad would be okay with sending me out to live in the wild. I thought they'd lost their minds."

"When Mom told me where you'd gone, I couldn't believe it either. I thought she was joking. And when I realized it was for real, I was like, whoa. Mom and Dad don't mess around."

Ashley laughed.

"It was weird you not being here," AB said after a moment. "I went in your room, like, a million times to ask you a question or tell you something, and then I would be like, *oh yeah, she's not here.*"

Ashley laughed again. "Awww, you missed me."

"I will never admit that in public, but yes. I missed you."

"I missed you too, AB."

Part of me felt guilty for listening in on their conversation. But more of me was happy to know that these kinds of conversations happen.

However, I'm not saying things are perfect. They're definitely not. Ashley is still a teenager, after all. She's fighting for her independence, and I've been a little hovering, like those helicopter moms you read about on the internet. I can't help it. To me she seems like a baby bird just learning to fly. You wouldn't let a baby bird jump out of the nest without first having flying lessons, would you? I think not.

A couple of days after she returned from the mountains, she asked to borrow the car.

"Where are you going?" I asked her.

"I don't know. I just want to get out of the house and drive around." She sounded defensive.

A familiar uneasiness began to bubble up inside me. She was being too vague. "Well, can you be more specific? Like, are you going to see someone or go to the mall, or what?"

"God, Mom. I don't know. I'll probably go to Starbucks and get a Frappuccino and then to CVS to buy tampons. Is that specific enough? You're treating me like a prisoner. I'm not going to do anything wrong, okay?"

Ashley's face had turned red, and I backed off. Maybe I am a little intense. I gave her the keys. She was back in forty-five minutes.

I'm learning to trust her again and give her the space she needs without giving her enough rope to make a noose. The last thing I want to do is suffocate her. I'm walking such a fine line. I yell to her every morning as she heads out the door, "I'm here if you need me! I'm on your side!"

She waves me off and says, "I know, Mom. Thanks." Sometimes I think I hear her faintly call me a weirdo under her breath. Oh well, this weirdo is here for you, girl.

We're trying our best to navigate this new territory. It's a newly paved road that no cars have driven before. *Are there barricades? Steep inclines? A bridge still under construction?* I'm traveling extra slow and have my hands planted squarely at ten and two. I don't want to take a curve too quickly and careen off the side of the cliff.

Dr. K loves all my new analogies and, even better, my sunnier outlook on life. She's encouraged me to write about my recent experiences. I mentioned to her that I'd kind of done that already. That day I sat in front of my computer the words just came pouring out of me, as a kind of catharsis. I did feel better. She liked hearing that, but is pushing me to do more—maybe write a book. I'm not sure I want to, but I've promised her I'll keep an open mind. Maybe someday, when all of this is way back in my rearview mirror, I'll consider it. But not now.

I'm superstitious in a way. If I were to write about how everything was terrible, but now it's great, it could backfire on me. I don't have another forty thousand dollars to spend on someone else's recovery. I'm only half kidding when I say this.

Still, Ashley seems focused on graduating from high school and is looking forward to her eighteenth birthday, which is just around the corner. We're planning a trip to New York City to celebrate both milestones. Annabelle's added in her two cents, insisting we see *Wicked* while we're there, and we've invited Daniel and his daughters to join us.

His girls and mine have been spending some time together lately, and it isn't as awkward as I'd imagined it would be. They have a lot in common because they're all so close in age. Seriously, all you have to do is bring up a TV show like *Scandal* and they're all, "Oh my God, did you see last week's episode? Is she a psycho or what?" That lasts until something else they're all knowledgeable about comes up.

YouTube videos and viral Tumblr sites are also good for conversation. Daniel and I happily take this as our cue to leave the room.

Steven pops over every couple of days to check on Ashley. I'm so used to it now, it doesn't even phase me to see his car in my driveway. He takes the girls to dinner at least once a week. It's the most attention he's given them their whole lives. I'm not even exaggerating. He would agree with that statement. I think the girls enjoy spending time with him; they look forward to it.

He leaves Monica at home for the most part. "Baby steps," he said to me when I asked. I guess things are better with them. I have no idea, nor do I really care. After his mini breakdown on the phone from the hospital, he's never said another word about it—not to me anyway. Perhaps when he bashed his head on the ground he knocked himself into submission.

He still hasn't broken the news to the girls about the pregnancy—I guess that's another "baby steps" situation—but the wedding is this weekend. I think he'd rather buy both girls new cars than tell them he's having another baby. It was hard enough telling them he planned to marry the twat; I can't imagine what it will be like to tell them he impregnated her too.

Boy, do I wish I could be there when he springs it on them. No, scratch that. If I was present, he'd try to have *me* tell them. I'm a little surprised he hasn't already asked me to do it. I can see the girls and me at breakfast one morning before school: "How do you want your eggs, girls? Fried, scrambled, or fertilized and growing in Monica's uterus?"

I told him he'd better not wait too long to tell them. They're going to notice her baby bump soon. I hope she gets fat. *Really* fat. Speaking of Monica, she is under the impression that since I spoke to her briefly and allowed her in my home, we are going to be friends. She said as much to Steven, who then mentioned it to me.

Do I even need to elaborate on this?

I've spent the day folding laundry, and Daniel called earlier and invited the girls and me to dinner. Ashley has a paper due, but she seems fine with putting it off for a couple more hours. Some things never change. Annabelle has driver's ed until six thirty, so we agreed to meet at the restaurant.

We're going to Delphino's, a really expensive steak house. I've never been there, but I remember Steven having many client dinners there over the years. He brought me a leftover crab cake once. It was divine, even cold and soggy.

I asked Daniel if this was some special occasion I wasn't aware of, but he laughed and said he just wanted to take all his girls out to dinner. Keeper. That's what he is.

CHAPTER 36

Daniel

"Griffin, party of six," the hostess says.

We stand up and follow the tiny little blonde (who looks twelve years old) to the table. Sarah is beautiful in a form-fitting black dress and heels. The rest of the girls are dressed in jeans and cute tops. I guess that's what you call them. Tops. I wear shirts, but Emma refers to her shirts as tops. Whatever. We're all wearing clothes. That's all you really need to know.

The hostess places a menu in front of each of us and tells us to enjoy our dinner before walking back to the front.

"Order anything you like," I announce to the table.

I look over at Sarah, and she raises her eyebrows. I smile at her and run my palms over my pants legs. My hands have never been this sweaty.

She reaches over and puts her hand on my upper arm. "Are you okay? You seem jittery. Did you guzzle a bunch of caffeine today?"

Now everyone at the table is staring at me.

"I'm fine. Really fine. Where's the waiter?"

And then he appears out of nowhere. "Good evening, folks. Welcome to Delphino's. My name is Eduardo, and I will be taking care of you tonight. May I offer you a cocktail or an iced tea?"

One by one the girls order: Water. Water. Water. Diet Coke.

I turn to Sarah and ask if she'd like a glass of wine.

"I think I'll be wacky and order champagne," she says.

"Champagne for the lady," I say. "And a vodka tonic for me. Extra limes."

"Very well, sir. I'll be back with your drinks in just a few minutes."

I'm dying over here. My coat feels too tight. I can't breathe. Someone is cutting off the circulation to my brain. I gotta get this over with. Uh, I mean, do this now so I can enjoy my dinner. Otherwise the anxiety is likely to kill me before the appetizer course.

I place my hands on the table and stand up. Five sets of eyes watch my every move. I push the chair out of the way and bend down on my left knee.

"Oh my God," Sarah says.

I'm hoping this is a good *Oh my God* and not a bad *Oh my God.* At any rate, I keep going. I hold her hand in mine and stare into her beautiful brown eyes.

"Sarah Elizabeth Lange, will you do me the honor of becoming my wife?" *Please say yes. I will die right here in the middle of this overpriced, uptight restaurant if you don't.*

She puts her free hand over her mouth and nods. Tears fall down her cheeks as the girls clap and cheer.

The applause spreads to the next table. And the table next to that. Soon, most of the diners plus the wait staff are watching. It's a scene out of a chick flick. I want to be embarrassed, but I'm too busy directing this movie.

She leans toward me and kisses me hard on the mouth. "Of course I'll marry you," she says. "I would be crazy not to."

I reach in the pocket of my sport coat and pull out a square red box. Sarah takes it from me before I have a chance to open it and opens it herself. She gasps when she sees the oval diamond ring. So do the girls, who are practically lying on top of the table trying to get a better look.

I don't even have to put the ring on her finger. She does that herself too. I can't help but laugh. This is part of the reason I love her. She's nothing you expect her to be. This is one of the best moments of my life.

The rest of the engagement evening is filled with laughter and happy tears, overpriced meals, and perhaps one too many vodka tonics.

I was so relieved to be done with proposing that I knocked back my first drink before Sarah had a chance to take a sip of her champagne. And not that I was too concerned, but all our girls seem really excited that we're getting married. I'm one proud man.

CHAPTER 37

Steven

I sit at my dining room table, staring at the amber-colored liquid in the bottle. I've reasoned that it's okay to drink at ten in the morning on a Saturday morning if it's a special occasion. My hands are shaking. I pour another two fingers of the scotch Monica's dad bought me and throw it back. It burns like hell as it rolls to the back of my throat, and heat spreads down into my chest.

I close my eyes for a moment, willing words that aren't there to form and reveal themselves to me. I'm startled by the sound of the doorbell.

"They're here!" Monica yells from the bedroom.

I put the glass on the table and get up to answer the door. I open it to find two of the most gorgeous women I've ever laid eyes on. They're not little girls anymore. They're women.

"Look who it is, my beautiful daughters. And right on time too." They're wearing matching dresses that Monica picked out especially for them. I was honored (and relieved) when they agreed to stand next to me during the ceremony. This can't be easy for them. Or maybe it is. I don't fucking know anymore.

Ashley and Annabelle both smile and make faces at me. I open the door wider and gesture for them to come in.

"Dad, you texted me, like, six times to remind us what time to be here. Did you think we'd be late even if we wanted to?"

I'm glad to see Ashley's still the same girl she's always been. Forever the smart ass.

I laugh and lead them into the living room. "Well, no. It's just a big day for me, that's all."

"For both of us, baby." The sound of Monica's voice causes me to jump. I wasn't aware she had entered the room.

Her eyes widen and she says, "Oh my gosh, Steven. Jumpy much? What do you have, wedding day jitters?"

I notice Ashley and Annabelle looking at each other. I can't tell what they're thinking.

"No, no, nothing like that. I just didn't hear you come in."

Monica gives each of the girls a hug. Is it awkward or am I just reading into it? I can't tell. I don't know as much about women as I'd like to think I do. The scotch is starting to kick in, so I sit in the chair. The girls sit down opposite me on the sofa, and Monica stands next to me, placing her hand on my shoulder. Is she squeezing me too hard or am I imagining it? It feels a little like a straighten-the-fuck-up kind of squeeze. Maybe I need another scotch.

"So girls, here's the plan for today," she begins. "We'll all go to my parents' house together in your dad's car. I'll probably have to drive because it appears he's had a few drinks. Brunch is at eleven-thirty, so we need to get going soon. After brunch, the guests will go to the lawn for champagne, and to find their seats and whatever, and then right around one o'clock, the string quartet will play music and the ceremony will begin."

After a short pause, Annabelle is the first to speak. "Sounds great. Your dress is gorgeous."

Monica waves her off. "Oh, thanks, but this isn't what I'm wearing to get married. This is my arrival slash brunch outfit. I'll change into my wedding gown and get my hair and makeup done while everyone is eating. God knows I can't look at food right now. Morning sickness is brutal."

Fuck. Me.

Ashley and Annabelle look at each other. I know I need to say something. I just need to let it all out and get it over with. I mean, it's not like there's anything I can really do about it. Monica is pregnant with my kid, and we're getting married today, and I can't keep it a secret forever. Or make it go away. Believe me, I've thought about it from every angle.

I sit up straight, slap my hands on my knees, and dive in. "Girls, here's the thing. Monica and I are going to have a baby."

They both gasp and look from me to Monica and back.

"She's four months pregnant."

"Five," corrects Monica.

"Five months pregnant, and we haven't told you before now because…you know…we've had a lot going on lately. Plus, we needed to figure some things out."

There's complete silence. If not for the drinks, I'd probably be hyperventilating, so thank God for alcohol.

Ashley breaks the silence. "What are you having?"

I exhale. "We don't know yet."

"A boy," says Monica.

A boy? I'm having a son? I stand up and grab Monica's hand. "I didn't know you knew."

She makes a kind of pouty face like her feelings are hurt. I can feel the girls' eyes on us.

"Because you haven't wanted to know, Steven. About anything. You've been so weird and distant—and frankly kind of mean—for a few months now. I've almost walked away a couple of times. I can do this on my own if I have to. I don't want to, but I can. I had a life before you too, you know."

Monica turns to the girls and says, "I'm sorry. We shouldn't be having this conversation in front of you. I didn't mean to go there just now." She laughs a little. "It must be my hormones."

"It's okay," Annabelle says.

"Yeah, totally okay," Ashley agrees.

My eyes fill with tears, hot and stinging. "I'm sorry. I'm an asshole. I probably don't deserve any of you."

The three of them suddenly wrap themselves around me in a tight hug. It's the most relaxed I've felt in a long time.

Annabelle lifts her head and says, "I've always wanted a little brother. He's going to be so cute."

"Super cute," adds Ashley.

We laugh, which is a relief considering that I saw this playing out much differently in my head, and Monica looks at the time.

"Shit!" she says. "We have to leave now or we'll be late for our own wedding."

The four of us scramble to get our things. Ashley helps Monica with her bag, and Annabelle grabs my bottle of scotch from the table.

"I think you're going to need this, Dad."

Atta girl.

CHAPTER 38

Sarah

I've decided to sell my house, and Daniel will sell his, and we're currently looking for a place that's just ours. It was not an easy decision to make. I love my house. I've pictured being cremated and having my ashes sprinkled under the magnolia tree out front. Well, maybe not exactly, but I seriously love this house. Daniel says he's fine moving in here with me, but I know he's just being agreeable. That's the kind of man he is. It would also be hard to find enough room for all the girls. I talked it over with Ashley and Annabelle, and they agreed. We need a fresh start in a different house. It's going on the market next week.

Annabelle is turning sixteen this month and will officially be a licensed driver. She's growing up so quickly—in the blink of an eye, really. I'm going to be needed less and less. I guess I'll have to focus all my attention on Daniel. Poor guy.

Daniel's daughter, Bridget, has decided to go to Mercer University in Atlanta to study nursing. He is so proud of her, and so am I. I'm fumbling my way through this blended family we've created. It doesn't always go smoothly. Sometimes it still feels awkward being affectionate in front of the girls. Not just Daniel's girls, but mine too. Sometimes he's holding me in an intimate embrace when one of them walks in the room. I'm not sure who's more uncomfortable, us or the girls. Two of them — one of mine and one of his — have made the comment, "Gross, get a room," on different occasions.

A few other times it's been the interactions between his girls and mine that have made for an uneasy feeling. I've asked Ashley to invite Bridget if she goes to get coffee or to the mall. They're the same age and like the same kinds of things. I think Bridget really wants to hang out more with Ashley, but the feeling is not always mutual. Ashley doesn't seem to be picking up on the cues. I try to push a little, to help Bridget, but Ashley keeps to herself more now that she's home. I think she's still trying to figure out where to from here. Daniel isn't bothered by the Ashley-Bridget thing, but it kind of eats at me. I really want the girls to get along and maybe even become best friends. He gently, and repeatedly, reminds me that they don't have to be best friends and has suggested, on numerous occasions, that I just stay out of it. Basically it's a nice way of saying *butt out.* I'm trying.

I want to be as close to Bridget and Emma as they'll allow me, but they already have a mom — I know that. From what Daniel has told me about Jackie, she's a good mom, too. So I'm not here to swoop in and take her place. But I do want to play an active role in their lives. They're a part of Daniel, and I want every part of him, so there you go. Do the math.

Plus, I care about Bridget and Emma. I even love them. Every day we spend together I learn something new. Bridget is smart — off-the-charts smart. She's one of those people who really listens when you speak, never breaking eye contact or getting distracted. She has the same eyes as Daniel. They're so blue, almost cerulean. When I first met her, I was sure her eyes were green. I even remarked about them. But they're a spectacular blue. She's kind and has been open to the idea of me since the very beginning.

Emma is more reserved, but not in a negative way. Of the two girls, she is more like me. She happens to be a really good writer, which, of course, I love. She's shared some of her short stories with me lately, and reading her work and talking about it with her has really formed a bond between us — a kind of sisterhood. Daniel told me she's never let him read her writing, so I feel truly honored. I can see Emma writing a national bestseller. It wouldn't surprise me if she does it before she's twenty.

Whatever part I'm supposed to play in their lives, I hope they know I want them to be happy. I try to let them know how I feel about them through my actions. I know Emma likes my chicken and rice, so I make it when I know she'll be around. I even comment about giving her the biggest helping. And Bridget loves the shampoo I use. Sometimes I make a special trip to Ulta to get some for her.

I want all of us to be happy. I want the fairytale ending. I'm going to get it this time.

I smile as I fold my clothes for our trip for New York City. Everyone is ready to go but me. Daniel is a planner and has had his bag packed for a couple of days now. And I think all four girls packed their suitcases almost immediately after we told them we were going. Me, I'm a last-second packer. I basically just take everything I own and hope for the best.

I'm just getting my bag to the front door when it opens.

"Hey, babe," Daniel says before leaning in to kiss me. "I told you I would carry your suitcase down. Why didn't you wait?"

I make a face.

He laughs and says, "I know. You can do it all. I realized what I said after I'd already said it. At least let me carry it to the car."

"Deal."

Bridget and Emma come in as he's on his way out. "Hey, Sarah," Emma says and hugs me.

"Are y'all ready to go?" asks Bridget.

"Yes," I tell her. Then I turn and shout, "Ashley, AB, let's go!"

Minutes later we're all piled into Daniel's truck, headed toward DFW airport. I turn to smile at the four girls squished together in the backseat. Ashley and Annabelle are double-buckled, which isn't the best or safest idea, but this is our first time in the car as a family of six. It's strange, but nice. Once we're parked near Terminal A, we lug our bags inside to the check-in kiosks. The girls are chatting nonstop.

"What are the chances we'll run into a celebrity, just out walking on the street?" Emma asks.

"Oh, I have this friend at school, and she went to New York over Christmas break last year and saw Channing Tatum coming out of a Starbucks," Annabelle answers.

Emma squeals. "Oh my God, I would die."

Daniel leans over my shoulder and says, "I thought his name was Tatum Channing."

This makes me snort and laugh out loud. "That's because you're old and out of touch. But if I'm being honest, I think I did too."

Ashley is quiet as we stand in line at security. While the other girls are laughing and plotting their attack on the city, she seems to be somewhere else.

"Everything okay?" I ask her. I put my arm around her shoulders and pull her to me.

"Yes," she says. "It's just the last time I was here I was headed to Utah. I was thinking about that."

A feel the smallest twinge of pain in my heart. "I'm sorry about that. But look where you are now. You're so different—better. I really see big changes in you. And I love it. I love where you're headed."

She smiles at me. "I'm not sorry. I'm grateful. It just made me think about the mountains and some of the kids there. That's all."

I look at Daniel and he mouths, "*Everything okay?*"

I nod and smile. Yes, I can honestly say it is.

We land at LaGuardia and retrieve our suitcases at baggage claim. I think about the first time I did this with Daniel. God, I was a lunatic. How I got him to fall in love with me is anyone's guess. Oh, and how is this for nostalgia? I woke up this morning with a giant cold sore on my top lip. I can't even make up this shit. When I pointed it out to Daniel, he shook his head and asked, "Want me to take your picture?"

The girls still won't stop talking. They have the entire weekend mapped out already. It mostly involves locating where celebrities hang out, followed by a carriage ride through Central Park, finding the fountain where the opening credits of *Friends* was filmed, and then seeing *Wicked* on Broadway. I'm exhausted already.

We get in a mini-van taxi cab and head toward our hotel in Times Square. After checking into the Marriott, we ride the elevator to the thirty-first floor and our adjoining rooms. Since Daniel and I aren't married yet, when we started planning the trip, we weren't sure how to handle the sleeping arrangements. We didn't want the girls to be uncomfortable with us sharing a room.

Then one night at Daniel's house we were sitting around eating pizza and one of Daniel's girls (I think it was Bridget) said, "It's going to be so fun staying right in Times Square. The four of us can stay up all night and watch people walk up and down the street and order room service and pay-per-view movies. Dad and Sarah will be in their room asleep at nine o'clock."

They all laughed, and Daniel and I kind of looked at each other like, *I guess we just figured out the sleeping arrangements.* It was that easy.

Inside the rooms, the view out the windows is spectacular. You can feel the energy of the city. Daniel likes to unpack, but the girls aren't having it. "Dad, let's go!" Emma says as she comes jumping up and down into our room. Annabelle changes out of flip flops and into running shoes. She's the sensible one of the group. A few minutes later, the six of us are back on the elevator. I've never seen teenage girls this excited.

Since none of them has been to New York City before it's so fun watching their reactions to everything: the noises, the smells, the masses of people everywhere, the constant horns honking.

We started Saturday off by taking them on the subway. We ate lunch at Serendipity, where they tried to convince Daniel to order the Golden Opulence Sundae that costs a thousand dollars. You can probably guess he said no to that one. Plus you have to order it forty-eight hours in advance.

After lunch, we walk through Central Park and visit the 9/11 Memorial. The weather is perfect. We end the day with orchestra seats at the Gershwin Theatre for *Wicked*. The girls are excited to see a Broadway play. Daniel is being a good sport, but I can tell this really isn't his thing. He brings me a glass of wine, and the girls get Peanut M&Ms and Twizzlers. As he hands me the wine, he whispers, "Four things of candy and two wines was forty bucks."

Poor Daniel. He is a selfless man. I make a mental note to volunteer to do something he's interested in, like go to MotoCross or a professional soccer game. Thinking about doing that already bores me, but luckily the lights go down signaling the show is about to begin. Annabelle squeals and claps her hands together, causing a couple of M&Ms to fly across her lap and onto the cement floor. The theater is quiet except for the sound of the crashing candy. We all laugh, and somebody behind me shushes us. It's pretty hilarious.

It was a glorious (and tiring!) first day. We didn't hear a peep out of the girls after we got back to the hotel late that night, and we were all up early and ready to do it again on Sunday.

By the end of the weekend, we had accomplished everything on our list, including two celebrity sightings: Tina Fey and Derek Jeter. Sadly, we did not see Channing Tatum. Or Tatum Channing. Whatever.

CHAPTER 39

Ashley

Dear Ashley,

We are pleased to inform you that your application for employment has been reviewed and accepted. We welcome you as the newest New Horizons team member. Per our previous conversations, we would like to offer you a position as Counselor In Training for a period of 12 months. After successful completion of the 12-month training period, and pending evaluation, you will then be eligible for full-time employment as a Group Leader. Our target date for your training to begin is September 1, 2015. Prior to then, you should relocate to our field office and housing site in Emery, Utah.

Please see the enclosed medical release form to be completed by your primary physician. Also, you must be current on all vaccinations and have a valid driver's license.

Please contact me or Ken Fisher with any additional questions or concerns.

Again, we welcome you and look forward to your arrival.

Bitsy Kline
Assistant to Ken Fisher, Director

I read the letter three times before it sinks in. This is really happening. I have the opportunity to go to work as a counselor! I don't know whether to cry, jump for joy, or shit my pants.

I haven't mentioned this—even that I applied—to anyone except Annabelle. She's said she thinks I should do it, if I get accepted. And now I have. I mean, it's not like I have a lot of other big plans. If I stay in Fort Worth, I'll most likely go to community college and get a part-time job until I figure out what I want to do with my life. And let's face it: I haven't given that much thought.

When I got home from the mountain, I was scared to go back to school. I hadn't seen or heard from any of those people in months. The person I was most freaked out about running into was Russell. That first Monday back, my stomach hurt so bad I threw up in the bathroom outside the counselor's office. The bell rang, and I quickly rinsed out my mouth and checked the mirror to make sure no vomit got on me. When I opened the door to head down the hall to Spanish, I literally crashed into Russell. His shoulder bumped mine and knocked my backpack to the ground.

"Hey. Sorry. I didn't see you coming out of there." Russell looked as freaked out to see me as I felt about seeing him. He bent down and picked up my backpack.

I couldn't make eye contact with him. "It's okay. It was my fault. I heard the bell and didn't want to be tardy."

I caught a glimpse of him, and he was smiling at me. "Dude, you're totally tardy. That *was* the tardy bell."

Oh. The first bell must have rang while I was puking.

"So you're back," he said.

I was glad to see he's still a genius.

"Yep. I'm back."

He went to say something else, then stopped. It was so awkward I was beginning to feel nauseous again. Lucky for me, the vice principal, Mrs. McAllister, approached us.

"Get to class, you two. There's no reason for being in this hallway unless you want to visit my office, Russell."

"No, ma'am, Ms. Mac. Peace." Russell handed over my backpack and jogged down the hall away from us.

"Slow down, sir." Mrs. McAllister let out a sigh and turned to me. "You're looking well, Ashley. Glad to have you back. My advice? Steer clear of boys like Russell. Now get to class."

Yes, ma'am, I thought. *Will do.*

When I got back to school, everyone was talking about where they were going to college. A lot of people had applied to universities out of state, which kind of blew my mind. I'd never considered moving that far from home. If I hadn't been forced to go to Utah, I might never have known what life was like somewhere other than Texas. It's just nothing my mom and dad ever gave as an option.

My mom would never suggest an out of state (or even out of the area) college for me. Honestly, we hadn't gotten around to discussing my future plans. Mom and Dad were in the middle of a separation and divorce toward the end of my junior year. Then I went through all my shit and was sent to rehab. I wonder if things would be different if I hadn't gotten in trouble. Would I have spent my weekends visiting colleges and writing essays? I really don't think so. I'm not like Annabelle. I don't like school that much.

After we got back from our trip to New York last month (which was a blast, by the way), I was super motivated to do something else I hadn't done before. So I went online, pulled up the New Horizons website, and searched for the employment application. I printed it, filled it out, signed it, drove to the post office near the square, and mailed it.

A few days later, the director, Ken, called me. He was really nice on the phone. He told me my name sounded familiar so he'd looked in the files to see if I'd been a camper. After he found my folder and reviewed the notes inside, he called Gail on the walkie-talkie and asked her about me. Of course Gail loves me and gave me a stellar review. And so they decided to hire me. That's what this letter is all about.

Now I just have to figure out how to tell my parents that this is what I want to do. What's that saying, there's no time like the present? Well, here goes nothing.

I find my mom in the kitchen chopping an onion. She's sniffing and wiping her eyes.

"Are you okay?" I ask.

"Yes. It's these darn onions. They get me every time."

I dig deep to build up my courage. I'm not sure I can do this. I have no idea how she will react.

"Hey, can I talk to you about something?"

She stops chopping, puts down the knife, and washes her hands in the sink. "Sure," she says as she grabs a dish towel off the counter. "What's up?"

I'm feeling a little light-headed all of the sudden. "Do you care if we sit down?"

Now she's concerned. I can see it on her face. Maybe I should just abort this mission.

"What's wrong, honey? You can tell me."

We sit on the sofa, facing each other. "It's not that something's wrong. In fact, it's something good. Well, at least I think it's good."

Her shoulders relax. "Great! What is it?"

I'm looking at her face, trying to decide how to start. I get an idea. "Hold on!" I say as I leap off the couch and head to my room. I'll get the letter and let her read it. That way I don't actually have to say the words. She'll be able to figure it out on her own.

Mom starts to protest, but I'm already off and running. I grab the letter off my nightstand and rush back to the living room. She's still sitting in the same position as when I left her. Her mouth is open, but she's not saying anything.

I thrust the letter in her lap. "Read this, but please don't freak out on me."

I watch as her eyes move across the page, reading the words. She puts the letter on the coffee table and looks up at me. Oh God, there are tears forming. Please be the onions making her cry.

She throws her arms around me and sobs into my neck. This is worse than I imagined. Just as I'm trying to come up with something to say, she pulls back and wipes her nose on her shirtsleeve. Kinda gross, but whatever.

"Ashley…" She sniffs. "This is so great."

What the what?

"This is fantastic news. I'm so happy for you. What an honor for them to want you to go back up there and work with kids who are struggling. I couldn't be more proud of you!."

Now I feel like crying. "Really?"

"Oh, baby, yes. Really."

"I thought you would be upset if I left." I'm starting to choke up. This is getting ugly.

"Of course I never want you to leave, but that's not realistic. Besides, you'll be back. You can't stay away from me for *that* long."

We both laugh.

"And this is a wonderful opportunity. Who knows where it will lead? Come here."

She pulls me in for another hug. It's the best feeling in the world.

Looks like I'm moving to Utah.

CHAPTER 40

Daniel

You know what no one ever tells you? That packing up your kid and moving her far away from home is one of the hardest days of your life. I'm on the verge of falling apart, and we're hardly across the Texas border into Louisiana.

When Bridget got accepted to Mercer, I thought, *Okay, Atlanta isn't that far away. Georgia is a southern state that practically neighbors Texas.* Boy, was I dead wrong about that. Atlanta is eight hundred and eighteen miles from Fort Worth, straight across Interstate 20. It will take us more than eleven hours to get there, give or take a few pit stops. By my calculations, Georgia may as well be a country in Europe.

When I said as much to Bridget, she said, "Actually, Dad, Georgia *is* a country in Europe."

Damn. Why does she have to be so smart?

Jackie is sitting up front with me, reading something on her Kindle, and Bridget is in the back, eyes closed, headphones on. I look at her in the rearview mirror. She doesn't seem to have a care in the world, nor does it seem to faze her that she's moving to a place where she won't know anyone—not even her roommate, really.

If you don't have a roommate picked out, you get something called *potluck*. And then you're stuck with whoever the university chooses for you. Veronica—that's the roommate's name—seems nice enough. She's from somewhere in Florida, and she's a nursing major like Bridget. The two of them have talked on the phone for the last month or so, getting to know each other. They've planned out how they want to decorate their dorm room, so I had to take Bridget to find the right bedding.

Jackie did most of the work getting her what she needed for college, but lucky me got to go to Bed, Bath, and Beyond to look for something called a *pin-tuck duvet.* It's white, which in my opinion was a big mistake. Won't be white for long. But no one seemed to care about my two cents, so Dad did what Dad does a lot: kept my mouth shut.

Sarah went along on the shopping trip, too, which I thought was a great idea until she started pointing out a hundred other things Bridget "had to have." The two of them together are dangerous. I'll remember that when it's Emma's turn to go to school.

The thought of her leaving too in a couple of years makes my heart ache. Maybe I'll insist she go to college closer to home.

It's now four hours into the drive, and the three of us have hardly spoken to each other. We pulled into a McDonald's outside Shreveport and communicated in the way of them telling me what they wanted to eat and me repeating it into the speaker in the drive-thru line. Jackie ordered her usual, a Filet-O-Fish. How anyone is okay with the fact that the fish is square-shaped is beyond me. It also stunk up the entire cab of my truck.

It's a little weird spending so much time with Jackie in such a confined space. I thought it would feel normal, seeing how I've known her for more than half my life. But she's become a stranger to me. I feel like I don't know her at all. I look over at her at the same time she looks up at me.

"Is this awkward to you, us riding in the car together halfway across the country?" she asks.

I nod and then chuckle. "I was just thinking the same thing. Why is this weird?"

"A lot has changed in the last year or so. We're not the same people we once were, I guess." She turns and looks out the window.

I reach over, grab her hand, and squeeze it in mine. "Hey. Let's not let it be weird, okay? We're not horrible people. We're both just trying to be happy, and it looks like it's turning out that way. Right?"

Jackie nods.

"We were good together for many years, and we got two great kids out of it."

Jackie looks in the backseat at Bridget and smiles.

"What?" Bridget pulls the ear buds out of her ears.

"Nothing. Just checking on you," Jackie answers.

"Like I can get into a lot of trouble back here, Mom. Don't be weird, okay? Seriously, you and Dad get a grip and stop acting like me moving to Atlanta is the end of the world. Y'all are getting on my nerves. The whole time Dad was loading the truck, he looked like he was about to lose it. I will come back, you know. So just stop acting like weirdos."

"Yeah, Mom, don't be a weirdo," I chime in.

Jackie jerks her hand from mine and tries to pout, but she can't. She starts laughing, and I start laughing, and pretty soon we cross over into Mississippi and it doesn't seem so bad after all.

All the lights are on inside as I pull into the driveway of Sarah's house. I was never happier to see the sign for Fort Worth city limits. Jackie stayed behind in Georgia to spend a couple more days getting Bridget settled into her new surroundings, so I made the drive back to Texas solo. She'll catch a flight back later in the week. I was actually kind of glad when Jackie told me she wouldn't be riding back with me. Bridget had served as a kind of a buffer, even if she mostly ignored us.

It's been a long weekend, and I'm looking forward to a hot shower and a beer. But first, I have to go see my girl. Normally I would have taken a different highway to my house in Irving, but my truck just seemed to navigate its way to Sarah's. It's funny how meeting the right someone can make you do things you never thought you would. If Jackie hadn't wanted a divorce, I'd probably have lived the rest of my life not knowing what I was missing—that feeling of loving someone so much that you physically ache.

I open the front door and find Sarah in the middle of the living room floor, surrounded by what seems like a hundred cardboard boxes.

She sees me, jumps up, and runs into my arms, knocking me off balance. "Hi there," she says, nuzzling her face in my neck. Her hair is tied up in a ponytail. It tickles my nose.

"Hi yourself. What in the world are you doing, crazy lady?" I look around the room. If you told me a tornado had just passed through the front door, I'd believe you.

"Oh. I've started packing. I didn't mean to...well...I just planned on going through some of the cabinets in the TV hutch, and...next thing I know, I'm at Lowe's buying moving boxes and tape. Please don't leave me." She makes the cutest face when she says this.

"Yeah, right. Like you could get rid of me that easily. The only thing I ask is that you don't expect me to help you—not tonight. I'm dog-tired."

I'm suddenly realizing how exhausted I am. Driving to and from Atlanta in less than forty-eight hours, unloading and unpacking boxes, setting up a TV and internet, and stocking a dorm refrigerator is my limit, I'm finding out.

"Oh, you poor baby. Of course you're tired. You're a superhero and a sweet daddy." Sarah leads me to the sofa and motions for me to sit down. "I'll be right back. Bud Light okay?"

It's like she's reading my mind.

"Perfect," I say as I lean my head back and close my eyes.

I don't remember ever drinking the beer. I only remember waking up around two in the morning and joining Sarah in her bed.

CHAPTER 41

Ashley

It's bizarre going back to the mountain. It feels way different this time—still scary, but in a different way. When I was sent to Utah before, I had no idea what to expect. This time I'm going because it's what I choose. I'm not a kind of prisoner living out a sentence. Call it therapy or rehab all you want. I was practically in jail. The mountainside was the cell, and the fear of people-eating wild animals and Gail were the bars. Saying it this way probably makes me sound angry or resentful, but I'm not at all. I know my parents did what they thought was best for me. And it definitely was. I'm not the same girl I was before. The mountain changed me.

The car ride is long. No airplanes this time. We're caravanning the twenty hours: me, Mom, Annabelle, and Daniel in one car; Dad and fat Monica in the other. She insisted on coming even though she's in her third trimester. Only six weeks until I have a baby brother. That's weird to say out loud. I'm still getting used to the idea of Dad being a dad to someone other than AB and me. I'm not sure I'll be home to see the baby when he's born. I'm not sure of anything these days. All I know is me and my stuff are moving to Emery, Utah, to train to become a counselor at New Horizons. It's crazy.

Mom is happier than I've ever seen her, and Daniel is responsible for that. They're so into each other it's gross. Don't tell them I said this, but I hope one day to have what they have. I just hope I don't have to wait until I'm in my forties to find it. Maybe I'll be lucky and find the right guy the first time. No offense to Dad, but he's the last type of man I'd want to be married to. I love him and all, but he and fat Monica sort of deserve each other.

We stop in Albuquerque for the night at a Holiday Inn Express. It's not the nicest hotel I've ever seen, but it's also not the worst. I lived outside on a mountaintop in the snow, so I'm probably not the most critical when it comes to places to crash for a night.

Dad helps Monica out of the car. She's complaining that her back aches, and I notice right away that her ankles are super swollen. I mean, they are huge—like giant sausages.

I elbow Annabelle.

"Ouch! Why'd you do that?!"

I make a face at her and, with my eyes, point at Monica's feet.

She opens her mouth. "Oh, holy crap," she says.

"Oh, holy crap what?" my mom asks. She's grabbing her overnight bag out of the back of the SUV.

Annabelle quickly responds, "Nothing. I thought I forgot my phone charger, but it's right here in my hands."

"Right," says my mom. Then I see her notice Monica's ankles too.

I know she thinks it's awesome that Monica is big and fat. And she most definitely hopes she stays that way after the baby's born. I know my mom pretty well.

We all walk toward the hotel together. Dad and Daniel are up ahead of us a little bit. They seem to be getting along pretty well, talking and laughing about something. It hasn't been as awkward a trip as I thought—

"Steven! Wait up!" Monica yells at my dad. She waddles a little faster toward him.

—well, except she's here. So there's that.

Dad and Daniel are at the check-in desk, apparently arguing (not in a mean way) over who's going to pay for what. Dad's trying to pay for all of it, and Daniel insists on chipping in. My mom finally says, "How about you two split the three rooms down the middle? That sounds fair. Jesus Christ already, Steven. You need to get Monica to a room, pronto, so she can elevate her legs before her ankles explode."

No, she didn't. And now my mom is pointing at Monica's sausage legs.

Monica looks down at her ankles. We all look at Monica's ankles. The guy behind the counter looks at Monica's ankles.

Monica bursts into tears. "Oh my God, Steven. Look at my feet!"

It is so hard not to laugh.

Steven throws my mom a nasty look, takes a room key and his credit card off the counter, and goes to Monica to try to calm her down. She's really crying now. She's mumbling something about being fat and hungry and tired and does he think they have Three Musketeers in the vending machine. Dad pats her on the back and steers her toward the elevators. The rest of us stay behind in the lobby until we're sure the elevator doors have closed. Then we laugh so hard I worry I might pee my pants.

Just after seven the next morning, I ride the elevator down to the lobby to get coffee, leaving Annabelle asleep in the bed next to mine. When the doors open, Dad is standing in front of the coffee pot, pouring a cup.

"Good morning," I say.

"Good morning, baby. How'd you sleep?" Dad smiles at me. He looks tired, and his hair is messy. He definitely didn't look in the mirror before he left the room.

"Okay, I guess. I think I'm nervous about going back."

We find a table near a window and sit down. The sun is already so bright you almost need sunglasses.

Dad takes a sip of his coffee. "I think it's normal to feel scared or nervous. This is a big step. You're moving to a new place and getting a real job. And you're not going to have your family breathing down your neck anymore."

"That is one of the positive things about moving to Utah," I tease.

He gets a serious look on his face and says, "I haven't told you enough, but I'm proud of you."

"Thanks, Dad."

He smiles at me. "You're welcome, kiddo."

He gets up and pours another cup of coffee. When he sits down again I ask, "How's Monica this morning? She okay?"

"She's fine. She kept me up most of the night with her snoring."

The thought of Monica snoring makes me laugh on the inside. I don't dare let on to Dad that I find it hilarious because…well… because of what happened last night with her.

I get up to grab a banana when Dad puts his hand on top of mine. "Ash, let me ask you something, between you and me."

"Okay."

"Your mom, she's happy, isn't she?"

I nod. I'm not sure what to say.

"Daniel seems like a great guy," he says.

On one hand this is a conversation I'm uncomfortable having. But on the other, he asked. "He's a really great guy. He's been great for Mom. She's her old self again."

My dad makes a kind of face. I'm not sure how to read it.

"Sorry, Dad."

He shakes his head and says, "Oh, babe, there's no reason to apologize. I'm happy for your mom. I really am. Remember, I'm the one who fucked up."

True.

"Well, you're happy too, right?" I ask. "I mean, you're married to a girl you're in love with, and you're having a baby boy. Life is good, am I right?"

My dad smirks. "You're a piece of work, you know that?"

I say nothing. I just smile. *Yep*, I think. *Just like my mom.*

After we share a banana we ride back up the elevator. I wake up Annabelle and then go back out in the hall and knock on Mom and Daniel's door. Daniel answers a few seconds later.

"Nobody's home," he says and smiles. His face is scruffy. He hasn't shaved in several days. I like him with hair on his face. He looks rugged and handsome.

"Is that Ashley?" I hear my mom ask.

"No. It's someone from the Mormon church. He wants to share God's good news."

I cover my mouth to keep from laughing out loud.

"Oh, it is not," she says as she pushes him out of the way. She sees me and smiles and hugs my neck. "Come in, sweetie. I'm just finishing packing my bag."

Thirty minutes later, we're loading up the cars and getting back on the road. I make a point to speak to Monica and get her a yogurt and a banana from the breakfast buffet. She looks like she's about to start crying when I hand them to her. I want to say, "Look, lady, it's just breakfast, not a marriage proposal," but I don't.

She looks at the yogurt and says, "But I don't have a spoon."

This is what I get for being nice.

I run back into the hotel and grab one—and a handful of napkins—and then rush back out to the car.

A minute later, we're on the road again.

When we cross the border into Utah four hours later, I get butterflies in my stomach. The radio is fuzzy again; we're between cities, so the reception is bad. Mom has spent the last few minutes scanning the dial, trying to find a good station—or any station. It's hard picking music we can all agree on anyway, so I'm not really sure what the point is. Daniel likes classic rock. Mom likes eighties music. Annabelle likes top forty and country, which makes me gag. I prefer singer-songwriter types like Courtney Barnett and indie bands like the Dum Dum Girls. You've probably never heard of either of them. That's cool. It's not for everybody.

For the first few hours of the trip, I listened to music on my phone, but after we got out of Texas, I took off my headphones and tried to be part of the group. Daniel made up goofy road games that would probably have annoyed me a few years ago. But it was fun shouting out the answers before Mom or AB had a chance. Daniel is the funniest person (besides my mom) I've ever known, and he tells the best stories. Annabelle thinks so too. She's constantly saying, "Daniel, tell us again about the time you hit a cow." You'd think a story about accidentally killing a cow with your truck is going to be tragic and awful, but not the way Daniel tells it. I mean, you feel bad for the cow, but it's also hilarious.

Finally, after being in the car for more than twenty hours, we turn off the main highway onto a familiar road. I'm so nervous, I really think I'm going to puke. Daniel follows Dad's car down the long gravel driveway until we park in a spot right by the front door of the cabin. I can't help but think about the last time I pulled up in front of this building. It was only six months ago, but it might as well be ten years.

When we get out of the cars, I'm the first to walk up the steps. The door opens, and a familiar face greets me with a smile. It's Marcus.

"Well, look who it is. The girl who eats more than me!" He pulls me close and hugs me.

I suddenly forget how scared I am. "It's so good to see you, Marcus." I stand back and look up at him. He's taller than I remember. "How's Beverly? How's everything? Still snatching kids from their beds?"

He laughs. "You know it. But not for much longer. Bev and I are expecting a baby, so we're going to hang up our kid-snatching hats. I will probably go back to teaching."

The rest of my family is standing around me now. Marcus shakes my dad's hand, and then Daniel's.

"I didn't know you were a teacher," I say.

Marcus nods. "Yep. I taught fifth grade for ten years before I started working here."

I can totally see that. If I'd had teachers like Marcus, I might have liked going to school.

Mom touches Marcus on the arm. "I want to thank you for taking care of our girl. You made a difficult situation not so terrible. I wish you all the best."

Marcus smiles and looks down at the ground. He puts his hands on his hips and looks up at me again. "You got one special girl here. I knew it from the first minute we met. Ashley, I'm so happy you're going to be working up here. You're going to make a great counselor. And just know you always have a friend in me and Beverly. Let's keep in touch."

Annabelle, who's been quiet up until now, chimes in. "Maybe she can be your babysitter."

"Hey, now that's a good idea!" Marcus says.

We walk inside, and Marcus writes his phone number on a Post-It note for me. "All right. I've gotta run, but I mean it. Keep in touch."

"I will. I promise."

He leaves, and the rest of us stand at the counter. I'm not sure what I'm supposed to do.

Just then Maggie comes out from behind a closed door. "Ashley Lange, it is so good to see you." She walks around the counter and hugs me. Then, one by one she greets everyone else. Maggie. Still wearing her goofy sweatshirts. This one has Winnie the Pooh on the front.

For the next hour or so she goes over the counselor-in-training program with me and my family. Monica is with us, of course, but she's quiet today. She mostly sits in a chair next to the front door and reads magazines. I can't tell if she's pouting or just not interested in any of this. Either way, I don't really care.

After reviewing everything, Maggie gets ready to take us to the counselor bunk house. It's a short drive up the hill. She says we can walk or ride in the golf cart.

Annabelle answers for all of us: "We want to ride in the golf cart."

"Great. Wait out front while I get the key." Maggie motions toward the door, and everyone walks outside but me. I follow her behind the desk.

"Hey, Maggie? I've been wondering about something," I say.

"What is it, love?" She's digging around in the desk drawer.

"There was a kid in my group. His name was Seth. I never knew his last name, so I couldn't search for him on Facebook. But I've wanted to get in touch with him—to see how he's doing. Do you remember Seth? Do you have an email address or something?"

Maggie stops messing with the drawer and looks up at me. Her face changes. She looks back toward the office she came out of earlier. She leans closer to me and says, "Yes, honey, I remember Seth. Cute as a bug, that one."

She takes my hands in hers. "Honey, when Seth left here and went home—wasn't too long after you, if I remember correctly—he hanged himself in his closet."

Suddenly I'm nauseous. I feel the vomit rising in my throat. Maggie must notice too because she reaches under the desk and pulls out a trash can. I lean over it just in time.

I'm crying and gagging, and Maggie pats me on the back. "I'm so sorry. It's just awful. That poor boy."

So much is going through my head. *What happened? Why did he kill himself? Why didn't the program work for him? Why didn't he get better? Does this even work, or did I just get lucky? What if I'm not able to help other kids?* I squeeze my eyes shut and shake my head before I turn and run around the desk to the front door.

Outside everyone turns to look at me. I know I look (and smell) awful. My mom rushes over.

"What's wrong, Ash?" She's strokes my hair.

I'm not sure I can say the words. But I try. "It's this kid, Seth. We were friends when I was here. He was such a great guy. Annabelle, you would have been in love with him. He was so cute."

They're all standing around me in a circle. Maggie is outside now too. She's across from me, holding a walkie-talkie and the keys to the golf cart.

"Anyway, Seth blamed himself for his girlfriend's drug overdose. He couldn't get over it. When I left, I didn't have a way to get in touch with him." I point to Maggie. "I just asked Maggie about him and she told me…"

I feel tears in my eyes again.

"What, baby?" asks my dad.

"He killed himself," comes a voice from behind me.

I turn and it's Gail, my old group leader. She walks over and grabs me by the shoulders, looking right in my face. "You listen here. I know what you're thinking. We all think it when someone does something like this. What could we have done differently? Do we really make a difference? The answer is yes. Look at you, Ashley. Look what the mountain did for you."

I start to really cry now. She grabs my chin and forces me to look into her eyes.

"This works for most kids," she says. "And for some it doesn't. But don't ever doubt yourself, okay? You're going to be a great counselor and a great leader. These kids will be so lucky to know you."

My mom is rubbing my back. Daniel and Dad and Annabelle seem frozen in time. Of course Monica is speechless.

"You got me?" Gail asks.

I wipe my eyes on my shirtsleeve and nod. I can't deny what this place did for me, and I have to try to do that for someone else. But

I also have the same thought I had the first time I heard Seth tell his story. *Some things stay with you forever.*

"Good," Gail says. "Now get over to the bunkhouse and get settled. We leave for the campsite at seven."

I take a deep breath, do as I'm told and spend the next couple of hours unpacking my stuff. Then I tell my family goodbye.

CHAPTER 42

Steven

I had an eerie feeling this morning when I got out of bed, and not because it's Halloween. It was just after six when I opened my eyes and checked the clock on the nightstand. I reached over to Monica's side of the bed, but she wasn't there. And the pillow was cold like she'd been gone for a while. After slipping on a T-shirt, I made my way down the hall toward the kitchen. All the lights were on, and I found Monica standing in front of the stove, making pancakes.

I look around for a moment and notice a plate on the counter with a stack of about fifteen, and there are six more on the griddle.

"Good morning," she says.

"Back atcha."

I walk over and kiss her cheek. I look down at her stomach, which is so big she has to stand two feet back from the stove to keep from bumping into it. She's wearing a short nightgown that barely covers her stomach and ass. The whole scene is strange. One, it is odd for her to be up this early. Honestly, sometimes I call her from work around eleven, and she's still in bed. Two, there are enough pancakes here to feed a football team. I've never known Monica to eat even one pancake.

"What's going on in here?" I ask. "You having some kind of breakfast meeting I'm not aware of?"

She laughs and puts down the spatula. "No, nothing like that. I woke up to pee about two hours ago, and on the way to the bathroom, my water broke."

Panic sets in. "What the fuck are you talking about?" I look at the floor under her. She's right. There's a small puddle of something, and I notice more trickling down her legs. "Your fucking water broke?! Jesus Christ, Monica! We need to go to the hospital! Why didn't you wake me up?"

She picks up the spatula and flips the pancakes.

"*Stop making pancakes!*"

Monica covers her eyes and starts to cry. She drops the spatula on the floor.

I didn't mean to yell at her, but this is insane. I turn off the stove and pull her close. She wraps her arms around my waist, and I see snot coming out of her nose and running into her mouth. She's a fucking mess.

"Let's get you to the car. We need to go now."

She lets me lead her toward the garage. We're nearly to the door when she stops suddenly.

"I can't do this, Steven. I don't know how to be a mom. I can barely handle being a wife. And your kids hate me. I'm scared, and I just want to take it all back. I've changed my mind. I don't want to have a baby."

I take her in my arms again. She's hysterical. "Baby, everything is going to be okay. I promise. You're going to be a great mom. And the girls don't hate you. They're just teenagers is all. They don't like anybody. You'll see. Everything will work out. But if we don't get going, we risk having the baby in my Porsche."

This makes her snort and laugh. I didn't intend to be funny. I'm actually quite serious.

"Okay, let's go," she says. "But Steven, you might want to put on pants first."

I look down. I'm in boxers and a T-shirt. *Shit.*

I get Monica into the car as fast as humanly possible. Then I rush back into the house, grab two towels from the laundry room, and take them out to her. I place one under her and one in her lap. She has no pants or shoes on, but I don't really give a fuck.

I run back in the house and into our room. I'm sweating like crazy, and I probably should put on deodorant—but Christ, who has time for that? I pull on a pair of jeans I find laying across a chair and slip on tennis shoes, no socks. I scoop up my wallet and keys from the dresser, along with the bag Monica packed weeks ago for just this very occasion. I take one last look around and rush back out to the car. This is really happening.

A minute later, we're backing out of the driveway, headed to Methodist hospital.

On the way, Monica starts complaining of stomach cramps.

"Those are contractions," I tell her. How does she not know those are contractions? I've seen her read every pregnancy book out there. "Just try to breathe in through your nose and out your mouth."

There's a stop sign, but I don't come to complete stop. As I make a right turn, for some reason Sarah's face pops into my head. I think about the two other times I've done this...Sarah knew what to do and was the one calming *me* down. I've never had to be the calm one before. I don't much like it.

I'm so deep in thought that I almost drive right past the hospital entrance.

"Turn here!" Monica yells.

Startled, I press on the brakes, hard. The car screeches, and I check the rearview mirror. Luckily no one is behind us or they would have run into me.

In between "stomach cramps," Monica looks at me and says, "Oh my God, Steven, you're sweating."

No shit, Sherlock. I'm stressed.

I park near the emergency entrance, jump out, and run inside to get help. I see a nurse (she's wearing scrubs, so I assume she's a nurse) and point toward my car outside. "My wife. She's pregnant. Her water broke." It's only now that I notice how winded I am. I'm feeling lightheaded. I reach for the wall to try to steady myself.

"Okay, sir," she says. "I'll get a wheelchair and meet you outside."

Just then I see Monica walking through the glass doors. Although, she's not really walking. She's hunched over and dragging her left foot, kind of how you imagine a zombie would walk.

"Steven!" She screams. "I think the baby's coming."

I go to her and try to help her stand upright. "I know, baby. The nurse is getting a wheelchair."

"No. I mean the baby is coming right noooooooooow!"

Oh God. The screaming. It's so loud and intense. Monica is on the floor now, on her hands and knees—well, one hand and two knees. Her other hand is holding mine in a death grip.

"Help!" I yell to what seems like no one. Where the fuck is everyone? Shouldn't there be people around? Doctors, nurses, patients waiting in the lobby? It's like the apocalypse has happened, and we're the only two people left. I don't even see the nurse who went to get the wheelchair. "*Help!*" I yell again.

A man in a white coat appears (a doctor?) and leans down next to Monica. "Hello. What's your name?"

In between screams she says, "Monica."

"Monica, okay. I need you to try to slow down your breathing. Can you do that?" he asks.

She does as he's asked. Her grip on my hand eases.

"Good," he says.

The nurse who went to get the wheelchair finally returns. "Doctor Wilhelmson, Room Two is ready."

Doctor Wilhelmson is kneeling behind Monica now, his hands on what I can only assume is her vagina. "No time. Bring me the tray and a couple of blankets. The head is out." The nurse runs in the opposite direction.

"Okay. Monica, listen to me," the doctor says. "I need you to turn over and put your head in your husband's lap. Try not to push until I say, okay?"

Monica yells out in pain, and then together we get her turned over on her back in the middle of the emergency room floor.

"That's good," he says.

Several people have walked by since the good doctor showed up. First was a guy with a blood-soaked shirt wrapped around his arm, then a woman carrying what appeared to be about a five-year-old girl. The girl asked, "What's wrong with that lady?" to which the woman replied, "It's not nice to say things like that out loud."

Within seconds the nurse is back with supplies, and the doctor covers the current business part of Monica with a blanket. He's putting on gloves when I see the baby's head.

The doctor says to Monica, "Okay, push now."

And she does. That's all it takes. One push and my son is born. Seven thirteen AM on Halloween.

Hours later, I leave Monica's bedside to make some calls. She's sleeping so soundly she's snoring loud enough to be heard from the hallway. I close the door and walk toward the nursery. After he was born, the doctor suggested baby Charles (named for my father) be taken there for observation and antibiotics since he was born in less-than-sterile conditions. Monica hardly put up a fight. As soon as we got her changed and into the bed, she practically fell unconscious.

I phone her parents first. Joanna answers, and when I tell her the news, she screams in my ear. Then she yells for Jerry, and they put me on speaker so we can all talk at once. Joanna starts crying and is obviously disappointed she wasn't here to witness Charles' birth. I try my best to assure both of them that there really was no time to let them know it was happening. After I explain that we barely made it through the hospital doors before the baby made his grand entrance, they seem to calm down.

At the end of the conversation, they inform me they've been in the car and driving for the last twenty minutes. They will be here soon.

Next I call Sarah. It's not that I think she'll want to know or even care about this, it's just that my phone always seems to dial her number on its own. She answers right away.

"Hey there, Sarah."

"Hi, Steven. What's up?"

She does this a lot now. There's never small talk with her anymore. She wants to know why I'm calling the second she hears my voice. I feel a sharp pain in my chest.

"I wanted to tell you we had the baby this morning."

Her voice immediately changes. "Oh, Steven, that's wonderful! I'm so excited for you. What's his name?"

"Charles." I feel a knot forming in the back of my throat.

"After your father. He would be so proud."

I hate that she always knows what to say. Makes it that much harder to be without her. *You fucked it up*, I remind myself.

She's right, though. If my dad hadn't died from lung cancer ten years ago, he would be so in love with his grandchildren. He got to be there when the girls were born. *Wouldn't have missed it for the world*, he said. And he visited the girls as often as he could. It was hard for him to drive from Oklahoma. His eyesight was failing and he was often ill. I tried to move him in with us, but he refused, saying he wanted to stay in Tulsa to be close to my mom's grave.

When Annabelle was five, we found out about his cancer. Four months later, he was dead. The last conversation we had, he told me to be a good man and always do right by my family. Another sharp pain stabs me in the chest.

"Steven?" Sarah says.

"Yes? Sorry. I was thinking about my dad."

"Oh. Should I bring AB to the hospital in a little while?"

"That would be great. Thank you, Sarah."

"Are you okay?" she asks.

"I think so. Just a little overwhelmed, I guess. It happened so fast. I mean, he was almost born in the car."

Sarah gasps. "Oh my God. You would have died if that happened."

She's the only person who really knows me.

"Instead Monica gave birth on the floor in the middle of the emergency room."

"Holy shit!" she yells. "How crazy is that? Wow. But is everybody doing okay?"

"Yes. Monica's sleeping. The baby is in the nursery. I'm standing right outside the window. I'm hoping to get to see him after we hang up."

"Well, go! We'll be down soon," she says.

Just then I see familiar faces. "Yeah, okay. I gotta hang up now. My in-laws are here."

She laughs. "Oh dear. At least my parents are dead, right? Never had to deal with in-laws before now."

I laugh and end the call. Joanna and Jerry hurry toward me. We hug, and then for the next ten minutes or so they pelt me with questions: *How is Monica? Where is the baby? What did the doctor say? Why didn't you get her here sooner? Why is baby named after your dad and not Jerry?*

After rattling off answers, I finally put my hands on Jerry's shoulders. "Did you bring any of that good scotch, Jer?"

His face lights up. "What do you think I am, a fucking asshole? Of course I brought the good scotch."

Maybe we *should* have named the baby after Monica's dad instead of mine.

CHAPTER 43

Sarah

If you'd told me a year ago that in 2015 I would meet the man who would change my life and ultimately save me, I would have said you were crazy. Seriously, there was no way I saw this coming. And yet, here it is: December twenty-first, my wedding day. It feels so weird saying that.

After Daniel proposed, we talked about getting married in early fall, but with so many changes in all of our lives, we couldn't make it work.

Two weeks after Steven and Monica welcomed baby Charles into the world, we moved into our new house. I love it. It's so different from my 1920s Spanish Tudor. This house is a modern ranch-style, all one story, that's been completely updated. It also sits on an acre of land, so Daniel is in yardwork heaven.

That's something I've learned about him. He's quite the landscaper. We spent the first month tearing out the existing plants and putting in hydrangea all along the front. The house faces north, so we don't get any direct sunlight in the front or back, which is ideal for shade plants in the Texas heat. Daniel also planted a couple of red oaks and a willow tree. We have a lot left to do—there's talk of building a swimming pool—but so far we love it here.

Annabelle has adjusted well. With Bridget at Mercer and Ashley living and working in Utah, she and Emma pretty much have one side of the house to themselves. She also loves being a big sister to Charles. I have to admit, I'm kind of a sucker for that baby myself. I've even babysat a time or two. How crazy is that?

Emma stays with us a lot of the time. Jackie and Daniel are great co-parents. We even had Jackie and her girlfriend over for a barbeque last month to celebrate Emma's birthday. Emma and AB have become really good friends and have their own inside jokes. Daniel is pretty sure that most of them involve making fun of the way he uses lines from Seinfeld in his everyday speech. It's true. He does this a lot. At least once a week he tries to work "These pretzels are making me thirsty." into a conversation. He never fails to make me laugh.

Steven seems happier these days, which, despite everything, is all I really want for him. He and Monica seem to be working out the kinks in their relationship. I had a feeling that for a time in there Steven had regrets. He's not that good at hiding his emotions, no matter how hard he tries to convince himself. As for Monica, I'm learning to accept her for the flawed woman she is. When it comes down to it, she's actually not that bad. I know, Dr. K is as surprised to hear me say that as you are.

However, Monica is totally clueless about motherhood. She calls me at least once a week for advice. *Charles won't stop crying. Do you think something is wrong? Charles's penis looks funny. Can you take a look at it? Charles is crying again. Maybe I should take him to the doctor?*

Daniel thinks I should be sainted. Perhaps he has a point.

Ashley is doing great at New Horizons. She's really set her mind on becoming a full-time counselor. We talk and FaceTime as much as we can, but it's hard communicating sometimes because she's living on the mountain three to four days a week. She's so passionate about the kids. I can hear it in her voice. I get emotional when I think about how far she's come in such a short amount of time.

Bridget loves school and has made lots of friends. She was home for Thanksgiving and spent a few days with us. She's a lovely young woman.

Since the move we've settled into an even newer "new normal." My life is so different now that sometimes I still wake up and ask myself, *Is this real?* It's like we were traveling down the same stretch of road over and over again, and then out of nowhere it changed direction.

One night after dinner on the back patio, Daniel turned to me and said, "How about a Christmas wedding? Right here in our home. Does that work for you?"

So that's how we came up with December twenty-first. I wish I could say we picked it because it's a meaningful day, filled with good memories or marking some anniversary like our first date or our first kiss. Honestly, it was one of the only free Saturdays on our calendar. No joke.

Now I'm sitting in our bedroom, having my makeup applied by a professional makeup artist. She's actually a friend of Monica's. I know. It just keeps getting weirder and weirder. All four girls are with me. Ashley was able to take some time off to come home for the wedding and Christmas.

I have to say, it's wonderful having everyone home and under the same roof again. Ashley wasn't here when we moved in, so it was fun taking her on a tour of the house and watching her expression as she saw everything for the first time.

The girls are beautiful today, all decked out in dark red silk. They insisted on getting authentic bridesmaids dresses. They even picked the color: Christmas red. I chose an off-white floor-length silk gown with pearls on the bodice. It was more money than I wanted to spend, but the girls gasped when they watched me try it on. I couldn't disappoint them. And I have to admit, I look damn hot in it.

There's a knock on the door. Annabelle answers, and I see my brother, Benny, who's going to give me away.

"Can I come in?" he asks.

The makeup artist is just finishing dusting my neckline with bronzer. "Of course."

He comes over and awkwardly half-hugs me like I'm a Faberge egg. "You look beautiful, sis."

I almost start crying. He hasn't called me sis since we were kids. "Thank you, Benny. I'm so glad you're here."

"Me too."

It's so nice having my brother back. After all the trouble with Ashley we kept in touch. We met for lunch several times, talking and laughing and getting to know each other again. I want him to be a permanent fixture in my life now. I think he wants that too.

When the ceremony begins, I see Daniel standing near the willow tree he planted. The sun is shining, and the temperature is a comfortable sixty degrees. Our friends and family are seated in neat little rows, all wearing smiles, and Christmas music plays softly in the background. I can't remember being happier.

Benny holds out his arm, and I loop mine through.

"Are you ready?" he asks, and I want to scream out, "I've never been more ready for anything in my life!" But I don't. I just nod my head and smile at him.

Steven and Monica are here. My friend Kate is here. Even Daniel's ex-wife, Jackie, and her girlfriend are sitting on the groom's side. Isn't life funny?

As I walk toward the man of my dreams, I study each of the beautiful young women who are right now, at this moment, looking at me with love in their eyes. Together they tell a story of hope, and of second chances, forgiveness, and new beginnings. They tell the story of my life.

I'm learning that families are made of all kinds of people: New husbands. Ex-husbands. Homewreckers. Long-lost brothers. Teenagers. And sometimes even a new baby.

All this is my family. It's not perfect. It might not seem ideal. It's probably too scary a climb for some people. Along the way, it sometimes seemed too scary for us. There were twists and turns and obstacles that seemed insurmountable.

Now that's all just part of the landscape. We're survivors. We *own* that fucking mountain.

Hope our story helps you get there too. See you at the top.

THE END

ACKNOWLEDGMENTS

I want to say thank you to anyone who had something to do with this book. I know a blanket thank-you sounds generic, but I started this book three years ago and I can't remember everyone who helped me along the way. Is this what Alzheimer's feels like?

I do know some of the people who lent a hand, like Mike Ferry. He's a really important and smart dude who I bugged over and over for information regarding legal shit that I hardly understand and that also made my head hurt. So thank you, Mike. Mike's not reading this book, I can assure you. No important person in his right mind will bother. It's okay, Mike. I don't blame you.

My lovely friend, Brittany Gibbons, played a big part in this book getting finished. Many times I called her and screamed things like, "I MEAN IT THIS TIME. I'M REALLY THROWING MY LAPTOP OFF THIS BRIDGE AND I'M NOT EVEN GOING TO BE SORRY." Brittany was instrumental in talking me off the literal ledge whilst I cussed and threatened to jump. Brittany, thank you. I think. Let's see how this thing pans out first. Also? You have pretty hair.

A gigantic thank-you goes to my editor, Jessica Royer Ocken. There would be no book without her and that is the God's honest truth. She had to reassure me over and over again that the story wasn't complete horseshit. And I do mean over and over and over…I don't know if you know this about me, but I can be annoying. Lucky for me I had the most patient editor ON THE PLANET. Her insight and suggestions were so on point and boy does she know how to work a red pen. She never came out and said some things I'd written sounded stupid, but I could tell she thought so. I am forever grateful that she pushed me to dig deeper, go farther, tell more of the story. It was hard sometimes, and I wouldn't have been able to do it without her. Jessica, I love you. I feel like we're sisters now. Or at least a neighbor I would check on if I hadn't seen her out and about after a week or so. Seriously though, there's no book without you. I'll say it a thousand times if I have to. THANK YOU.

I want to thank my husband, Jeff Jones, for sticking by me through this long process. I was mean and bitchy sometimes, and he probably absorbed most of that. And by probably I mean definitely. Look, marriage is hard enough without seeing your wife's head spin around while she screams MURDER, MURDER, MURDER, on a continual loop. Anyone who knows him personally is going to relate the character Daniel with him. Is he Daniel? Everyone will ask. I don't know, is he? This is not a trick question. Daniel is a pretty perfect guy in the story, and while Jeff is a lot like Daniel's character, he's not perfect, but close. Daniel is meant to be my love letter to Jeff. But also, he's a blueprint for becoming more like this fictional perfect man who doesn't really exist. This is starting to sound bad so I'm just going to end it here. Thank you, Jeff. And thank you for loving me anyway.

My children deserve big praise for helping this book come to life. Each one of them in their own way (Presley, Riley, Harley, Ethan) has attributed to the shaping of the characters. I don't want to exploit them any more than I already have, but I will say this. You all got the very best parts of me, and none of the bad. You're all better versions of me. We'll call you Me 2.0. Thank you, thank you, thank you, thank you. I love you more than you'll ever know because I'm not going to tell you because you'll just become arrogant little shits and then all my hard work will have been for nothing. Don't do drugs.

And lastly, I want to thank you, the reader, for humoring me and reading my book. It took way longer to write than it should have, but because of the personal nature of the story (you know parts of it are based on true events in my life, right?) it gutted me at times and I had to walk away from it. Sometimes I was gone for months and months. Then I would open it back up and be like, oh good God, this it total shit. And then I would start drinking and rewrite it until I was convinced the shit had been extracted. Jessica deserves another shout out here because I would email her and be like, *hey, remember me?* And she would have to dig in her trash folder to locate my manuscript she deleted because she assumed I had jumped off the bridge or said screw it to the whole thing. Jessica, we did it!

Now that you've made it all the way to the back, feel free to close the book and start that Netflix series you've been putting off. I'll be over here starting my next book I've already titled *The Year I Lost My Mind*. I know this sounds like a joke, but I swear to God it's not. It's seriously the name of my next book. Stay tuned. Love you, mean it.

ABOUT THE AUTHOR

Shauna Glenn is writer and interior stylist in Fort Worth, Texas. She began her writing career as a blogger for numerous online outlets and as a columnist for *Fort Worth Texas* magazine. After years of blogging on her personal website and building her brand on social media, she gave it all up to begin a new chapter in her life: interior design. While having no formal training, she landed a job at a design firm, learning from one of the best interior designers in Texas. Her passion for color and global textiles set her apart from other stylists. What started out as a part-time gig ended up blossoming into a second-chance career. When she's not writing books (which let's be honest, are few are far between) she's working with clients, bringing pops of color and eclectic style with her.

Her Instagram account, @shaunaglenn, has nearly 60,000 followers and counting.

She can be reached at shaunaglenndesign@gmail.com. Visit her website at shaunaglenndesign.com.

Made in the USA
Lexington, KY
16 October 2017